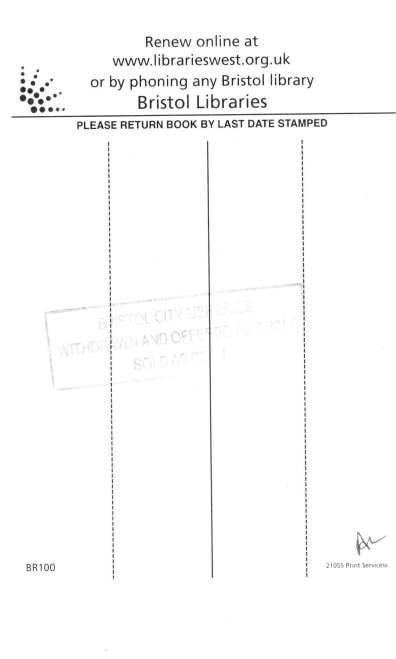

How to Read Spook's Symbols

Boggarts

Beta for Boggart

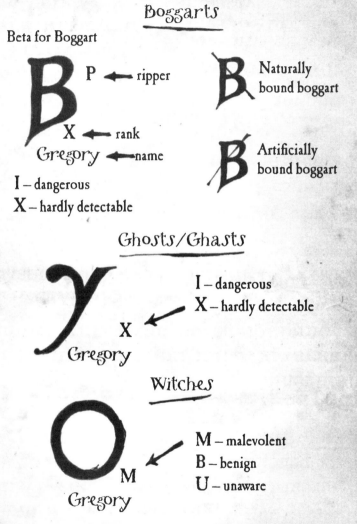

P ← ripper

X ← rank

Gregory ← name

I – dangerous
X – hardly detectable

Naturally
bound boggart

Artificially
bound boggart

Ghosts/Ghasts

I – dangerous
X – hardly detectable

X

Gregory

Witches

M – malevolent
B – benign
U – unaware

M

Gregory

CHARACTER PROFILES

TOM

Thomas Ward is both the seventh son of a seventh son and the child of a powerful lamia witch. He has abilities beyond those of a regular spook: as well as being able see and hear the dead, he can also slow down time to aid him in battle. For more than three years he has trained as an apprentice to the local Spook, and now as the wielder of the Destiny Blade he may be the world's only hope of defeating the Fiend.

THE SPOOK

The Spook is an unmistakable figure. He's tall and rather fierce-looking. He wears a long black cloak and hood, and always carries a staff and chain. For over sixty years he has protected the County from things that go bump in the night, but his long battles have left him weary. Tom fears that the days when he can continue to rely on his mentor may be numbered.

ALICE

Tom can't decide if Alice is good or evil. She is related to two of the most evil witch clans (the Malkins and the Deanes) and was trained as a witch against her will. While she counts herself as an ally of the light, she has increasingly been forced to rely on dark magic to save her friends. Tom fears that each time she does it will draw her closer and closer to the dark.

MAM

Tom's mam always knew he would become the
Spook's apprentice. She called him her 'gift to
the County'. There always were quite a few
mysterious things about Mam, but even Tom never
suspected the truth: that she was a lamia witch, and
that she had planned for Tom to battle the Fiend
since before he was even born. Tom's mam fell in
the battle against the Ordeen, but he hopes that
she might still be watching over him somehow...

GRIMALKIN

Grimalkin is the current assassin of the Malkin
witch clan. Very fast and strong, she has a code
of honour and rarely to trickery. Although honour-
able, Grimalkin also has a dark side and is reputed
to use torture. Recently she has forged an unlikely
alliance with Tom Ward against their
common enemy, the Fiend. But can a true servant
of the dark ever really be trusted?

THE FIEND

The Fiend is the dark made flesh, the most
powerful of all its denizens and the very oldest of
the old Gods. He has many other names, including
the Devil, Satan, Lucifer and the Father of Lies.
Together, Tom Ward and his allies managed to sever
the Fiend's head in battle, but their fight to destroy
him once and for all has only just begun ...

THE WARDSTONE CHRONICLES

BOOK ONE:
THE SPOOK'S APPRENTICE

BOOK TWO:
THE SPOOK'S CURSE

BOOK THREE:
THE SPOOK'S SECRET

BOOK FOUR:
THE SPOOK'S BATTLE

BOOK FIVE:
THE SPOOK'S MISTAKE

BOOK SIX:
THE SPOOK'S SACRIFICE

BOOK SEVEN:
THE SPOOK'S NIGHTMARE

BOOK EIGHT:
THE SPOOK'S DESTINY

BOOK NINE:
SPOOK'S: I AM GRIMALKIN

BOOK TEN:
THE SPOOK'S BLOOD

BOOK ELEVEN
SPOOK'S: SLITHER'S TALE

BOOK TWELVE
SPOOK'S: ALICE

BOOK THIRTEEN
THE SPOOK'S REVENGE

ALSO AVAILABLE

THE SPOOK'S STORIES:
WITCHES

THE SPOOK'S BESTIARY

THE SPOOK'S REVENGE

JOSEPH DELANEY

Interior illustrations by David Wyatt

THE BODLEY HEAD
London

THE SPOOK'S REVENGE
A BODLEY HEAD BOOK 978 0 370 33204 8

Published in Great Britain by The Bodley Head,
an imprint of Random House Children's Publishers UK
A Random House Group Company

This edition published 2013

1 3 5 7 9 10 8 6 4 2

The Random House Group Limited supports the Forest Stewardship Council (FSC®),
the leading international forest certification organization. Our books carrying the FSC label
are printed on FSC®-certified paper. FSC is the only forest certification scheme endorsed
by the leading environmental organizations, including Greenpeace. Our paper procurement
policy can be found at www.randomhouse.co.uk/environment.

Mixed Sources
Product group from well-managed
forests and other controlled sources
www.fsc.org Cert no. TT-COC-2139
© 1996 Forest Stewardship Council

Set in 10.5/16.5 Palatino by Falcon Oast Graphic Art Ltd

RANDOM HOUSE CHILDREN'S PUBLISHERS UK
61–63 Uxbridge Road, London W5 5SA

www.randomhousechildrens.co.uk
www.totallyrandombooks.co.uk
www.randomhouse.co.uk

Addresses for companies within The Random House Group Limited can be found at:
www.randomhouse.co.uk/offices.htm

THE RANDOM HOUSE GROUP Limited Reg. No. 954009

A CIP catalogue record for this book is available from the British Library.

Printed and bound in Great Britain by Clays Ltd, St Ives plc

for Marie

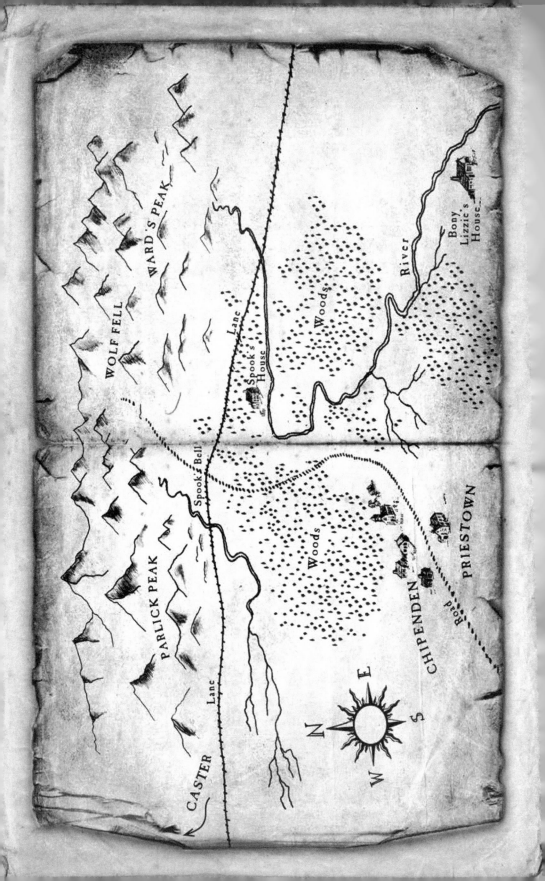

THE HIGHEST POINT IN THE COUNTY
IS MARKED BY MYSTERY.
IT IS SAID THAT A MAN DIED THERE IN A
GREAT STORM, WHILE BINDING AN EVIL
THAT THREATENED THE WHOLE WORLD.
THEN THE ICE CAME AGAIN, AND WHEN IT
RETREATED, EVEN THE SHAPES OF THE
HILLS AND THE NAMES OF THE TOWNS
IN THE VALLEYS CHANGED.
NOW, AT THAT HIGHEST POINT ON
THE FELLS, NO TRACE REMAINS OF WHAT
WAS DONE SO LONG AGO,
BUT ITS NAME HAS ENDURED.
THEY CALL IT —

THE WARDSTONE.

CHAPTER 1
ANOTHER WAY

I awoke from a nightmare, my heart pounding, and sat up in bed feeling sick. For a few moments I thought I was going to vomit, but gradually my stomach settled down.

In my dream I had been killing Alice – cutting away her thumb-bones.

At Halloween, now barely a month away, I would have to carry out this terrible ritual in the real world. It was what was expected of me. My mam wished it, for it was the only way to end the threat of the Fiend for ever.

But how could I do it? How could I kill Alice?

I lay awake, fearful of going back to sleep lest the nightmare resume. Painful thoughts continued to swirl through my head. Alice was a willing victim. She was prepared to be sacrificed. Not only that, but she had bravely ventured into the dark to retrieve the Blade of Sorrow. This was one of the hero swords – three sacred weapons to be used to destroy the Fiend; weapons that would kill her in the process.

The hero swords had been forged by the Old God Hephaestus; the first of these was the Destiny Blade, given to me by Cuchulain in Ireland. The second was called Bone Cutter, and now, if Alice had succeeded in her quest into the dark, I would possess all three.

At the moment the Fiend was bound to his dead flesh – his body impaled with silver spears in the Irish countryside; his head in a leather sack in the possession of Grimalkin, the witch assassin. She was on the run, fighting desperately to keep it from the Fiend's servants. If they got hold of it, they would reunite head and body, and the Fiend would walk the earth once more; and the ritual could not take place.

But Alice had still not returned from the dark. Perhaps something had happened, I thought. Maybe she would never come back . . .

I was also worried about my brother James, who had gone missing. The Fiend had said that his servants had cut his throat and thrown him into a ditch. I desperately hoped he was lying but I couldn't keep the terrible thought of it out of my head for long.

I tried to sleep again, but without success, and the night

dragged on. Then, just before dawn, the mirror on my bedside table suddenly began to glow. Alice was the only one who ever contacted me using a mirror. I sat up and grabbed it, looking into the glass, hardly daring to hope. For weeks and weeks I had been waiting for word from her. I had thought that perhaps I would see her just stroll happily into the garden, the Dolorous Blade – the Blade of Sorrow – in hand. But now Alice would be able to tell me that all was well immediately.

My heart soared with happiness as she stared out of the glass at me, a faint smile on her lips. She mouthed a sentence:

'I'm on the edge of the western garden.'

In the past I used to communicate with Alice by breathing on the glass and writing, but I had grown skilled at reading her lips. She had no difficulty at all in reading mine.

'Wait there!' I told her. 'I'll be down right away.'

I dressed quickly, then went downstairs as quietly as possible, trying not to wake the Spook. As I headed out through the back door, a thought struck me: Why hadn't Alice come into the garden?

The sky was growing lighter in the east, and as I passed the bench where my master sometimes gave me lessons, I saw Alice waiting at the edge of the trees.

She was clothed as I had last seen her – in a dark dress that just came down below her knees, and her pointy shoes. But what cheered me most of all was the smile on her pretty face. I ran towards her and she opened her arms, her smile broadening. We hugged each other tight and rocked back and forth.

'You're safe! You're safe!' I cried. 'I never thought I'd see you again.'

At last we broke apart and stared at each other silently for a moment or two.

'There were times when I thought I'd never escape from the dark,' Alice said. 'But I did it, Tom. I got in and out safely and I have the blade. Glad to see you, I am.'

She pulled it from her pocket and held it out to me. I turned it over and over in my hands, examining it closely. It looked just like its twin, Bone Cutter: the same skelt with ruby eyes adorned the hilt, staring up at me; the skelt was a killer that hid in crevices near water before scuttling out on its eight legs to pierce its victims with its bone-tube and drain their blood.

I forced my eyes away from the blade and looked again at Alice, feeling a surge of happiness. I'd missed her so much. How could I ever have considered sacrificing her? Even the destruction of the Fiend surely couldn't justify it. It was clear to me now that I couldn't go through with it. Tears came to my eyes and a lump to my throat.

'You're brave, Alice. Nobody else could have succeeded. But I'm sorry – you did it all for nothing. I can't go through with the ritual. I won't sacrifice you. I wouldn't hurt you for anything. We'll have to find another way to put an end to the Fiend.'

'It's funny, Tom, but you're the second person to tell me that my going into the dark was unnecessary. Grimalkin thinks so too.'

'You've talked to Grimalkin? I haven't seen her in over a month.'

'Grimalkin's been helping me. She's found another way to destroy the Fiend – we're working on it together. I'm hopeful, Tom. I really believe we can do it without the need for such a sacrifice. Had to come and see you and tell you, I did, but I've got to get back now – there's work to do.'

I couldn't believe that Alice was already going off again. We'd been apart for so long, and now all we'd had was a couple of minutes together. It was so disappointing. I wanted to know more about Grimalkin's plan. How had she discovered a method that Mam had not been aware of?

'Come back to the house for a while, please,' I begged her. 'Tell me what's going on. And I'd like to know how you coped in the dark – I'm sure the Spook will have all sorts of questions to ask you too.'

But Alice shook her head firmly. 'That ain't possible, Tom. You see, Grimalkin's plan makes use of seriously dark magic. It's the only thing that'll work. Old Gregory wouldn't approve – you know that. He's bound to ask me questions about what I'm up to, and I'd have to lie to him. He's good at telling when people are lying. It's best that I go.'

'Then when will I see you again, Alice?'

'Ain't sure, but Grimalkin and I will return for sure . . . See you when we've succeeded.'

Alice looked just as I remembered her, but as she spoke now, she sounded different – completely confident of success. Was she being overconfident?

'Is it dangerous?' I asked nervously.

'I won't lie to you, Tom. Of course it's dangerous. But we've been in danger from the dark from the moment we met, and we've always come through safely. Don't see why this shouldn't be the same.'

Suddenly she rushed into my arms and kissed me fiercely on the lips. Before I could respond, it was over; she broke away from me and began to walk off.

I stared after her in shock. I was stunned. Why had she kissed me? Could it really be that she cared for me as much as I cared for her? I had never known. I desperately wanted to hold her in my arms again.

Alice turned, looked back and called out over her shoulder: 'Take care, Tom! Don't tell Old Gregory you've seen me. It's best that way.'

And then she was gone. There was so much I hadn't had time to ask her. What had it been like in the dark? How had she managed to survive and retrieve the blade I now held in my hand?

I walked back towards the house sadly. I was very relieved that Alice had returned safely, but now I had something else to worry about. What were Alice and Grimalkin about to attempt? No doubt there were great risks involved.

She'd asked me not to tell my master that I'd met her. One

part of me agreed with her; it was probably for the best to keep it from him – he'd only ask questions. But I'd kept too many things from him in the past. Now I'd have to hide the blade to make sure he didn't see it.

I'd been feeling increasingly guilty about such deceptions. Each had seemed very necessary at the time, but they had accumulated, and the more there were, the worse I'd felt. This was one more to add to the list, and I didn't like it.

The following day, late in the morning, the Spook and I were sitting at a table in his new Chipenden library. Opposite us sat a small thin man dressed in a black three-piece suit and a white shirt with a dark grey tie. He was a lawyer, a Mr Timothy Potts, who had made the journey south from Caster. He was taking notes as my master spoke.

The Spook was making his will. Or, to be more accurate, he was updating it.

As he did so, I looked around, only half listening. The house had burned down and been rebuilt, and now almost everything within it was new. The library smelled of fresh wood. The shelves were still mostly empty and probably contained fewer than three dozen books. It would take a long time to restore it, and much of what had burned was irreplaceable – especially the legacy of books written by former spooks, with their personal accounts of how they'd practised their trade. We dealt with ghosts, ghasts, boggarts and witches – all manner of things from the dark. So we relied on books and notebooks a lot. Our careful records were vital: we looked to the past in order to prepare for the future.

'So *those* are my wishes,' ended the Spook very firmly.

Mr Potts adjusted the glasses on the bridge of his nose and coughed to clear his throat. 'I'll read it back to you, Mr Gregory. Please interrupt if you have anything to add or feel that I have not accurately recorded those wishes.'

The Spook nodded, and Mr Potts began to read very slowly, with hardly a trace of a County accent. He sounded really posh. He was obviously an 'incomer' who had been born and educated down south.

'*I leave my two main houses, at Chipenden and Anglezarke, to my apprentice, Thomas Ward, including all fixtures, fittings, books and tools of the trade. They remain his, as long as he lives, on condition that he practises the trade of spook for as long as he is able. In his own will, he may only leave them to another spook, and on these same conditions.*'

I was sad to hear those words. It made me feel as if my time as the Spook's apprentice was almost over. But I took a deep breath and tried to think positively. Our time together might be drawing to a close, but surely we had another couple of years –

time to complete my apprenticeship properly and then perhaps continue when I was a fully trained spook, so that I could take some of the burden off his shoulders.

'I grant the use of my third house north of Caster, which I inherited from William Arkwright, to Judd Brinscall for as long as he practises as a spook in that location. In the event of his death or early retirement from the trade, that property with its library will revert to the owner-ship of Thomas Ward on the same terms stipulated for my other properties.'

Bill Arkwright had died fighting the dark in Greece. Now Judd Brinscall, a previous apprentice of the Spook, had taken up residence in Bill's old water mill and was attempting to deal with the water witches there.

Mr Potts gave a little cough. 'Is that correct, Mr Gregory?'

'Aye, it's correct,' my master confirmed.

'What about your other financial affairs? Have you any income to dispose of?'

The Spook shook his head. 'There is nothing significant, Mr Potts. This is not a trade that makes a man rich. But if money is in my possession at my death, I leave that to my apprentice, Master Ward.'

'Very well.' Potts made a further short note before packing up his papers, pushing back his chair and rising to his feet. He took his pocket watch from his waistcoat and glanced at the time before tucking it away again. 'I will write this up in the proper manner and return here next week so that you may sign the document.'

The two men shook hands, and then it was my duty to escort the lawyer through the garden and off the premises – otherwise he would have been in danger from the Spook's pet boggart, which guarded against intruders, both human and otherwise.

After setting Mr Potts safely on his way, I returned to the library to find my master still sitting in the same position. He was slumped in his chair, staring down at the tabletop. He had aged a lot during the past two years; his beard was now totally white and his face gaunt. He probably felt that his life was drawing to a close. That, no doubt, was why he wanted to put his affairs in order. He certainly did not look happy.

In a few moments he was going to feel a lot worse.

Alice had asked me to keep her return and work with Grimalkin secret. But I'd been feeling guilty about it: my master was planning to entrust me with his property and his work after his death, whenever that might be. There were important things that I had to confess; things that would anger and dismay him. And I felt that now was the right time.

'Well, lad, that's one more thing sorted out,' he said, giving me a weary smile.

'There's something I've not told you,' I blurted before I could change my mind. 'I already know the details of the ritual for destroying the Fiend.'

My master stared at me for a few moments without speaking, looking far from pleased. 'In that case you've lied to me, lad. You told me that the details would only be revealed to you when Alice returned with the third blade.'

'I'm sorry. Yes, I did lie, but I did so for good reason. I didn't want to worry you until Alice got back and we knew we had the third weapon. And I needed time to think; to find a way of avoiding what's supposed to be done . . . because it's bad – really bad.'

'Lying to your master is also bad. I'm disappointed, lad. I've left you my property because I want you to follow in my footsteps after I've gone. And how do you repay me? Yes, I'm disappointed; and hurt too. After years of working together in mutual trust, speaking the truth to each other should be second only to breathing. And time's running out. Halloween is approaching. Is there any news about the girl yet, or have you been hiding that from me too?'

'No.' I shook my head, telling a new lie.

'Well, lad, I'm waiting. Get it off your chest. Spit it out. Tell me about the ritual and don't leave anything out.'

'I won't be carrying out the ritual,' I told him. 'I can't. There has to be a sacrifice. To make it work, I have to kill Alice.'

'Why does it have to be her?' the Spook demanded.

The next words were very hard to utter. My master had always mistrusted Alice because she had been trained as a witch. He also thought that a spook should devote his entire life to the trade and not marry. To get too close to a girl was, in his eyes, a dangerous distraction.

'To carry out the ritual I have to sacrifice the person I most love on this earth. That's what Mam told me. So it has to be Alice.'

12

The Spook closed his eyes and gave a deep sigh. There was a long silence. At last he spoke, his voice hardly more than a whisper.

'Does the girl know?'

I nodded. 'The victim has to be a willing sacrifice. Alice *is* willing to die in order to destroy the Fiend. But it's too horrible – I won't do it. Here!' I said bitterly, reaching into my pocket and pulling out the piece of paper that gave the details of the ritual. I held it out. I'd been carrying it around waiting for the right time to reveal all this to my master.

He shook his head. 'My eyes are tired. Each day I'm finding it more and more difficult to read. So do it for me, lad. Read it aloud slowly.'

So I did as he said, but just read out the most important sentences:

'The destruction of the Fiend may be achieved by the following means. Firstly the three sacred objects must be to hand. They are the hero swords forged by Hephaestus. The greatest of these is the Destiny Blade; the second is the dagger called Bone Cutter . . . The third is the dagger named Dolorous, sometimes also called the Blade of Sorrow . . .

'The place is also important. It must be one especially conducive to the use of magic. Thus the ritual must be carried out on a high hill east of Caster, which is known as the Wardstone.

'First the blood sacrifice should be made in this precise manner. A fire must be constructed – one capable of generating great

heat. To achieve this it will be necessary to build a forge.

'Throughout the ritual the willing sacrificial victim must display great courage. If she once cries out to betray her pain, all will be lost and the rite will fail.

'Using the dagger Bone Cutter, the thumb-bones must be taken from the right hand of the victim and cast into the flames. Only if she does not cry out may the second cut be made to remove the bones of the left hand. These also are added to the fire.

'Next, using the dagger Dolorous, the heart must be cut out of the victim and, still beating, cast into the flames—'

'Stop!' cried the Spook, rising to his feet so suddenly that his chair overturned.

'But there's more,' I protested. 'I have to—'

'I don't want to hear any more!' he exclaimed. 'I've put my own affairs in order because I know that I'm approaching the end of my time in this world. But there's one further thing that I want to do – use the last of my strength to destroy the Fiend for ever. We need to pay him back for all the suffering and misery he's inflicted upon the world. But you're right, lad, in not wanting to use that ritual. We've already compromised with the dark in order to get this far. You and the girl – you've used a blood jar to keep the Fiend at bay, and we've had a long-standing alliance with Grimalkin, the witch assassin. Those were bad enough, but this is something far worse. It's more than just cold-blooded murder. It's barbaric. Do that and we're not fit to call ourselves human. The ritual is out of the question.'

The Spook righted his chair, sat down again and glared at me across the table. 'Now I want to ask you a few questions. You learned of the ritual from your mam when you visited Malkin Tower?'

'Yes.'

'She appeared to you?'

I nodded. Mam had died in Greece fighting her mortal enemy, the Ordeen. But her spirit had survived; it was still strong – and was trying to help us finish off the Fiend.

'What form did she take?'

'At first she looked like a fierce angel with claws – just as she appeared in Greece. But then she changed into the Mam I remembered – the woman you talked to at our farm soon after you first took me on as your apprentice.'

The Spook nodded. He seemed to be deep in thought.

'Where did that piece of paper come from?' he asked, taking it from me.

'Mam appeared to Slake and dictated the instructions. She wrote them down.'

Slake was a lamia witch – one of Mam's 'sisters'. She was still in control of Malkin Tower, keeping the local witches from repossessing it.

'Well, lad, we've some serious thinking and talking to do. What's the job for us today? I heard the bell ring early this morning. It must be important if somebody walked through the night to reach us.'

The bell was at the withy trees crossroads, not far from the house. When somebody wanted the Spook's help, they went there and rang the bell and waited.

I wondered why the Spook was suddenly so interested in our work again. For weeks he had just sat in the garden or in the library, dreaming. The heart seemed to have gone out of him. Mostly, he'd just left me to it, not even asking who'd come for help or what their problem was.

It had been hard work dealing with the dark alone – there had been more spook's business in the last week than normally came to us in a month. It seemed that it was becoming more active. Perhaps it was something to do with the approach of Halloween and the coming ritual?

'No, he didn't journey through the night,' I replied. 'He lives locally – south of the village. It's only half an hour away at most. He's accused someone of using dark magic against him. He claims she's a witch.'

'Who made the complaint?'

'A man called Briggs. He lives at number three Norcotts Lane.'

'I'll come with you, lad,' said the Spook, nodding his head. 'It'll give us a chance to talk things through.'

I smiled at him. It was good to see him taking an interest in the trade once more.

Within the hour we had left the house and garden and were walking across the fields. I was carrying both bags.

It was just like old times!

The sun was shining and there was hardly a cloud in the sky. It was warm for late autumn, but that wouldn't last. In the County, more often than not, we had rain and winds blustering in from the west. By November the wet weather would really have set in.

At first the Spook seemed to be enjoying the walk, but after about ten minutes his expression became grim. I wondered if his knees were bothering him. He'd started to complain about them more frequently, claiming that too many chilly and wet County winters had destroyed the joints. But today's warmer, drier weather should have been making him feel better.

'Are you all right?' I asked. 'Do you want to slow down a bit?'

'Nay, lad, this pace is fine. I'm just thinking things through, that's all.'

So it was the thoughts in his head that gave him that grim expression. I wondered what was bothering him.

We continued in silence until we came to a row of three small terraced houses set on the edge of a large grassy meadow, fronted by a low hawthorn hedge. They had been built many years earlier for farm labourers and their families, but were now in a bad state of repair. The windows of the middle one were boarded up and the small front gardens of all three were unkempt and overgrown.

Only the nearest house had a number – a crude 3, carved high on the top left-hand corner of the front door.

'Well, lad, you go and talk to Mr Briggs and I'll go for a little walk. See you in about five minutes!'

To my astonishment, the Spook headed off along the row and disappeared round the corner of the last house. His manner had seemed almost flippant. This wasn't like him at all. I felt disappointed. My master of old would have been eager to sort out the problem. After all, this was spook's business – I thought that was why he'd decided to join me.

I walked up to the front door of the house and rapped on it three times. Within moments I heard footsteps approaching and the door was eased open. A scowling face peered out at me. Then it opened fully to reveal the old man I'd talked to earlier at the crossroads. He had a bald head, a large red bulbous nose and a fierce, angry face.

'Good afternoon, Mr Briggs,' I said.

'Where's Gregory?' he demanded. 'When I spoke to you earlier, I told you quite clearly that I wanted your master to deal with the situation, not a stripling still wet behind the ears.'

'He's sent me in his place,' I told him politely. 'I've been working alone for weeks now and getting each job completed successfully. I know exactly what I'm doing and I'm capable of sorting out your problem. But first you need to tell me a little more about it.'

'There's nothing more to tell,' he cried, his face contorting with rage. 'The old witch used a spell to stop my chickens laying. When I went to complain, she just laughed in my face, and the day afterwards my dog dropped stone dead right in front of me!'

I couldn't just accept what he said without looking into it more closely. I had to be sure that he really was a victim of witchcraft. The Spook had taught me that there were four categories of witch: the Benign, the Malevolent, the Falsely Accused and the Unaware. The first were usually healers; the second was the largest category – those who used dark magic to increase their power and hurt people; the fourth were extremely rare – those who used magic without knowing that they were doing so. But it was the third category I had to consider here. Anybody could accuse a person of witchcraft. An innocent person couldn't be made to suffer because of someone's mistaken belief. I had to be sure.

'Did this happen recently?'

'Yes – this week.'

'And when did your dog die?'

'Are your ears made out of cloth? *This week*, as I told you!'

'But *which* day?'

'Yesterday evening. I came to see you at first light.'

'Could I see the dog, please?' I asked.

It was a reasonable request, but Mr Briggs didn't seem to be a reasonable man.

'Don't be daft! I buried it, didn't I?' he exclaimed.

'Even so, we might have to dig it up,' I warned him. 'How old was it?'

I'd no intention of digging up a dead dog, but I needed to prod him for information.

'It was witchcraft! Haven't you listened to a word I've said?'

I was being polite, but he wasn't, and I was starting to get annoyed.

'How old was your dog?' I persisted.

'Sixteen years, but it was fit and healthy.'

'That's old for most types of dog. It could have died of natural causes . . . Where does the woman whom you accuse live?' I took a slow, deep breath to keep myself calm.

'There!' he shouted, jabbing his finger at the only other occupied house. 'That's where you'll find her. She calls herself Beth, but no doubt she goes by another name after dark.'

Then, his face red with anger, he went back inside and slammed the door in my face.

What he'd said was nonsense. Some people believed that the witches in a coven had special secret names for each other, but it was just superstition.

I walked along the front hedge that separated the small front gardens from the track, and went down the path of the first house in order to talk to 'Beth'. I was about to knock on the door when I heard the sound of voices. One of them sounded like my master's.

So I strolled round the side of the house. My first surprise was that there was a large, well-maintained back garden; an area of lawn bordered by flowers, and beyond that an extensive vegetable and herb garden. Two people were sitting on a bench sipping tea from small cups. One was indeed the Spook; the other was a dainty white-haired woman. I liked the look of her immediately. She was old, yet there was something extremely youthful about the joyful expression in her laughing green eyes.

It was good to see the Spook looking so relaxed and at ease. It was a rare sight these days.

'Well, lad, you certainly took your time!' he exclaimed. 'Come here and meet Beth.'

'Hello, boy,' said the old lady. 'I've been hearing all about you. Your master tells me you're a good apprentice. But let me judge for myself. Come closer and tell me what you think. Am I a witch or not?'

I approached her as she beamed up at me from the bench. There was no feeling of coldness to warn me that I was dealing with someone or something from the dark. That wasn't always a factor, but I was almost certain that she wasn't a witch.

'Well, lad, speak up!' commanded my master. 'Don't be afraid to talk in front of Beth. Is she or isn't she?'

'Beth isn't a malevolent witch,' I answered.

'On what do you base that judgement?' he asked.

'I have no feeling of warning coldness, but more than that, I trust my instincts. They tell me that Beth isn't a servant of the dark. And Mr Briggs didn't offer any real evidence. Anyone can accuse someone of being a witch for their own reasons. Some witchfinders do that, don't they? They burn someone as a witch just so they can confiscate their property.'

'That they do, lad.'

'What am I supposed to have done?' Beth asked, still smiling.

'Mr Briggs's hens won't lay and he says his dog dropped down dead after he complained to you.'

'She was a very old dog and not in good health,' she told me. 'And there could be lots of reasons why his hens have stopped laying.'

'Aye, I totally agree,' said the Spook, coming to his feet. 'Thanks for the tea, Beth Briggs. You make the best in the County!'

I glanced at them both in astonishment. She had the same name as her accuser . . . What was going on? Was my master testing me in some way – trying to see if I could quickly get to the root of a situation that he was already familiar with?

With that, the Spook led me out of the garden and back along the front hedge towards the house where Mr Briggs lived. He rapped hard on the front door.

The man opened it and scowled at us aggressively.

'Beth isn't a witch,' asserted the Spook, 'as you well know! This isn't the first time she's been falsely accused by you. So let that be an end to it. Don't waste my time or that of my apprentice again. Do you hear?'

'Scratch *any* woman, and just beneath the skin you'll find a witch!' said Briggs with a sneer.

The Spook shook his head. 'Well, you should know, you old fool! After all, you were married to Beth for thirty-eight years! So she must have used some pretty powerful magic to tolerate being close to a malicious idiot like you for so long!

'Come on, lad!' he said, turning to me. 'We have more important things on our minds.'

Soon we were striding back across the fields towards Chipenden, my master setting quite a pace. His joints did indeed seem better today.

'They were married? So what was all that about?' I asked.

'Beth finally got sick of him, and when her mother died and left her the other cottage, she left him. No doubt she'd prefer to be twenty miles further away, but it's better than sharing a house. It's the third time he's accused her of witchcraft since they parted, and that was my third visit here. I just thought I'd come along and see how you handled the situation. Not all spook's business involves dealing with the dark.

'But you did well, lad,' he continued. 'And there was another reason why I came along. I wanted to stretch my legs, get a bit of pure County air into my lungs and do a bit of clear-headed thinking. I've spent too much time brooding recently – worrying and doing little. Now sit yourself down and listen to what I've got to say,' he said, pointing to a stile we were approaching.

I set our bags down next to the hedge, took a seat and watched the Spook pacing up and down in front of me, his boots flattening the long grass. It reminded me of our lessons in the pretty western garden behind his house, where there were no bound witches or boggarts. It was a long time since we'd done that, and I missed it. Nowadays he usually taught me in his new library or at the kitchen table.

'We've already agreed that we can't use the ritual – it's barbaric. But we need to ask ourselves some serious questions.' The Spook came to a halt and looked me straight in the eye. 'I asked you what your mam looked like when she appeared to you in Malkin Tower. You said she was like a fierce angel, but then she changed into the woman I spoke to at your farm – the woman we accompanied to Greece to fight the Ordeen. I remember her well. She had an honest, open face. I sensed a tremendous strength in her and, above all, goodness. That woman would never ask you to sacrifice Alice – never mind kill her in such a cruel, inhuman way. So my conclusion is this, lad.

You've been deceived. That *wasn't* your mam. Someone or something was impersonating her.'

I could understand why the Spook said what he did. But this time his instincts had let him down. I still knew things that he didn't. Now was the time to tell him more.

'Just before she left me, Mam turned back into that cruel angel. She's very old, and only a very small part of her existence has been in human form. She became Mam for two reasons. One was because she loved my dad and wanted to repay him for rescuing her when she was chained to a rock, about to perish in the sun's lethal rays. The other reason was so that she could have me – a seventh son of a seventh son. I would be her son as well as my father's, so I would inherit some of her gifts, such as the ability to slow or halt time – the gifts that have helped us come through some dangerous situations and bind the Fiend. She had me so that I would be a weapon to be used against the Fiend. That was why I was born. She would do anything to put an end to him. And if it means killing Alice – then she would do that too.'

'I'm still not convinced, lad.'

There was nothing for it. I had to tell him the whole truth, something I'd always hoped to avoid.

'Mam was the first Lamia,' I told him. 'She was the mother of them all.'

CHAPTER 4

THE UNEXPLAINED

The Spook stared at me for a long time without saying a word. Then he turned, bowed his head and started to walk slowly away. He'd almost reached the gate at the far end of the field before he stopped and began to pace back towards me.

'This seems to be a day for truths,' he said quietly. 'Let's get ourselves back to the library.'

I stood up, allowing my master to climb over the stile first, then picked up our bags and followed him miserably back to the Chipenden house.

Once there, he led the way up to the library and pointed to my usual chair at the table. I took a seat while he went to get a book from the almost empty shelves. I knew which book it would be.

The Bestiary.

There was an entry that the Spook had made in this book, which was the only one that had survived the fire. I knew it almost word for word because it was so important and painful to me personally. He set the book down in front of me, open at the page I'd predicted. The heading was:

Lamia Witches

'Read the full entry – not out loud, because I remember what I wrote. I just want to be sure you know what you're saying about your mam.'

Feeling more and more despondent, I read the account silently.

The first Lamia was a powerful enchantress of great beauty. She loved Zeus, the leader of the Old Gods, who was already married to the goddess Hera. Unwisely, Lamia then bore Zeus children. On discovering this, the jealous Hera slew all but one of these unfortunate infants. Driven insane by grief, Lamia began to kill children wherever she found them, so that streams and rivers ran red with their blood and the air trembled with the cries of distraught parents. At last the gods punished her by shifting her shape so that her lower body became sinuous and scaled like that of a serpent.

Thus changed, she now turned her attentions to young men. She would call to them from a forest glade, only her beautiful head and shoulders visible above the undergrowth. Once she had lured her victim close, she wrapped her lower body around him tightly, squeezing the breath from his helpless body as her mouth fastened upon his neck until the very last drop of blood was drained.

Lamia later had a lover called Chaemog, a spider-thing that dwelt in the deepest caverns of the earth. She bore him triplets, all female, and these were the first lamia witches. On their thirteenth birthday they quarrelled with their mother and, after a terrible fight, tore off her limbs and ripped her body to pieces. They fed every bit of her, including her heart, to a herd of wild boar.

The three lamia witches reached adulthood and became feared throughout the land. They were long-lived creatures and, by the process of parthenogenesis (needing no father), each gave birth to several children. Over centuries the race of lamia witches began to evolve and breeding patterns—

'Are you past the third paragraph?' the Spook interrupted. I nodded.

'Then that's enough,' he said. 'It's a terrible tale. But according to that, Lamia was slain by her own children.'

'The information is wrong. Yes, she did quarrel with her children, but they did her no physical harm. You once told me that not everything in your Bestiary can be verified, and that some things are definitely wrong. And we make notes and corrections as we find out more, don't we?'

'That's true enough,' said the Spook, nodding. 'Well, how did you find this out, lad?'

'Mam told me herself when we were in Greece. It's true. After the terrible things she did, Mam repented and started to fight against the dark. Her greatest wish is to destroy the Fiend, but you have to realize that she isn't *just* the woman you met at the farm. She has spent most of her long life as Lamia, and she is ruthless. She sacrificed herself to destroy the Ordeen. She loves me – but would ask me to sacrifice myself if it proved necessary. She is also willing to sacrifice Alice. She'll do anything to destroy the Fiend. She really does want me to carry out that terrible ritual.'

As I said this, I wondered if I'd have been brave enough to sacrifice myself if Mam had actually asked me to. Would I be as brave as Alice?

'Despite all you say, I still find it hard to believe,' said the Spook. 'I trust my instincts. The woman I met wouldn't ask you to do that.'

'She'll do anything to destroy the Fiend. She wants me to sacrifice Alice. She's no longer the woman you knew. It's as simple as that.'

'Well, we'll agree to differ, lad, but it changes little. You can't carry out that ritual. So in that case, we need another plan. Let's both get our thinking caps on and try to come up with some alternative method.'

I nodded and resolved to try – though I wasn't optimistic. How could I hope to do better than Mam, who had lived so long and knew so much about the Fiend?

The following morning, just after dawn, I headed for the area in the western garden that we used for training. There was a dead tree, which was useful for practising with our staffs, and a post over which I would cast my silver chain. I remembered the first time I'd managed to cast it successfully one hundred times. My master had warned me against complacency, pointing out that a witch wouldn't oblige me by standing still; after that I'd had to cast on the run and from a variety of angles.

Now I was competent with both chain and staff, but still practised here three times a week in order to maintain those skills. The Spook had done the same until a few months ago.

I was surprised to find him using his staff against the trunk of the dead tree. He was driving the blade into the wood again and again, almost in a fury. The sweat was pouring down his forehead and he was breathing hard.

In fact, so great was his concentration that I stood watching him for a couple of minutes before he stepped back and looked round, as if becoming aware of my presence for the first time.

'Well, lad, that's just about enough for one day – for me, that is. Now it's your turn to sweat a bit. I'll get back to the house.

I'll see you at breakfast. We need to talk again.'

With that, still panting after his exertions, he strode away through the trees. I did my routine training, and after about an hour followed him back, wondering what he wanted to say to me now.

It was a good breakfast. The boggart had done us proud. The toast was crisp and brown, and our plates were heaped high with bacon, eggs and mushrooms.

The Spook nodded, and I nodded back; then, without further preamble, we tucked in and didn't say a word until we'd finished every last mouthful. Only then did my master ease his chair back from the table and fix his gaze firmly upon me.

'I'm sorry, lad,' he said. 'I've been neglecting my duties and letting you do all the work. What's worse, I've not been training you.'

'It's been a very difficult few years,' I said. 'We've travelled a lot and faced great dangers; we've both been lucky to survive. Recently, you've needed time to recuperate and gather your strength – I know that. So there's no need to apologize. You've been a good master; but for your help and training I'd be dead by now.'

'It's kind of you to say so, lad. But I'm going to try and make up for the past weeks. Do you remember what I said we'd be studying in your fourth year of training?'

'Yes – it's something that you called the "unexplained"; you told me to look in the back of your Bestiary.'

'And did you do that?'

I nodded, not mentioning the fact that my master had failed to follow it up with the expected lessons.

At the end of the Spook's book there was a short section called 'Mysterious Deaths in the County'. One account told of a woman called Emily Jane Hudson, who had died under very strange circumstances. There had been puncture marks in her neck, but she hadn't been drained of blood. Instead, the blood had been forced in between her flesh and her skin, as if to store it there. The incident had remained a mystery. Who or what had done that to her?

'So you do have an idea what you'll be learning. It will take us right to the edge of what we know. It's a higher level of study: rather than me just passing on my acquired knowledge to you, we'll be carrying out research together. We'll hopefully be able to expand our knowledge and record what we learn. Some of it will be just speculation, but we will also search for likely causes. We'll begin today with a journey to a location that's mentioned in that terrible ritual – the place where you were bidden to perform it. We're going to journey across the fells to the northeast. It's time for me to show you the Wardstone.'

'Is it a big stone or just the name of a hill? I remember once seeing it marked on one of your maps, but that wasn't clear.'

'It's a big hill *and* a big stone, lad – one of the highest in the County.'

'And what we see when we get there – will that be part of our study of the unexplained?' I asked.

'Aye,' replied the Spook. 'It certainly will. And I'll tell you something else. You'll be the first apprentice I've ever shown the Wardstone. Despite some deceits – or shall we call them "failings of trust"? – you really have become the best apprentice I've ever trained.'

CHAPTER 5
THE WARDSTONE

Within the hour we had set off from Chipenden, heading north across the fells. I was carrying both bags as well as my staff, and I also had an extra burden – a bundle of firewood tied to my back. There were no trees up there and we planned to cook supper.

I went with mixed feelings. On one hand it was good to be travelling with my master, who suddenly seemed invigorated and enthusiastic. I was also intrigued by the Wardstone. Was it just coincidence that it shared my name? I wondered. I remembered noticing that when I'd first spotted the place on the Spook's map.

However, one part of me would have preferred to stay close

to Chipenden. That was where Alice would go if she managed to defeat the Fiend using magic. I was desperate for news; desperate to see her again. I'd even tried using a mirror to contact her – something that would have infuriated my master. But although I'd called her name repeatedly, she hadn't responded. Why couldn't I reach her now? That failure made me even more worried. But I'd had no choice but to leave with the Spook.

It was good walking weather, chillier up on the fell-tops, but the sun was shining and the breeze was light. There were curlews swooping down to glide low over the tufts of grass, and fresh rabbit droppings, suggesting that supper wouldn't be too difficult to find. Out to the northwest I could see the light blue waters of Morecambe Bay sparkling in the sunlight. We had trekked this way many times together; we would often bypass Caster, with its ancient castle, keeping well to the east. If there was a witchfinder operating in the County, this was where he was usually based. And most of them believed spooks to be fair game. We dabbled with the dark, and that was as good an excuse as any to hang us.

But this time, instead of continuing past Caster, we turned directly east and went deeper into the fells than I'd ever been before. The Spook was still setting a lively pace and seemed to know exactly where he was going. By now the breeze had become a chill wind battering us from the west. Clouds were racing overhead and I could smell rain.

'You've visited the Wardstone before?' I asked.

'Aye, lad, I certainly have – twice, to be exact. The first time I came as a young spook, soon after the death of my master. He'd told me a bit about it, and I was curious enough to want to see it for myself. The second time was soon after your mam wrote me that letter. You remember which one I'm talking about?'

'The one she wrote to you in Greek just after I'd been born?'

'That's the one, lad. It stuck in my memory: I can still recite it word for word! *I've just given birth to a baby boy*, she wrote. *And he's the seventh son of a seventh son. His name is Thomas J. Ward and he's my gift to the County. When he's old enough we'll send you word. Train him well. He'll be the best apprentice you've ever had and he'll also be your last.*'

The final sentence made me sad, but I had to expect that unless something happened to me, I *would* probably be my master's last apprentice. Once again I had a sense of things coming to an end, but I shook it off and tried to think positively. My master and I probably had years left to work together.

'I remember you telling me about it just after you'd taken me to the haunted house in Horshaw to see if I was brave enough to become your apprentice. You seemed angry about the letter.'

'It annoyed me at the time because of its presumption,' the Spook explained. 'I'd never met your mam then, and I wondered just who she thought she was – to decide who my apprentice would be. Not only that: there was an element of prophecy in her letter – and as you know, I believe in free will; that we shape the future ourselves with our daily choices.'

'But that letter made you want to visit the Wardstone again? Is that right? Was it something to do with my name and the name of the hill being the same?'

'Curb your curiosity and practise a little patience; it's a quality that's very useful when studying the unexplained. You'll find out when we get there, lad,' my master retorted. 'Now the sun will be going down in a couple of hours, so I think we've gone far enough for one day. Why don't you catch us a couple of rabbits for our supper?'

I was hungry and only too pleased to nod in agreement. The Spook found us a hollow in which to shelter from the wind, and I was glad to put down our bags and my staff and remove the bundle of wood from my back. My master was already laying the fire as I set off to hunt for our supper.

A couple of hours later we were eating the rabbits I'd caught and cooked. We didn't speak much, but we were both enjoying ourselves. It was just like the early days, when I first became his apprentice and we used to walk across the fells a lot. I'd been nervous about the job and sometimes scared too. But there'd been a sense of everything just beginning. Things had seemed so simple, I realized; now everything was much more complicated. Sometimes it was just good to appreciate being alive and not worry about the more problematic things ... though the delicious rabbits put me in mind of Alice. She usually did the hunting and cooking when we were travelling and the thought tempered my happiness a little.

The rain began just before dawn and woke us. By then, the wind had become a gale, driving the rain almost horizontally above us so that mostly we remained dry in our hollow. But we could hear it drumming on the ground above and I knew that the second phase of our journey to the Wardstone would be delayed.

'We'll sleep late, lad,' said the Spook. 'It'll be wet enough up on yonder hill without turning ourselves into drowned rats before we even begin.'

It was almost noon before the rain finally stopped and we were able to continue our journey east. The wind had died away almost to nothing, but the visibility was worsening.

'I'll carry my own bag,' the Spook told me. 'The going gets difficult soon and you'll need the support of your staff.'

He was quickly proved correct as we left what he told me was Grit Fell – to follow a meandering muddy track through clumps of reddish grass.

'Keep to the path, lad,' he warned. 'The ground on either side is not just soggy. There are deep pools of stagnant water, no doubt swollen by the recent heavy rain. It's worse where the grass grows tallest.'

Without the Spook to guide me, I'd probably have blundered into the bog. He knew the County like the back of his hand, and still had lots to teach me about travelling across it, particularly remote places like this.

Finally we reached the summit of the Wardstone. Here we were shrouded in low cloud and unable to see that we were walking across one of the highest places in the County.

'There it is!' The Spook pointed ahead of us. Through the mist I could see a gigantic rock to which the name 'Wardstone' was also given. There were smaller rocks surrounding it, half buried in the ground.

My master walked right up to it and put his left hand against the wall of stone that rose into the sky before him. 'Place your palm against it too,' he commanded.

I obeyed.

'Tell me what you feel,' he said.

'It's warm to the touch.'

It was strange but true – there was no doubt. Despite the chill, damp air, the rock seemed to be radiating heat.

'And what else, lad? There's something else. Can you tell what it is?'

At first I couldn't work out what he meant, but then I became aware that everything seemed very still. I was breathing very slowly – unnaturally slowly. I could feel the pulse of blood circulating through my body too. It was so slow that I thought for a moment that my heart had stopped.

I snatched my hand away from the rock, and immediately my breathing and heart-rate returned to normal. When I put my hand back on it, everything slowed again. The Spook beckoned me away from the Wardstone, and I followed him for about twenty paces.

'Did you feel it?' he asked, coming to a halt.

'It slows time. The Wardstone slows down time!' I exclaimed excitedly.

'And you can do that too, lad, can't you? But what's the difference here?'

My ability to slow down time was a gift that had saved my life on many occasions when fighting servants of the dark – most importantly the Fiend, who had the same power. I'd prevented him from moving for long enough for us to launch our attack on him.

But what *was* the difference here? I thought carefully before replying.

'When I use my gift, I'm in control. Everything slows down, but I'm free to move. Here, it's the Wardstone slowing time, affecting everything around it. But, of course, being a big chunk of rock, it can't move.'

'Can't it, lad? Are you sure?'

'How can a rock move?'

'Maybe it can move through time. I'm just speculating, but it's a possibility. I'll tell you the reason for my thinking. There are eye-witness accounts from some who've climbed to the summit of this big hill to find, to their astonishment, that the rock wasn't there. It had vanished. So where would it go, lad, but into a different time?'

'Were they reliable witnesses?'

'Some were fools, that's for sure,' the Spook answered with a smile, 'but others were sensible folk not much given to flights of fantasy. But it's a coincidence, isn't it: a rock that goes by your name also being able to affect time? And isn't it strange that this should be the location specified for the ritual? There's a lot needs explaining . . . Now I'm going to show you something that's also strange.'

My master led the way widdershins around the rock. He came to a sudden halt, staring at its surface, then moved closer. For a moment I thought he intended to place his hand against it again. Instead he pointed with his index finger.

'Read that,' he commanded.

I approached it, and saw that words had been carved into the rock-face. It looked a little like a poem, because it was set out in a pattern and not all the lines were of equal length. The inscription was partly covered in moss, making sections of it hard to read, so it took me a few moments to decipher it while my master waited patiently.

THE HIGHEST POINT IN THE COUNTY
IS MARKED BY MYSTERY.
IT IS SAID THAT A MAN DIED THERE IN A
GREAT STORM, WHILE BINDING AN EVIL
THAT THREATENED THE WHOLE WORLD.
THEN THE ICE CAME AGAIN, AND WHEN IT
RETREATED, EVEN THE SHAPES OF THE
HILLS AND THE NAMES OF THE TOWNS
IN THE VALLEYS CHANGED.
NOW, AT THE HIGHEST POINT ON
THE FELLS, NO TRACE REMAINS OF WHAT
WAS DONE SO LONG AGO,
BUT ITS NAME HAS ENDURED.
THEY CALL IT –

THE WARDSTONE.

'Well, lad, you've read it. What have you to say for yourself?'

'It might have been someone with my name who bound the evil, whatever it was,' I suggested.

'Aye, it might – that's a possibility. But the word *ward* also means something else. It's the old name for a district. So the stone might simply mark the corner of some plot of land whose ownership has long been forgotten; it might be nothing to do with your family name. Does anything else come to mind?' my master asked.

'Whatever happened here was a long time ago. How long ago was the last Ice Age?'

'Thousands of years, lad – I reckon it was thousands and thousands of years back in time.'

'That's a long time ago to have an ancestor called Ward – and language changes, doesn't it? You once told me that during an Ice Age, when it is difficult to survive, men forget knowledge and live in caves and hunt, concentrating on survival. How old is this inscription? It might not be that old – just somebody commemorating a legend.'

'It's hard to estimate its age, but it was there at least a hundred years ago because my own master, Henry Horrocks, saw it when he visited the spot as a new apprentice in the company of his master. The truth is, we'll probably never find out when that lettering was carved into the stone. It's one of the great mysteries – another example of the unexplained. However, I want to put something else to you, lad. What if this big rock really *can* move through time? If that were true, it would open up two possibilities. The inscription might be a record of something that happened long ago in the past. But what else could it be?'

I didn't have to think. It was as if a deep part of my brain had always known and now surrendered the knowledge to my conscious mind. When I opened my mouth, the words just fell out, as if they had been readying themselves to escape.

'It could point to something that's going to happen in the future. It could have been written in the distant future, looking back on events yet to happen in our time. It could be a prophecy.'

The Spook seemed deep in thought. He didn't believe in scrying – for him the future could not be fixed. But during my years of training with him I had seen that belief challenged over and over again.

'On the other hand, the Wardstone might go somewhere else but stay in our own time,' he suggested.

'What do you mean? Where else could it go?'

'Some folks believe that there are other worlds, invisible but very close to ours. You should know, lad: you've been to one of 'em yourself – the Hollow Hills, where you got that sword, is one example. Of course, that could be just an extension of the dark.'

'Could the Wardstone go to the dark?'

'Who knows? It's part of the unexplained, and another mystery to be solved.'

Then, without another word, my master led me off the fell and we headed back towards Chipenden.

CHAPTER 6
THE DOOMDRYTE

After spending another night outdoors, we arrived back at the Spook's house early in the afternoon. I was tired, but my master seemed bright and full of energy.

'That was just what I needed, lad. Despite the wet weather on the way there, the pains in my joints have gone. That walk has done me a power of good.'

I smiled and nodded. It was a relief to see the Spook's health and attitude so much improved, but I was feeling down again. I had hoped to find Alice waiting for me at the Chipenden house, but she wasn't there. Moreover, the Spook's suggestion that the inscription on the stone might be a prophecy troubled me.

It said that a 'man died there'. Who could that be ... the Spook? But I was turned sixteen now, so I probably counted as a man too – was the end in sight for me? Perhaps I wouldn't be the Spook's last apprentice, after all.

'Cheer up, lad!' my master said. 'Things have a way of sorting themselves out.'

I forced myself to smile back at him. He meant well.

That night I didn't sleep well. No sooner had my head touched the pillow than I was plunged straight into a nightmare. And in that dream I was re-living one of the scariest experiences I'd ever endured as a Spook's apprentice.

I was back in Read Hall, south of Pendle Hill, living moment by moment the night, years ago now, I'd been visited by the evil creature called Tibb. He had been created from the body of a sow by the Malkin clan, in order to see into the future. They needed a powerful seer because they were being challenged by young Mab Mouldheel, who had tremendous powers of prophecy.

I was lying in bed, paralysed by a dark magical spell. Tibb was above me, and I could hear the sound of his claws biting into the wood as he clung to the ceiling. He resembled a giant spider, but he had four limbs and his head hung down backwards from his long neck. The mouth was open wide and I could see his sharp teeth. In the dream I was just as terrified as I'd been then. Something fell from his gaping mouth onto my shirt. It was sticky and warm. At the time I hadn't realized what

45

it was, but now, despite the terror of the dream, I knew that it was human blood – Tibb had been in the next room feeding on Father Stocks. I had heard the poor priest crying out in anguish.

It was then that Tibb spoke to me – the terrible words of a prophecy:

'I see a girl, soon to be a woman. She will love you, she will betray you, and finally she will die for you.'

I awoke dripping with sweat, my heart racing.

Alice would be using dangerous magic, perhaps even at this very moment.

Had Tibb foretold her death?

Early in the afternoon I went to collect the week's groceries from Chipenden, visiting the butcher's, the greengrocer's and then the baker's, as usual. The village had been attacked during the recent war, a patrol of enemy soldiers killing some of the inhabitants and setting fire to several houses. I was pleased to see that things were almost back to normal.

Like the Spook's, most of the damaged houses had been rebuilt, and the main cobbled street that sloped down between the shops was bustling with housewives clutching shopping baskets. People came to Chipenden from distant farms and hamlets, for here they could find the best cheese in the County, and mutton and beef of the highest quality.

I threw the sack of provisions over my shoulder, and set off back towards my master's house. I was trudging up the lane towards the gate when I saw that I was being watched.

To my left, not far from the place where I had first met Alice, three people were standing underneath a large, wide-branched oak. I knew them of old, and automatically put down my sack and brought my staff up into the diagonal defensive position – for they were witches.

It was Mab, Beth and Jennet Mouldheel.

They came towards me, but halted about five paces away. I kept my staff at the ready.

Mab was a girl of about seventeen; despite her youth, she was a dangerous malevolent witch and the leader of the Mouldheel witch clan. I'd found out what she was capable of on my first visit to Pendle; I'd gone there with the Spook to rescue my brother Jack and his family, who'd been kidnapped. She had a strong personality, powerful magic, and was without a doubt the best scryer in the County. She was attractive too, with big bright green eyes and fair hair. Like the rest of her clan, she went barefoot, and her feet and legs and tattered skirt were spattered with mud. Her two younger sisters, Jennet and Beth, were twins and it was difficult to tell them apart. They lacked the good looks of their elder sister and had thin, pinched faces and hooked noses.

All of them were a little older than when I'd last seen them. They were taller, and their faces and bodies were now those of young women.

'You've taken your time! Been waiting here for you for almost an hour, we have. And you don't seem too pleased to see me, Tom.' Mab smiled. 'Should be glad, because we're here to help you again.'

I didn't trust her one bit. Before the battle on Pendle Hill, she had tried to force me to open one of Mam's boxes for her – the trunks that the Malkins had stolen after raiding the farm and kidnapping my family. When I'd refused, she'd threatened to murder Mary, my young niece. And I'd known instinctively that it was no idle threat. Mab was a blood witch, and would kill to get what she needed in order to practise her dark magic.

However, she had since formed an uneasy alliance with us. She had accompanied us to Greece to fight Mam's mortal enemy, the Ordeen.

'Help us to do what?' I demanded.

'Help you to finish off the Fiend, of course – destroy him near that big rock. Must make you feel really important to have a hill and a rock named after you!'

I felt cold inside. I'd thought that this knowledge was confined to just a few people – myself, the Spook, Grimalkin, Alice, and the lamia witch Slake.

Mab gave me a wicked smile. 'I suppose you thought it was a secret! But nothing stays hidden from me for very long. It was easy-peasy to scry what you're up to. And I know others will find out too, and at Halloween they'll all head for that hill where you're supposed to kill Alice! Many will be servants of the Fiend: you'll need our help to fight 'em off, so don't you scowl at me like that. I thought you liked me once.'

'He was a bit soft on you, that's for sure!' Jennet said. 'Once Alice is dead he'll soon come round to that way of thinking again.'

Of course, it wasn't true. Mab had used dark magic to make me kiss her, hoping to sap my will and control me. But her attempt was doomed: when we first knew each other, Alice had gripped my forearm so tightly that her nails pierced my flesh, leaving scars. She'd told me it was her 'brand'. And it meant that no witch could control me in that way. So Mab had failed. I'd never felt anything for her but anger and revulsion.

'Should I tell him about Alice?' she said, smiling slyly at each of her sisters in turn.

'Yes! Yes! Tell him now. I want to see the look on his face,' Beth gloated.

I thought I knew what was coming. No doubt she was going to claim that she'd scryed Alice's death again. Had she seen me slay her as part of the ritual? If so, she was mistaken: I wasn't going to do it. And for all her power, Mab had been wrong about Alice before.

Scrying could be uncertain. In Greece, Mab had predicted Alice's death. But when she'd been seized by a lamia and dragged deep into its lair, I had saved her with a spell – a 'dark wish' given to me by Grimalkin.

But what Mab now told me came as a real surprise.

'You saw Alice, didn't you?' she said. 'Well, guess what – she'd been back for nearly a week before she bothered to contact you! She can't care that much about you or she wouldn't have let you go on worrying, would she?'

I just stared at Mab, wondering if she was simply lying to hurt me.

'Tell him the rest, Mab!' said Jennet. 'I want him to hear all of it!'

'Alice has found another way to finish off the Fiend. Grimalkin is helping her,' Mab gloated.

'I know that already,' I snapped angrily. 'She told me what she was doing.'

'Did she now? Well, I bet she didn't tell you everything. Alice is going to use the *Doomdryte*,' Mab crowed.

That word – *Doomdryte* – was like a blow. I couldn't hide my feelings, and all three girls grinned at the dismay on my face.

Grimoires were books full of dark magic spells. And the most notorious and dangerous of them all was the book Mab had just referred to – the *Doomdryte*. It contained one very long spell. It had to be recited perfectly, without even the slightest pause for rest or mispronunciation of a single syllable. That task had never been accomplished. Every mage or witch who had attempted the incantation had failed.

And the price of failure was death.

I didn't know what to say. My master and I had found that grimoire in a private library in Todmorden while fighting witches and daemons from Romania. I had been unconscious for three days and nights, then confined to my sickbed for two more weeks after almost dying in the grip of Siscoi, the vampire god. While I lay helpless, Grimalkin had killed or driven away the remaining vampiric entities. She said she had searched for the *Doomdryte* – but in vain. But if what Mab Mouldheel said was correct, I knew exactly what had happened.

Grimalkin must have found that deadly book, hidden it away and then taken it to Alice when she emerged from the dark. It was no wonder Alice hadn't come to see me at Chipenden right away! She'd waited a whole week and then visited me on the edge of the garden without my master present. And she'd told me only half a tale. The Spook and I would have been in full agreement: it was madness to even attempt the incantation. I was hurt, really hurt, by Alice's failure to confide in me.

My master considered the *Doomdryte* to be totally evil. He had wanted to burn it. Alice would surely die attempting such an impossible task. And even if she did succeed, what would be the result? Would it help her destroy the Fiend? My fear was that, in using that evil grimoire, she would finally become a fully-fledged malevolent witch.

Alice would have joined the dark.

'Do you know where Alice is now?' I asked Mab. 'Could you take me to her?'

As I uttered these words, I remembered the last time Mab had taken me to her. It had been a trap: Alice had already been a prisoner of the Mouldheels.

'She's too well hidden,' Mab retorted. 'Must have used an incredibly powerful cloaking spell to hide from me.'

'So she's too strong – you can't scry her whereabouts?'

It was a measure of Alice's tremendous power that not even Mab could find her.

'I wouldn't go looking for her anyway!' snapped Mab. 'Me

and Alice never did see eye to eye, and she wouldn't thank me for meddling in her affairs.'

'So you won't help?'

'Can't – and wouldn't if I could. There's Grimalkin to worry about too. It doesn't do to cross her. Anyway, it's been nice talking to you, Tom. We're off to visit the Wardstone. Need to learn the lay of the land so that we'll know what's what at Halloween.'

'You're wasting your time, Mab. I'd already decided not to carry out the ritual, and now that Alice is using the *Doomdryte*, I won't even be there at Halloween.'

'Don't be so sure about that, Tom. Scrying is difficult – sometimes the future changes from minute to minute – but I do know one thing. Something really big and powerful is going to happen near the Wardstone this Halloween. Creatures of the dark will be drawn to that spot – some to fight for the Fiend, others to oppose him. There'll be witches of every type, ab-humans and other dark entities. The outcome of that conflict will change the world. And guess what! You'll be there too – that's one thing I'm sure of.'

With that, Mab gave me a wave of farewell, turned her back and led her grinning sisters off into the trees.

I stayed in the same spot for quite a while, deep in thought. My instincts told me that Mab was correct in at least one thing. Even without the ritual, something significant would happen at Halloween, and I felt certain that the Wardstone would play a part.

My mind returned to Tibb's prophecy again; to the part that came before *and finally she will die for you.*

I remember what had preceded it: Tibb had claimed that *she will betray you . . .*

Isn't that what Alice had just done? She'd been back from the dark for almost week before bothering to tell me that she was safe, that she'd survived. And she'd known that I'd be desperate for news. Not only that; she'd gone off to use the *Doomdryte,* knowing that it was against everything my master and I believed in.

Wasn't that a betrayal?

CHAPTER 7
A TERRIBLE SCENE

The following night I didn't dream at all. It was a wonder, because I'd enough worries and anxieties to conjure a dozen nightmares.

There was no nightmare.

It was something far worse.

Well before dawn, I suddenly awoke in a cold sweat, certain that something was terribly wrong. I got out of bed, trembling from head to foot, full of dread and a terrible sense of loss. I felt sure that somebody close to me had died – or at least been badly injured.

My master!

I ran downstairs. The Spook was in the kitchen. He didn't sleep in his bed every night. Sometimes his back felt stiff and sore of a morning, so he dozed upright in a chair. He was in his armchair now, close to the embers of the fire. He was very still.

Was he breathing?

I walked very slowly across the flags towards him. I was expecting the worst, but suddenly he opened his eyes, stared up at me and scratched his beard.

'What's wrong, lad? You look as white as a sheet.'

'There's something not right. Something's happened to someone, I feel sure – something terrible.'

'Perhaps it's nothing, lad.' My master rubbed the sleep from his eyes. 'Maybe you just woke from a bad dream and carried the feeling of unease back with you. That happens sometimes.'

'I wasn't dreaming.'

'Dreams can be forgotten at the instant of waking – you can't be sure of that,' said the Spook.

I shook my head. 'I need to go outside,' I told him.

Full of apprehension, I went out into the garden. The dark sky was covered with uniform light grey cloud; it was starting to drizzle. I shivered. The feeling of dread and loss was stronger than ever.

Suddenly there was something like a flash of light right inside my skull, and a pain in the centre of my forehead. And now the wrongness had a direction. Its source was some distance away – in a southeasterly direction.

I heard the Spook approach and stand at my side.

55

'Whatever is wrong, it's over there . . .' I pointed through the trees.

'It could be dark magic,' said my master, 'luring you out into a trap. The servants of the Fiend will never give in. We must be on our guard.'

'It's strange. I've never felt like this before. I'm scared . . . But you could be right – it might just be a trap . . .'

I began to pace up and down, my stomach churning with anxiety while the Spook stared at me, clearly concerned and alarmed.

'Take deep breaths, lad. Try to calm yourself. It'll pass in a few moments.'

'But what if it doesn't?' I demanded, coming to a halt and looking him right in the eye.

All at once the need to go and investigate became over-whelming. 'I have to go!' I cried out. 'I have to see for myself what's wrong or I can never rest.'

The Spook stared into the trees for over a minute without speaking. Then he simply nodded.

Five minutes later we'd left the garden and were striding southeast. I was carrying both bags, as usual, as well as my staff. In addition to his own staff, the Spook had also brought a lantern, as dawn was still some way off. I didn't know how far we had to go.

The source of my unease proved to be much nearer than I expected.

Years earlier, when I first met Alice, she had been staying in the area with Bony Lizzie and an abhuman called Tusk. Lizzie's plan had been to rescue Mother Malkin from a pit in our garden, and also to kill my master, John Gregory. They had all been living in an abandoned cottage southeast of the Spook's house. Of course, they failed, and the cottage had been burned out by local people who were outraged by the proximity of a dangerous witch.

Now I could just glimpse that cottage through the trees, and the nearer we came, the more certain I was that this was the source of my fear.

The lantern-light showed us the first of the dead bodies: a man lying on his back, his eyes wide open; rain streamed down his face like tears. Blades were still clutched in both dead hands, but they had availed him not. His throat was cut from ear to ear.

There were other bodies closer to the blackened walls of the cottage – maybe a dozen or more. Most were female, and almost certainly witches. They were armed with blades, some lashed to the ends of long poles in the Pendle manner. All had died violent deaths. Their wounds were fresh and there was a lot of blood splattered on the grass.

All was silent, but I was drawn to the cottage. I led the way in, trembling at what I might find there. The doors and windows had been burned out years ago and never replaced. All at once, in the gloom, I saw someone propped up against a far wall. At first I thought it was another dead body. Could it be Alice? The thought made me tremble with anguish.

My eyes were slowly adjusting to the darkness, but when my master came in behind me, the lantern illuminated a terrible scene.

I saw that it was the witch assassin, sitting in a pool of her own blood. She was breathing hoarsely and her eyes were half closed. It was hard to tell whether she was conscious or not. Her body was covered in stab wounds that looked like open mouths.

She was still gripping a skelt dagger in her left hand. This was Bone Cutter, the blade I'd loaned her to help in her running battle with the Fiend's supporters. Additionally, her left leg had been broken just below the knee. I could see a piece of bone jutting through the flesh.

Of the leather sack containing the Fiend's head there was no sign.

I just stared down at Grimalkin helplessly, feeling emotions surge through me; a torrent of terrible possibilities churned through my mind.

I had never imagined a situation where she would be bested in combat. How could this have happened? I wondered. The servants of the Fiend had been hunting her for a long time. They were numerous and relentless, and a number of them were very powerful – it was perhaps inevitable that they would finally prevail. She had put up a good fight – as the dead bodies scattered around the cottage showed.

My heart sank even further as I suddenly remembered that Grimalkin and Alice had been planning to use the *Doomdryte*. Is this where they had been hiding and preparing for the ritual?

If so, where was Alice now?

My thoughts were still racing and I couldn't move. I stared dumbly as the Spook knelt close to the witch assassin.

'I'll make a splint for her leg,' he said, coming to his feet, 'but I can't do much for her wounds – she's lost a lot of blood. We're close to the western boundary of Clegg's farm. He has a cart. Run there and get him to bring it here. We need to get her back to Chipenden and a doctor. There may still be a chance to save her. Stop gawping, lad! Run!'

CHAPTER 8
ONLY YOU CAN DO IT

So I ran – but nothing proved to be straightforward. Clegg was a very sound sleeper and he apparently lived alone. I woke the dogs all right, but it was a good fifteen minutes before the farmer came to the door, bleary-eyed and cantankerous, wielding a stick.

'What time do you call this to come knocking on my door fit to wake the dead? Be off with you, before I give you a taste of this!'

'My master, John Gregory, sent me. Could he borrow your horse and cart? There's somebody badly injured over at the ruined cottage. We need to get them to a doctor.'

'What? Ye want my cart? Who's injured? Nobody lives in that cottage. It's a ruin.'

'Look, there's been a fight. People are dead. But there's one still alive and we can save her. We need your cart. Don't worry – my master will pay you well!'

At the offer of money, Clegg led me to an outbuilding; he found it locked and had to go back to the house for the key. At last we dragged the cart out and harnessed it to a horse.

By the time I'd got the cart back to the cottage, almost an hour had passed. I expected the Spook to complain about my delay, but he said nothing. He'd made a fire and boiled water in a small pan he'd found in the kitchen.

After cleaning up Grimalkin's wounds as best he could, he'd managed to push the bone back into place and had used two thin branches as rough splints on each side of the leg. He was binding them into position when I arrived. Grimalkin was still unconscious, her breath rasping through her open mouth. There were beads of sweat on her forehead and her upper body twitched as if gripped by a fever.

The dagger lay on the ground beside her. I picked it up and tucked it into my belt.

Carefully, we lifted her up into the cart and set off for the Spook's house. Once there, we carried her upstairs and put her in my bed. Then my master sent me off to fetch the local doctor. Fortunately he was at home and within half an hour was treating his patient.

When he took his leave, we walked him across the garden to the boundary, protecting him from the boggart. There he halted and shook his head. 'By rights she should be dead,' he said.

'As you saw, she's no ordinary woman,' the Spook replied.

'I've known you a long time, Mr Gregory,' the doctor said. 'The people around here owe you a lot. You've kept this village safe. The whole County is in your debt. So I won't ask why you're harbouring a witch.'

'I have good reason. I wouldn't do it if it weren't absolutely necessary for the good of us all. Now I need your opinion. Will she live, do you think?'

'If she survives the night, she has a chance. But even then she won't be out of danger. There's the risk of infection. And if she does survive, life will never be quite the same for her again. It's an extremely bad break. She'll have a permanent limp. Anyway, I'll come back tomorrow and see how she's doing.'

Poor Grimalkin, I thought. Much of her potency as a witch assassin relied on her speed – that whirling dance of death was what made her so formidable. She would no longer be such a powerful opponent.

'Come back at noon,' the Spook instructed. 'I'll meet you at the edge of the western garden.'

With a nod, the doctor went off down the hill.

We decided that Grimalkin would have to be observed at all times in case she took a turn for the worse. The Spook sat with her for the rest of the day; I volunteered to take over at sunset.

I sat beside the bed, staring at her anxiously and wondering what had happened to Alice. Grimalkin muttered in her sleep, and sometimes gave a low groan, but showed no sign of regaining consciousness. I felt helpless, but I did what I could, occasionally mopping the sweat from her brow or lifting her head and holding a cup of water to her lips – though each time this brought on a fit of choking.

Her breathing was hoarse and irregular. Sometimes it seemed to stop for almost a minute; each time this happened I thought she was dead. Then, about half an hour after midnight, there was a change. Grimalkin's breathing became steadier, and then she finally opened her eyes and looked at me.

She tried to speak, opening and closing her mouth, but no words emerged. Then her face twisted with pain and she attempted to sit up, so I pulled the pillows into position behind her back and helped her upright. I held a cup to her lips, and this time she was able to sip without choking.

She stared at me for a long time in silence. At last I could hold back no longer.

'Alice?'

Grimalkin dropped her gaze, as though unable to meet my eyes. Then she replied with one word: 'Lukrasta!'

I knew the name. Lukrasta appeared in the Spook's Bestiary in the section that dealt with mages. He was supposed to have been the dark mage who had written that grimoire in the first place, taking dictation from the Fiend! Despite this, he had died while attempting the full *Doomdryte* ritual. He'd supposedly made an error and been destroyed.

'Do you mean the mage who died?' I asked.

'No! No! Not dead,' Grimalkin protested, struggling to speak, her voice very faint; I had to lean over the bed and bring my ear close to her lips. 'When Alice opened the grimoire to begin the ritual, he appeared before us, right out of thin air. He took us by surprise. Blasted us with power. Later the Fiend's servants attacked.'

'Where's Alice?'

Grimalkin shrugged. 'I was stunned. Befuddled. Far less than what I am ... Too many to hold off ... Didn't see what happened to Alice ... Think Lukrasta has her.'

Alice was the prisoner of Lukrasta! What exactly had happened? I *had* to know.

Grimalkin began to cough, and I brought the cup to her lips again. This time she drank greedily, draining every drop.

'They have the Fiend's head,' she continued. 'They'll try to return it to Ireland ... Reunite it with the body ... You have to go after them. Bring it back!'

'Which direction did they take? Did they go west?'

'I didn't see – but, yes, I expect they'll have gone west towards the coast. No doubt they'll follow the river ... It's up to you to find them.'

With the help of the kretch, a creature fathered by a daemon, the Fiend's servants had seized the sack from Grimalkin once before. They had boarded a boat north of Liverpool, but had been thwarted by Alice, and Grimalkin had recaptured the Fiend's head. Would they make for the same place again or go north to the main County port, Sunderland Point?

'How many are left?' I asked.

'A dozen or more – certainly enough to have slain me had they pressed home their attack. Others will surely join up with them later.'

I wondered what I could do alone. By now they could have reached the river estuary and headed south, or maybe crossed by the Priestown bridge and gone north.

'They'll probably have too much of a start on me,' I said. 'They'll have set sail before I can reach the coast.'

Grimalkin seized me fiercely by my collar and drew me close so that our noses were almost touching. Wounded as she was, I could feel the strength in her grip. Her eyes blazed into my own.

'Only you can do it!' she hissed. 'If they cross the sea to Ireland, then you must do the same. Follow them as far as is necessary! You're not a boy any longer. You're a man. You have the sword. Was Bone Cutter still in my hand?'

'Yes, it's safe.'

'I know Alice gave you the other dagger, Dolorous. You have all three blades now, and the gifts from your mam. What's more, you're a seventh son of a seventh son. So go and do what's necessary. Kill anyone who stands in your way, but bring back the Fiend's head!'

CHAPTER
9
THE AMBUSH

Grimalkin collapsed back against her pillow, fighting for breath, her eyes closed. The effort had exhausted her.

I quickly left the room and went to find the Spook. As I expected, he was sleeping in his chair in the kitchen, close to the embers of the fire.

'My turn is it, lad?' he asked, opening his eyes at the sound of my boots crossing the flags towards him. He thought I'd come to wake him for his turn to watch over Grimalkin.

I realized I had to make my mind up about how much to tell him. I decided to leave out any reference to Alice and Grimalkin's use of the *Doomdryte*. He would have considered that unforgiveable, and the greatest of follies. I just concentrated on the need to recapture the sack and its contents.

I shook my head. 'Grimalkin said I had to go after those witches and try to recover the Fiend's head.'

'The odds against you are very great, lad. You might well be going to your death.'

'It's death and worse for all of us if those witches reunite the head with the body.'

I thought my master would protest more, but all he did was apologize.

'I'd go with you if I could,' he said sadly, 'but I haven't the speed for such a pursuit. You'd never catch them with me dragging at your heels.'

As quickly as I could, I prepared for my journey. I didn't take my bag because it would only hinder me. I wouldn't need my silver chain – I wouldn't be taking any prisoners to bind in pits. Salt and iron would also be an unnecessary encumbrance. So I wore the sword and the two daggers in their sheaths and, carrying my staff, prepared to set off into the night.

The Spook was waiting at the door. He had a small parcel of cheese for me, which I stuffed into the inside pocket of my cloak.

'I fear for you, lad,' he said, patting my shoulder. 'If anyone else were setting out alone after them, I'd think it a hopeless task. But I've seen what you can do.'

Then he did a strange thing: he shook my hand – something that happened very rarely, because nobody wanted to shake hands with a spook. Even when my dad and John Gregory had agreed the terms of my apprenticeship, they hadn't shaken hands. He'd certainly never taken mine before.

It made me feel strange. In one way it was as if he was treating me as an equal – a fellow spook rather than just the apprentice that he was training. Yet I felt a chill in my heart. It seemed like the end of something.

I headed west at a fast walking pace. When I came to the river Ribble, I had to make a decision: which bank should I follow towards the sea? Had they gone north or south? Soon the river would become too wide and deep to cross. If I got it wrong, I would have to go into Priestown, a place where spooks weren't welcome, and cross the bridge there. It would mean several hours' delay.

I found no evidence of tracks to the north, so I took a chance, crossed at the next ford, opting for the south bank of the Ribble. Then I pressed on, breaking into a jog. Those I hunted had almost an entire day's start on me. Would they have made camp for the night? That was surely my only real chance of catching them before it was too late.

According to Grimalkin, there were over a dozen of the Fiend's servants, with perhaps more joining them on their journey. But such a large group would draw attention, especially as many of them were witches. So would they split up into smaller units? After all, their main objective would be to get the Fiend's head to the pit where his body was bound –

Kerry in the southwest of Ireland. One person could do that. They could all converge later.

Soon after dawn I had my first piece of good luck. Beside the path was a pond; the earth around it had been churned into mud by cattle – and there were a dozen or more fresh tracks; the majority clear imprints of pointy shoes.

I could find no trace of a man's boot. I thought Lukrasta might be with the witches, Alice his prisoner, but I knew Alice's tracks well and saw no sign of her either. That made my heart drop into my boots – I'd hoped that in following the witches I would also find Alice.

Half an hour later, I faced my first threat. But it wasn't witches.

As I passed a farm, a big farmer suddenly stepped out from behind a barn into my path. He had broad shoulders and well-muscled arms, but a bulbous belly hung down over his leather belt.

'You a spook?' he demanded belligerently.

I nodded.

'Well, where were you last night when you were needed?'

He was angry and unreasonable, so I tried to placate him.

'On my way here,' I replied calmly.

'Well, you're too late to be any use to me. There were witches here last night – dozens of 'em. Helped themselves to three pigs and most of my hens. What are you going to do about it? You owe me compensation. It's your job to stop things like that happening.'

Most people are nervous in the company of a spook. They think that we're contaminated by the dark. But very occasionally we get angry reactions such as this. The man's livelihood had suffered, and he wanted to take it out on someone. I looked young and I was smaller than him, so I would do.

With a snarl, he stepped towards me, hands outstretched, intending to grip my shirt front. I dodged to the side and ran towards the gate that led to the next field. I could hear his heavy boots pounding across the grass behind me. He was fast for a big man: he would catch me as I clambered over the gate.

I didn't want to hurt him, but I had to do something. I spun quickly and rapped him twice with the base of my staff: one blow to his left shin; the other to his right forearm. He dropped to his knees with a groan, which gave me a chance to climb over the gate. I ran on, and when I glanced back he was still on the other side, shaking his fat fist at me.

Soon it started to rain, a cold wind blustering into my face from the west. If anything, this drove me on faster. I ran all morning, pausing to catch my breath only briefly. Twice I found the tracks of those I pursued. They were still together, and three or four new witches had joined the group.

The third time I found their tracks, it was at a crossroads. They were heading south. Liverpool seemed the most likely port for a boat to Ireland. Would they have already arranged passage? They'd been hunting Grimalkin for many months. It could well be that plans were already in place to return the Fiend's head to Kerry.

By noon I was exhausted and desperately in need of rest, so I sat on the edge of a ditch in the lee of the wind and the rain, and nibbled at the cheese my master had given me. I remained there no more than five minutes. After slaking my thirst with the icy-cold water of a nearby stream, I ran on.

All morning, desperate thoughts had been churning around inside my head – mainly fears for Alice. Perhaps I'd been mistaken, and her pointy shoe prints had simply been obscured by those of her captors? That made me run even faster.

I'd also speculated about the Wardstone and what might happen on Halloween. What was it Mab had said about something that would change the world?

Finally, as the late afternoon gave way to evening, I ran on without thought, numb and weary, driving myself on in pursuit of my enemies. I thrust to the back of my mind the fear that when I caught up with them I would achieve nothing. It was all very well for Grimalkin to send me off after them; to say that only I could retrieve the Fiend's head. But the odds against me were too great. How could I defeat so many? How could I hope to rescue Alice as well? I began to wonder if they knew that I was following them. Witches could long-sniff the approach of danger; this didn't work against seventh sons of seventh sons, so I was safe from that, but of course they might have a scryer with them. Someone with even half the ability of Mab Mouldheel would see that I was on their trail. Then again, there were many non-magical means of protecting themselves against pursuit.

Once the witches knew that they were being followed, they might wait in ambush. A couple of them would peel off to the side and make their way back towards me. It would be impossible to tell that this had happened until it was too late.

That's exactly what they did.

But there were more than two.

Five witches lay in wait for me.

The rain had stopped and the clouds were in shreds. The sun had dropped below the horizon; soon the light would begin to fail.

I was now moving at a slow jog. Before long I would have to stop and snatch a few hours of sleep. As I moved into a forest, I immediately sensed that something was wrong. It was too quiet. The birds should not have been roosting yet. Seconds earlier, the countryside had been filled with song. Now, in the deeper gloom beneath the branches, all was silent.

Out of the corner of my eye I saw someone running towards me from behind and to my left. Without breaking stride, I swung hard, widdershins, with the base of my staff. There was a dull thud, and the satisfying feel of contact with a skull. My attacker went down and I ran on.

However, I'd made a mistake and I knew it. I heard the voice of Grimalkin in my head; a fierce rebuke filled with scorn. *Fool! Fool!* that imaginary voice cried. *That one will get up and attack again. You are greatly outnumbered. Kill or be killed!*

That was what she would have said. Now I had one enemy

behind me as well as many ahead. So I pressed the button on my staff to release its blade. Next time I would show no mercy.

Suddenly a long-haired witch burst out of a group of saplings close by; she attacked, shrieking like a banshee, scattering dead leaves with her pointy shoes. She wielded a blade strapped to a pole and I saw that her lips were flecked with foam. She looked demented; insane with hatred and anger. I barely had time to lift my staff, but somehow I parried her blade and then flicked it upwards so that it arced away from her.

She ran to retrieve her weapon, but I came round in a circle and attacked quickly, thrusting the blade of my staff under her ribs and into her heart. She screamed and fell, and I ran on. I needed to get out of the trees so as to see other attackers earlier.

When I emerged from the forest, three more witches were waiting. They were Pendle witches; their brown garb, long skirts and leather jerkins marked them out as Deanes. They waited in a line, their eyes watchful, confidently wielding their long blades. They looked much more formidable than the previous two.

'You're a fool to follow us, boy!' the tallest one jeered.

All three began to cackle.

'I'll drink his blood!' one cried.

'I'll take his thumbs!' shrieked another.

The third one drew her finger across her neck. 'I'll cut off his head,' she said softly, her voice hardly more than a whisper. 'That will please our master!'

I thrust my staff blade-first deep into the soft ground and

drew the sword and a dagger – the Bone Cutter. They were more flexible weapons.

The ruby eyes in the skelt hilt of the sword seemed to glow in the gloom under the trees. Then both eyes began to drip blood. The sword was hungry.

A second later the dagger also began to bleed.

I concentrated, waiting for them to make a move.

Let them come to me . . .

They did. All three attacked at once.

CHAPTER 10
THE PURSUIT

The battle was fast and furious, and I had no time to think. All I could do was react as they pressed home their attack. More by luck than skill, I managed to kill two of them: a slash with my sword against a neck; an upward thrust with the dagger, and it was done.

The third witch ran back into the wood.

I followed. She was fast, and by the time we came out of the trees again, I hadn't managed to close the gap. She had thrown away her weapon in the interests of speed and was heading back in the direction we'd been travelling. Then I saw the witch I'd previously stunned, perhaps two hundred yards ahead, also running away.

They were scared.

I came to a halt and sheathed my sword and dagger, waiting for a minute to regain my breath and composure. Then I turned to head back through the trees and reclaimed my staff. My whole body was trembling, a reaction to the fierce fight and having taken three lives. I felt more and more nauseous, until eventually I came to a halt and was violently sick.

It was getting dark now, so I decided to rest for a few hours. I found a copse on high ground – a little knoll that would give me a good view over the surrounding countryside. After a while a half moon rose above the eastern horizon and I used its pale glow to search for my enemies. Nothing moved. I was exhausted and settled down with my back against the trunk of a tree and my staff across my lap.

After a while I dozed, then awoke, suddenly terrified that I was under attack. But still there was no threat and the moon was much higher. Each time I nodded off, my sleep was deeper and longer, until finally I had a strange dream.

It was one of those dreams where you know that you're dreaming. I was back at the farm. Mam was facing me across the hearth, smiling from her rocking chair. She looked exactly as she had the night before I left the farm to begin my job as the Spook's apprentice. Her skin was pale, but her eyes were bright; apart from a few grey streaks in her black hair; she looked far too young to have grown-up married sons.

'I'm proud of you, son,' she said to me. 'Whatever happens, I want you to know that.'

'I'm sorry, Mam, if I let you down. But I could never perform that ritual. I couldn't sacrifice Alice.'

'There's no need to apologize, Tom. It was your decision to make, and what's done is done. Maybe the Fiend can be destroyed in other ways. Nothing is certain. At the moment everything hangs in the balance. You must draw upon your strengths: some came from your dad, because you're a seventh son of a seventh son; others came from me, for lamia blood courses through your veins. You are already aware of some of those gifts, but more will become apparent as you grow up. There is one you need now; one that would not normally have emerged for many years. But I reached out to bless you with it earlier. It is a gift that a hunter needs – the ability to know the location of his prey!'

Mam began to rock back and forth on her chair, smiling at me all the while. So I smiled back, hoping the moment would never end. But the dream began to fade. I could still see her smile, and I wanted to hug her, but then she was gone . . . I woke up to the sound of a distant cock crowing and the eastern sky pink with the promise of sun. The dream was vivid and real in my mind. My head was whirling with thoughts. Was it more than just a dream? I wondered. Could it really have been Mam talking to me?

If it was, she seemed to have forgiven me for not being prepared to carry out the ritual she had decreed. She had also used the word 'hunter' – I would receive the gift that a hunter needs. In the first year of my apprenticeship she had told me that one day I would be the hunter; then it would be the dark that would be afraid.

Mam had been giving me important information. She said she had reached out to unlock the gift. Somehow it all made sense. That was why, lying in my bed in the Spook's house, I'd had the strange feeling that something was wrong. And, yes, I'd known exactly which direction to take. My new gift had led me to the cottage where Grimalkin lay gravely injured. It was lovely to think that I might really have been talking to Mam, and for a while I was filled with hope. But as the seconds became minutes, the dream seemed less substantial; soon I felt it was merely wishful thinking. What was I doing fooling myself and wasting time? I sat up and cursed myself for sleeping right through the night. The witches would be even further ahead now. Wasting no time, I ate half the remaining cheese and set off west again. This time I didn't run; I would save that for later. My legs felt stiff, and I contented myself with a fast stride to loosen them up.

I thought about Lukrasta again. He had abducted Alice – Grimalkin had been unable to do anything to stop him. What had happened when he attempted the ritual with the *Doomdryte*? And more importantly, what might Alice be suffering now? I thought fearfully. I felt helpless. He could be anywhere, and even if I could find him, what could I hope to do against such a mage?

By late morning I was getting worried. I hadn't found the witches' tracks again; I was now crossing meadows and rough pasture rather than following lanes and tracks. This meant they could already have turned and headed for the coast. I estimated that I was presently about four miles from the sea, heading south, somewhere between Formby and Liverpool.

I came to a halt, filled with uncertainty. Then, very suddenly, there was a flash of light behind my eyes and a pressure on my forehead – and I knew precisely where they had gone. It was something very similar to the feeling I'd had back in my bed-room in Chipenden – the conviction that something was terribly wrong. Now I felt that certainty again. I knew where the witches were – the direction they had taken with the Fiend's head. This was surely the gift that Mam was talking about in the dream – the gift that a hunter needs: the ability to track a prey without signs, to pinpoint its location.

They hadn't gone west to the sea. They were continuing south and were passing east of Liverpool. Where could they be bound? In my mind's eye I tried to conjure up the maps I'd studied in the Spook's library, all of which had perished in the fire. Beyond Liverpool lay the County border, and beyond that, county after county – over two hundred miles to the south coast.

That made no sense at all. They needed a port on the west coast to take a boat over the Irish Sea.

I began to run again. Wherever they were heading, I would eventually find out because I could sense their location in my head. For a while they seemed to have changed direction and were heading east, but after a few hours they veered back towards the coast and continued south again.

I came to a wide river, which I guessed was the Mersey: as I forded it, I wondered how the witches had managed to cross over. One possibility was that they had witch dams in place; in Pendle these were used to temporarily hold back running water. They would have had to make a detour east to where the river was narrower. That explained their earlier change of direction. The delay meant that I was closing in on them once more.

After a while, in the far distance, I saw a walled city with a castle and the tower of a cathedral. We were beyond the County border now and, again drawing on my memories of the Spook's maps, I guessed that the city was Chester – though I'd never travelled this far south over land. If that were the case, it also had a river called the Dee.

Sure enough, I sensed my enemies head east again, no doubt to use another witch dam. I simply forded the river, which meant that I was drawing near to my prey. Beyond the city the witches turned directly west.

Soon I saw mountains ahead, and glimpsed the sea in the distance to the north. We seemed to be following a coastal plain, a wide strip of flat land between the mountains and the water. And now I was on a track that eventually gave way to a wide road. It was muddy, so I slowed down and walked on the grass verge. The occasional cart trundled past, its wheels adding to the deep ruts, but nobody gave me a second glance.

Eventually I came to a large sign that had been nailed to two posts proclaiming:

CYMRU

I remembered that word from my master's maps. It was in another language: the name for the country that we called Wales. I was entering a foreign land, with its own customs, language and – no doubt – dangers.

I sensed that the witches were no longer moving; they had made camp for the night. I had two choices. Catch up with them now and attack under cover of darkness, or wait one more night and rest to gather my own strength.

I decided on a compromise.

I would rest for a while and then press on. I moved some distance from the road and settled down as best I could. I didn't have time to set traps for rabbits, so I finished off the rest of my cheese and drank some cold water from a stream. I intended to sleep for about three hours before setting off west again.

I awoke suddenly after just one hour, immediately fully alert. Although my physical senses told me nothing, I had a sudden flash of light inside my head and a pain above my nose.

Something was amiss. I sat up quickly and stared into the darkness. The moon was covered by clouds: I could see nothing and hear nothing. But danger was out there and it was creeping towards me.

I came up onto my knees and reached for the sword that I

had placed on the grass beside me before lying down to sleep. My gift was telling me *precisely* where my enemy was.

A witch was crawling stealthily towards me; she was now less than ten feet away.

No, not the Destiny Blade, I decided; a spook's primary weapon was more suited to dealing with this threat. So, leaving the hero sword where it was, I seized my staff, released the blade at its tip, ran straight towards the witch and stabbed downwards, piercing her back directly over her heart and pinning her to the ground. She had no time to scream, but I felt her body twitch beneath my staff, and she gave a little gasp.

I knew instantly that she was dead: the inner certainty I had of where she was simply ceased. It went out like a light. I wondered if it was the soul or life force I could detect? Whatever it was, I knew that I'd put an end to her.

I fumbled for my tinderbox and lit the candle-stub I always carry. I looked at the dead witch, holding the light close to her face. I was almost certain that she was one of those who had fled after the attack the previous day. That made me wary. Perhaps the other one had come back too?

I listened, but could hear only the sighing of the wind. My new ability to sense things at a distance no longer alerted me to any immediate danger. Those I pursued were some way ahead; I knew that they had still not broken camp. Nevertheless I didn't want to take any chances, so I extinguished the candle, gathered my things together, and continued steadily west.

Just before dawn I sensed that the witches were moving

again, but by now I knew that I was within a few miles of them. They were still out of sight, but my objective was to get close without being detected, and then, once night fell, move in quickly. My new ability seemed to be refining itself and getting stronger as I used it. I felt certain that even in the dark I would be able to go straight to the leather sack containing the Fiend's head, retrieve it quickly – fighting only if necessary – and then make my escape.

My only fear was the sea to the north, which was quite close now. At times I spotted big ships, their sails billowing in the wind. The danger was that the witches would rendezvous with one before I could intervene.

But they turned south, not north, heading inland towards the hills and taking me completely by surprise.

Less than an hour later, at the point where they left the road, I found their tracks. Puzzled, I followed them; I was no longer running, for I was exhausted.

How could they possibly manage to reach Ireland by heading away from the sea? I asked myself. It didn't make any sense.

I was following a narrow road, just as badly rutted as the main one that had led westwards. Once again I walked on the grass to the side. The land was beginning to rise; I could see wooded hills ahead and high mountains behind, with snow atop the highest, even though it was still autumn.

After a while I found myself in a dense wood where most of the trees had already shed their leaves. I was wary of another ambush and moved some distance away from the road. It was just a precaution – I was confident that my new ability would provide me with an early warning of any threat. It was as if, like a witch, I could long-sniff future danger.

Then the trees gradually changed, until I was tramping through a forest of tall conifers. I reached the summit of a hill and saw that the land fell away before rising again.

It was then that I glimpsed something in the distance. It stood on the summit of the next hill, rising high above the trees at the end of the muddy road.

It was a dark tower, and the sight of it filled me with unease.

CHAPTER 11
THE DARK TOWER

M y enemies had already disappeared inside, and now the
Fiend's head was in there too.

I studied the tower. Built from big blocks of grey stone, it was
an impressive structure, perhaps twice the height and at least
three times the girth of Malkin Tower, but square, with a flat top
but no battlements. Strangely, high up on the side of the tower
there was a wide balcony and a tall pointed door.

It had no moat, but any attacking force had only one point
of access: a narrow flight of stone steps – two hundred of
them or more – which led up a steep incline to a heavy metal
door. There were arrow slits as well as windows in the

high walls, and climbing those steps would be suicidal.

Hidden by the trees, I made a slow circuit of the building, keeping my distance, and was able to confirm that there was only that one door. Then, after setting some traps for rabbits, I made myself as comfortable as possible on the hilltop facing the steps, and watched and waited.

Late in the afternoon the big door opened with a grinding sound that echoed across the hills, and a party of eight witches emerged and descended the steps. Something about their manner and clothes suggested that they weren't from Pendle. Their skirts were short, hardly covering their knees, and their hair was pulled back from the forehead and braided into a single ponytail behind. They were probably from some unknown clan beyond the County.

Behind them the door closed and I heard heavy bolts being slid back into place.

For a while I was apprehensive. Had they somehow detected my presence? Were they coming for me?

One thing I was immediately sure of – they were not in possession of the head. They passed within half a mile of where I was hiding and continued north. How many did that leave in the tower? I had a sense of a largish group, but exactly how many I couldn't tell.

I had set four traps but, to my disappointment, only one held a rabbit – and a small one at that. I was hungry, but it would have to do. After dark, I descended the northern slope of the hill so that I was out of sight of the tower. Here I lit a small fire and cooked the rabbit, listening to the dripping juice sizzling on the embers.

It was delicious and, feeling better for having eaten, I climbed back up to my original position and kept watch. I intended to do so for just a couple of hours and then snatch some sleep.

As I stared at the tower, I considered what to do after that. My priority was to stop the Fiend's head being reunited with his body. Now that it was in the tower and not on a ship, there was no immediate threat of that happening. But I needed to reclaim it and take it back to the relative safety of Chipenden – which was easier said than done.

Firstly, I was alone. And even if I could somehow climb the steps undetected and reach the metal door, it was locked and bolted. But this must be just a temporary refuge, I thought – maybe while they waited for a passage to Ireland to be organized? Surely they would soon transport the head towards the sea?

I was just about to lie down and try to get some sleep when the moon came out from behind a cloud and bathed the tower in its silver light. Almost simultaneously I heard the sound of a door opening. It wasn't the harsh grating sound of the main door; more of a click – from the door that led out onto the wide balcony. Someone stepped out and approached the balustrade, resting their hands upon it and staring out over the forest.

For a moment I was too astonished to take in what I was seeing. But there was no doubt.

It was Alice.

I stared at her in amazement. Despite the lack of evidence in the tracks, I'd expected her to be held prisoner in the tower – brought here either by the witches, or by Lukrasta (using a different route). But her appearance was a surprise to me.

In the moonlight, she looked radiant, transfigured – almost happy. Her face and slim body had always been beautiful: I remembered the first time I'd seen her at the edge of a wood close to the village. She'd been wearing a tattered black dress tied at the waist with a piece of string.

Now she wore a long dress that seemed to flow down her body like water. It was hard to determine the colour in the pale glow of the moon, but I thought it was black or dark purple silk. Her hair was different too; whereas before it had hung down past her shoulders, now it was lifted away from her forehead and ears and fastened into a bun with a jewelled clasp that glittered in the soft light. And around her neck was a necklace with a locket that hung down over her heart.

She seemed to be looking towards me; I was tempted to wave but a sense of unease held me back. She was a prisoner and couldn't escape from that high balcony. Maybe there were others behind her – guards who were permitting her to take a little air.

Then, as I gazed at her, full of wonder and foreboding, another figure emerged from the open doorway and went to stand beside her on the balcony. It was a tall man with a long moustache that fell below his chin and hooked upwards like two horns. He wore a dark cloak and his long hair hung down his chest in two pigtails.

As he came alongside Alice, he put his left arm across her shoulder. There was something protective and fatherly about the gesture. But then she turned her face up towards his, and seconds later my whole world fell apart, shattered like an icicle falling onto a slab of granite.

They kissed.

CHAPTER 12
THE COFFIN

It was not a fatherly kiss. It went on for a long time, their bodies locked together.

Then the man lifted Alice, holding her under her arms and knees, and carried her back through the door. Moments later, it closed, and there was the distant click of a lock or bolt.

I felt as though I had been punched in the heart. All the breath left my body in a rush and I felt powerless to replace it. At the end of our last meeting, Alice had kissed *me*. I thought that meant something. And now, so soon afterwards, I thought bitterly, she was kissing someone else.

I had no doubt in my mind that I loved Alice; I'd believed

that she felt the same way about me. But I had never really thought about a future together. Spooks do not have wives. They are like priests, who dedicate their lives to God, putting their parishioners first. In the same way, a spook serves the people of the County; his duty is to protect them from the dark. That was what my master had taught me.

However, in some vague way I felt that I would find a way round that. Perhaps when I became the Chipenden Spook, we would marry . . . I had never thought about the future in those terms until now.

Until now, when she was clearly with somebody else . . .

Slowly my shock and bewilderment gave way to rage and jealousy. I couldn't bear the thought of her being in the arms of another. It took all my will power to stop myself from going directly to the tower and calling out a challenge.

After all, what would that achieve? I would get no chance to fight the stranger and take Alice away. Most likely I would lose my life on the steps – or be taken prisoner.

I paced up and down until, after a while, my anger subsided and I began to think about the situation and what it meant.

Was the tall stranger the mage Lukrasta? I had no way of knowing because I had never seen him. But he had put his arm round Alice and seemed to be controlling her. He was tall, powerful and imposing, and there had been an arrogance in his expression. I felt certain it was him.

In my head I began to work through the steps of what had

happened. It seemed to me that, with the aid of Grimalkin, Alice had prepared to use the *Doomdryte*.

Lukrasta was supposed to be dead, having failed to complete the ritual successfully. But somehow he was here, and had enchanted Grimalkin so that she had been unable to repel a simultaneous co-ordinated attack by hordes of witches. Afterwards, she'd been in no condition to give a coherent and detailed account of events, but I felt I could now piece together what might have happened.

Perhaps Lukrasta had used dark magic to control Alice and bring her to this tower? If he could overpower Grimalkin, I was sure he could do the same to Alice. She was not in her right mind. She was no longer in possession of her free will. That's what I told myself. Perhaps she'd had no choice but to kiss him . . .

That thought made me feel better. But it still did not tell me what I might do about the situation.

I tried to sleep, but I was raging inside and was still wide awake when the sun came up.

I felt sick inside, anything but hungry, but I went through the motions and set my traps anyway. Suddenly I remembered what my master had always believed – that it was helpful to fast before facing the dark. Well, this was surely my biggest challenge yet. I should keep up my strength for whatever lay ahead, but I would only nibble on some cheese.

I wondered again how I might get into the tower. Storming

the front entrance was impossible. But could I climb up to the balcony and gain access through the smaller door?

If, despite the odds, I managed to get inside, what would my priority be? It had to be the retrieval of the Fiend's head. But what about Alice? How could I just leave her there in the power of that monster?

Cautiously I moved through the trees and approached the tower, climbing a little way up the hill upon which it was built. I stared up at it. The crevices between the stones might afford hand- and foot-holds. But it would be difficult and very risky. The base was surrounded by boulders and scree. A fall from any but the lower sections of the wall would result in death or serious injury.

Chastened, I retreated down the slope and returned to my original position. There I thought about the stranger again, remembering his arm round Alice, the way they had kissed . . . Try as I might, I could not force the image from my mind. If it *was* Lukrasta, he was a powerful, dangerous mage. The Spook's Bestiary claimed that he had died while attempting the ritual, but it seemed that he had instead completed it.

This was why he had been able to appear before Alice and Grimalkin, taking them by surprise. His power was too terrible to contemplate.

He would have immortality, invulnerability and god-like powers.

Just after noon I saw a party of witches climbing the track

towards the tower. They were on foot, over a score of them, and they had a cart with them. They were making slow progress – the cart's wheels kept getting stuck in the mud, and each time they had to lift it clear.

The nearer they came, the more puzzled I became. The cart was being pulled by a team of six dray horses, which seemed a lot. Usually four heavy horses were sufficient to manage the heaviest loads of coal, stone or barrels of ale. The road was steep in places, and the track muddy and rutted; that might be the explanation, I supposed.

Then I looked more closely at the cart. It was long, with four wheels on each side. It looked as if it had been made specially. Perhaps two carts had been joined together . . .

It was only as it drew nearer that I saw what it carried: a long wooden box. The best materials had been used, and it had brass handles, six on either side, to allow it to be carried.

It was a coffin.

At that realization, my heart began to pound within my chest. This coffin was far bigger than necessary for ordinary human remains. It was at least three times the length of a tall man and twice as broad.

I knew what this meant, but at first my mind simply refused to accept it.

We had always believed that if the Fiend's head was ever recaptured, it would be taken back over the sea to Ireland.

But they had done the reverse.

For in that coffin lay the body of the Fiend.

CHAPTER 13
THE VAST DARK TIDE

E ven as I watched, it was being carried towards the dark tower where the severed head waited.

In some dark magical ritual they would join the head back to the body and he would return to our world, able to do his worst. No doubt he would deal with the Spook, Grimalkin and me first. After all, we were the ones who had hurt him so badly, cutting off his head and binding his body with silver spears. Or perhaps Alice would be his primary target – the daughter who had betrayed him . . . And she was a prisoner in the tower, near at hand.

I wanted to run down the slope and attack the escorting

witches. I knew I would not last long – there were far too many of them for one person to deal with. But at least I would die fighting, and then find my way through Limbo to the light before the agents of the Fiend could reach me. Bone witches could sometimes seize a soul after death as it moved through Limbo and hold it there, torturing it.

Wasn't it better to die now before the Fiend was returned to power? Back in Greece I'd promised him my soul in exchange for a chance to avert a future that would have led to the destruction of the County. Once whole again he would collect my soul on death and torment it for all eternity.

I was in danger. Both my life and my soul were at risk, and I was truly scared.

A surge of anger went through me – anger at myself. I remembered what my master had always told me: duty came first.

Stop thinking about your own situation! I told myself silently. *Think about the people of the County and the world beyond. Put first the interests of those you are bound to protect.*

Yes, I had to put all concerns about my own safety – and that of Alice – out of my mind. The shock of seeing the Fiend's body brought to this place, and the thought of how close he was to regaining power, had jolted me to my senses. I had to focus. I had to do the right thing.

The witches had now reached the foot of the stone steps and I watched as they gathered around the cart and struggled to lift the huge coffin.

I had to be calm and think logically, keeping my emotions at bay. I had to put the image of Alice and Lukrasta out of my mind.

The witches were carrying the Fiend's body up the steps now. The huge door was slowly opening to receive it, filling the air with the sound of metal grating on stone.

I took a pace forward and put my left hand on the hilt of my sword. I could attack and attempt to halt time. If only the head had been in their possession, I could seize it and run. But what could I do with that gigantic body? I could cut it into pieces – but would that make any difference? We'd always considered it too dangerous to destroy the head itself. The Fiend had remained bound because the two parts of his body had been kept intact but separate. According to the Spook, destroying either head, body or both might somehow free the Fiend, enabling him to return to the dark, where he would quickly gather strength and, with the aid of his supporters, return to our world more dangerous and powerful than ever.

As a warning to these supporters, Grimalkin had gouged out one of the Fiend's eyes. She had done it in the heat of the moment; looking back, I realized it had been a very risky thing to do: it might have brought about the very thing that the Spook had feared.

I watched the witches carry the coffin through the huge door. There was another grating sound as it closed behind them.

I had done nothing.

It was over.

The Fiend had won.

* * *

I walked in a daze through the trees, away from the tower, climbing hills and stumbling down into valleys. My mind was numb. I was unable to think. I had no plan, no idea of where I was going.

I had no clear sense of how much time had passed, but eventually I found myself at the summit of a bare, rocky hill, walking through a ruined building. At first I thought it was a farmhouse, but then I noticed a stone altar and a solitary arched window, the glass broken; I realized that this had once been a chapel. I glanced over my shoulder and saw a similar window in the opposite wall, next to where the door had once been.

I looked back at the altar and gazed through the window. I had never felt so low. Terrible things had happened during my time as the Spook's apprentice: the deaths of friends such as Bill Arkwright; threats to my life and, worse, my soul; moments of extreme terror. But somehow this seemed worse.

This was a final defeat – the end of everything.

The witches now had both parts of the Fiend in their possession. How long would it take to restore him?

What had Mab said about the Wardstone?

Creatures of the dark will be drawn to that spot – some to fight for the Fiend, others to oppose him. There'll be witches of every type, abhumans and other dark entities. The outcome of that conflict will change the world.

But for all her skill, she'd been wrong before and might be

wrong again. It could happen here and now in Wales, far from the Wardstone.

No doubt it would require some form of magical ritual. This could take days, hours, or might even be near completion now. The Fiend might come for me at any second. I might never even leave this ruined church.

I looked about me.

This was what some called a house of God. Was there a God? I wondered. A supreme creator? It seemed very unlikely to me. What was it that my master had once said . . . ? That there had been times during his life as a spook when he thought he was facing the end, when it was all up with him. But at these moments he had sensed something invisible standing at his side, lending him strength. That was the nearest he had come to admitting to any kind of faith.

Well, now I felt nothing; nothing at all – I was alone, with nobody to help or advise me.

A memory suddenly came to me: my dad standing in the farmyard, stamping his feet, spattering my breeches with manure and mud, facing the Spook with both bravery and impatience – the latter because he was eager to get back to the milking; the former because most people thought spooks were scary. This was our first meeting with the Spook. An agreement had been reached, and John Gregory had given me a month's trial as his apprentice. Little had any of us known that it would end like this.

What was it that my dad had once said?

Heaven helps those who help themselves.

Well, I'd done my best. I'd *tried* to help myself. But I wasn't getting any assistance in return. There was nothing to guide me, nobody to even offer advice. Entities from the dark banded together, sometimes in large numbers. And what did the light have? Just a few scattered spooks, helpless against the vast dark tide that would soon sweep all goodness aside.

I stared through the window. It was dusk, and the light was beginning to fail, but I could see a village in the distance. Through the trees was a church spire; another church – either an empty shell like this one, or a place where deluded fools banded together to offer useless prayers that were never answered.

I felt a surge of bitter anger, and stepped out of the ruins onto the rocky ground. Advancing a few steps so that I could see the grey slate rooftops below the spire, I spotted something else. It must be quite a large village, I thought – a small town, even; for I could now see another church spire just behind and to the right of the first.

I went forward a few more paces. My heart was starting to beat a little faster as an understanding started to form inside my head. Then I retraced my steps, went back into the chapel and looked through the window.

Once again I could see only one church spire.

That was because the other, more distant, steeple, was hidden *directly* behind it.

They were in perfect alignment.

I spun through 180 degrees and looked back in the opposite direction through the window at the rear of the chapel. I could now see the tower, dark against the red sky above the setting sun.

Now my heart was beating even faster as I turned towards the churches once more; towards the east, where the sun would rise tomorrow, filling the world with light.

Four buildings stood in a straight line: the tower, the ruined chapel and two churches. I knew what that meant. Churches and ancient buildings were often erected in such alignments.

They were ancient tracks; lines of power. Some called them ley lines.

I was actually standing on a ley line and it ran directly through the dark tower.

I *had* been given help after all; I had been shown what I could do.

I had thought myself alone and without any support. But this ley line changed everything.

I had a powerful ally, and the ley line would make it possible for him to reach me.

I could summon the Spook's boggart.

CHAPTER 14
THE SPOOK'S BOGGART

Boggarts used ley lines to travel from one location to another – though they could not stray far from these ancient tracks that crisscrossed the County.

But this tower *was* on a line.

And so was the Spook's house at Chipenden.

The Spook's boggart had left that house after the fire, its agreement with my master at an end. But I had been sent to search for it and issue a new contract. That I had done, and it had since successfully defended the house and garden against an attack by Romanian witches. What I had not told my master was that the new agreement had been made with *me*, not him, and that it had been necessary to offer the boggart more in return for its services.

The boggart had scratched its demands on a piece of timber: *My price is higher this time. You must give me more.*

I'd had to think quickly, but then I'd had a moment of inspiration.

In addition to killing dark things that try to enter the garden, I'd said, I have another task for you. Sometimes when I hunt out creatures of the dark I find myself in extreme danger; then I will summon you to fight by my side. You will be able to slay my enemies and drink their blood! What is your name? I must know your name so that I can call.

The boggart had thought for a long time before replying, and I'd wondered if it was reluctant to reveal its name to anyone. But at last it had scratched it on the wood:

Kratch.

When I am in danger, I will call your name three times! I had told it, and so the pact was made. I had never used its services since because I did not like to leave my master's premises unprotected. But this was an extreme situation: I felt certain that the Spook would agree with my decision to summon the boggart.

It was then, still staring at the alignment of churches, that I reconsidered my fear of imminent attack by the Fiend. I started to think things through carefully, step by step, using the brain I'd been born with.

Back on Pendle, the witches had summoned the Fiend, but they had only been able to accomplish this at a very special time, when dark magic was powerful; they had been forced to wait for Lammas, one of the four main witches' sabbaths. Similarly, they couldn't now simply put head and body together and reanimate him.

Our original plans for the ritual with Alice could not go ahead until a certain time of year; they too would have to wait to perform their own ceremony.

Mab was right after all.

They would have to wait for Halloween!

Circling the tower, I returned to my original position. Now I was free to choose the moment when I would attack.

I was hungry and went to check my snares. I had set four, and all of them held rabbits. I retreated to my previous spot, out of sight of the tower, and lit a fire. I abandoned my resolve to follow my master's advice and just eat cheese before facing the dark. My plans would require energy and physical strength. So I cooked and ate one of the rabbits.

The moon was rising in the east, sending shafts of silver light down through the trees. The moment was right: I summoned the boggart.

First I just whispered his name:

'*Kratch!*'

The air had been very still, but as I spoke, I heard a faint rustle; a breeze was stirring the fallen leaves. I called the name again – but this time much louder.

'*Kratch!!*'

Now the wind was whipping the branches, gaining in power. The last of the crisp autumn leaves fell to join the soggy brown mounds beneath the trees.

The third time, I shouted out the name of the boggart at the top of my voice like a priest calling out to the faithful. I cared nothing for the fact that it might be heard in the tower. Now it was my enemies who would be afraid. My voice resonated through the air so that it seemed to ring like a great bell.

'*KRATCH!*'

In response, the wind surged in from the west, howling like a banshee and almost throwing me off my feet. I staggered back and covered my eyes with my arm to protect my face from the fragments of wood, mud and stones that hurtled between the trees.

And then the gale dropped to nothing. There was silence, the air absolutely still.

Had the boggart responded? I wondered. Was it here?

The silence continued. I held my breath, listening hard.

Still there was nothing.

My heart began to sink into my boots. Had my summons failed?

But then I heard it: the very lightest of treads. Something was approaching from the west, moving very stealthily towards me.

I picked up one of the rabbits and cast it high in the air in the direction the sound was coming from.

I heard the low thud of the carcass hitting the ground. Then came a wet rending noise, as if flesh were being torn apart, followed by the crunch of bones being crushed by powerful jaws.

Now I heard footsteps approaching me again – louder now. *Pad! Pad! Pad!*

Then I heard the swish of a big tail.

I tossed over the second dead rabbit. It was devoured even more quickly.

Again those heavy padding feet, coming towards where I waited; the approach of a confident and deadly creature who didn't need to tread softly. Now only one rabbit remained, and that too I threw.

Why had I given the rabbits to the boggart?

Its reward for answering my summons would be the blood of my enemies, but the rabbits were a first offering to mark our first meeting under the new pact. I had also acted out of fear. I was afraid that the boggart might turn on me. This could well be the final approach of a predator stalking its prey, the moment before it sprang. Perhaps I was the next thing on the menu.

I was scared, and my knees shook violently because we were no longer in the Spook's house or garden; the old pact had endured for many years, made safe by custom and repetition. Now we were out in the open; this was a new and dangerous beginning.

I was truly afraid.

All at once I heard a deep purring and felt a furry animal rubbing against my legs. At this moment the boggart felt no bigger than a normal cat. This was the shape it assumed when carrying out its agreed domestic duties. Perhaps this was what suddenly made me feel brave . . .

I should probably have just spoken to the boggart, telling it what I intended; instead, without thinking, I did something very dangerous – something that would have shocked John Gregory.

He had always kept his distance from the creature.

But I acted from pure instinct.

I knelt down beside that cat-boggart and gently placed my hand upon its head. I could feel its fur, but the body was not warm like that of an animal. It was ice-cold.

Then, very slowly, I stroked it from its head to the tip of its long tail.

In response, the boggart stopped purring and became very still.

Unable to help myself, one part of me watching in astonishment at what I was risking, I repeated the action; once more I stroked it from head to tail.

This time the boggart gave a hiss; as I stroked it for the third time, I realized that its fur was standing up on end, its back arched.

What a fool I'd been. What had come over me? What madness had driven me to do such a thing? I remembered how irascible the boggart could be. On my first morning in the Spook's house I'd come down to breakfast too early and had soon received a blow to the back of the head. My master had warned me that it could have been worse.

What would happen now? I needed the creature on my side.

Gradually the boggart began to glow in the darkness until I could see it clearly. A livid scar ran across its left eye: it had been blinded defending us against a daemonic entity called the Bane. Its remaining eye was a vortex of orange fire.

Now it seemed to be growing larger. My sense of danger grew too. Salt and iron could be effective against such creatures, but I had none in my pockets. I had left everything in my bag back in Chipenden. I had been pursuing witches, and my chosen weapons had been staff, sword and dagger.

Suddenly the boggart struck me a terrible blow and I fell backwards. I was stunned, barely conscious, in pain. It was if a shock wave had passed straight through me.

I was lying on my right side, my left hand stretched out in front of me. I sensed the boggart looming over me. Now it seemed much larger than I was.

Then it struck my left hand. I felt its claws rake my skin. Pain seared into the flesh, running up my arm and into my chest; I feared my heart would stop.

I was rigid with agony. My hand had surely been mangled, the flesh torn, the bones crushed. But I saw in the light of the moon that it was intact, but for a single scratch running across from my little finger to the base of my thumb. As I watched, dark blood welled up from the wound and began to trickle down towards my wrist.

Why had the boggart turned on me? How could I ever hope to understand the motives of such an alien entity? It seemed likely that this was a reaction to my audacity in stroking it – though its response could have been much worse. My hand was still connected to my arm. Perhaps our pact had survived my recklessness?

Suddenly I felt the boggart's huge rough tongue begin to lick the blood from my hand. As it lapped, the pain receded from my body; I closed my eyes and fell into darkness.

I was dragged back to consciousness by a deep rumbling vibration that seemed to shake the ground beneath me. I was lying on my back and there was a cold, heavy weight across my lower legs.

I sat up very slowly and saw in the bright moonlight that the boggart had laid its huge head and paws across my body; the rumbling was its purr – a sound that in a normal cat indicated contentment. For a long time I didn't dare move my legs, even though I had cramp: any movement that disturbed the boggart's comfort might result in another violent reaction.

At last I could stand it no longer. I moved my legs very slightly. Immediately the weight vanished and the boggart disappeared.

I came to my feet and took a deep breath. Had it returned to Chipenden? I wondered. Had it abandoned me?

But then I heard a voice, harsh and sibilant, right inside my head.

I thirst! it hissed insistently. *The rabbits welcomed me, thank you, but were just morsels. Now I need to quench my thirst with human blood. I kept my promise and answered your summons. Now you must provide me with what I need!*

My previous communications with the boggart had been very different: I had spoken and it had understood, but it had scratched its replies on wood. Why had things changed now? Was this another gift inherited from Mam?

I reflected that it might well be connected with the fact that it had drunk my blood.

What are we waiting for? demanded the voice of the boggart. *No human has ever dared touch me before. You are brave! You are worthy to walk with me. Let us kill together!*

It seemed that it was happy with me after all. That was why it had been purring.

'Yes, we'll go together to the tower on the hill where my enemies are lodged!' I replied. 'Help me to defeat them and their blood is yours.'

So saying, I picked up my staff and set off. The boggart was still invisible, but I could hear it padding at my side as we climbed the final hill. I halted just short of the narrow stone steps and drove my staff into the ground.

'I'll climb up to the tower and fight those who emerge,' I told it. 'Then I will retreat slowly, drawing them forth. While I live, do not pass beyond this staff! If I die or fall, then you may attack at will. But when my retreat brings me back below this staff and as many as possible are in the open, that is when I wish you to attack. At that moment you may kill all those both within and without the tower – with the exception of one person. The girl, Alice, whom you know, is not to be harmed. Do you understand and accept?'

I knew that the boggart could enter through the arrow slits and slay the witches; but in the confines of the tower they might be able to combine their magic and fight it off. That was why I needed to surprise them out in the open.

Yes! hissed the boggart. *It is a good plan. They will be easier to hunt and kill out in the open. My thirst will be slaked more rapidly!*

I looked up at the dark tower and the narrow steps that led to the door. With my right hand I drew the sword; with my left the dagger called Bone Cutter.

I began to climb.

The steep stone steps were barely wide enough for two to walk abreast, and that would serve me well. On either side was a sheer drop to the rocks below, so it would be difficult for my enemies to surround me and come at me from behind. Their superiority in numbers would count for little.

I climbed at a steady pace, wondering if I was being watched. Were there eyes hidden behind the arrow slits? I did not expect to be fired upon – witches did not use bows themselves, though they sometimes employed servants to carry out tasks such as cooking . . . and opening the iron gate that I now approached (direct contact with iron was painful for a witch). They might have people to fight for them too – I just had to hope that none of these were bowmen.

Halfway up the steps, I started to wonder if Alice was still in the balcony room. At the thought of her alone in there with the moustached stranger, my anger flared. I tried to banish it from my mind. If I were to succeed in what I was about to attempt I needed a clear head.

I reached the door and paused before it, taking a deep breath to steady myself.

Then I struck it hard, three times, with the hilt of my sword.

The sound of each blow was loud enough to awaken the dead, echoing around from valley to hill again and again. But there was no response. Nothing seemed to be moving within that dark tower.

So I struck the door three more times – harder than before.

All was still and silent. What were the witches doing? Were they gathering behind the door, ready to attack? If so, they could not take me by surprise, for the door was heavy, and opened only slowly.

For the third time I beat on the door with my sword. And this time I shouted out a challenge:

'Come out and fight, cowards! Come out and die! What are you waiting for?'

Perhaps they were watching me through the arrow slits – surely thinking that I was touched with madness. Either that or I had reached such depths of despair that I desired death. For what could one person do against so many enemies? But they did not know about the boggart.

The boggart had defended the Spook's garden for many years. Early in my apprenticeship I'd been pursued by the witch Bony Lizzie and the abhuman Tusk – but I'd reached the sanctuary of the Spook's garden just in time, and the boggart had driven them away. Even a powerful witch like Lizzie had run from it in terror. It had also fought off that powerful daemon called the Bane and, more recently, Romanian witches. It was a force to be reckoned with.

I hoped it would take these witches completely by surprise. It was unlikely that they could discover the specific danger – though some of them had no doubt long-sniffed the future and sensed the threat of death. If this was the case, they might ignore my challenge and stay inside the tower. Then I would have to command the boggart to go in. It might be able to kill many of them before they could fight back with their magic. But that would not open the door for me. The Fiend's head would still be out of reach.

Suddenly there was a harsh sound – the grating of metal upon stone – and slowly the door began to move, no doubt dragged open by the witches' servants. I waited, my blades at the ready. When it was less than a third open, it stopped, and I stared into a darkness that the moonlight could not penetrate. There were eyes glowing in the gloom; the strange wide eyes of witches staring out at me.

All at once my confidence wavered. Fear seized me, filling me with doubts that I had previously thrust to the back of my mind. What if I couldn't carry out my plan? There might be skilled fighters here – perhaps even a witch assassin; someone with the ability to pierce my guard with ease and slay me on the steps.

While I stood there, the door began to open further, pulled by unseen hands. It was almost half open when the first witch attacked. Her hair was long and hung down over her face; it parted to reveal one baleful eye, a hooked nose and the slit of a sneering mouth. She ran straight at me, a long thin blade in her left hand.

I took two rapid steps: the first backwards, moving down; the second to the right.

Her wild swing missed my head by inches. Then I retaliated. I did not use a blade; I simply smashed my left elbow into the side of her head. That and her own momentum carried her over the edge of the steps. She screamed as she fell. Then there was a horrible thud as her body struck the boulders below. I glanced down and saw blood splattered on the rocks, black and wet in the moonlight.

Now my fear was gone. My objective was to retrieve the Fiend's head – and to do so, I first had to clear the steps of witches. Grimalkin had once told me that she fought within the present, living in each moment, without thought of the future. I had to do that now. So I concentrated and stepped into another place where all that mattered was the need to deal with each attack.

Almost immediately, two more witches came for me,

shrieking and spitting curses as they emerged through the door. This time I quickly retreated further down the stone stairs. Although there were two of them, their attack was uncoordinated and they posed little threat. Their blades were easily parried and I thrust quickly with my own. One fell away to the right; the other collapsed sideways across the steps, forcing the next attacker to step over her body.

I continued my descent, fighting my enemies in ones and twos, driving them back, parrying their blows. But inevitably, they started to advance in larger numbers – perhaps eight or nine emerged at once from behind the iron door. Faced with this, I turned and ran – though halfway down the steps I halted, spun suddenly and readied my blades. They were many and I was but one. Yet barely two could attack me together; the others must wait behind while I despatched their vanguard.

But they were not helpless; while I fought those closest to me, the others gathered their collective strength and began to use their magic. Their faces distorted and became daemonic; their hair clustered into coils of writhing snakes; forked tongues spat poison towards me. I knew it was an illusion – part of the common witch spell known as *Dread*.

A seventh son of a seventh son has some immunity against the dark magic of witches; but this is not totally effective. The illusions soon faded, but the force of their magic filled me with a fear that was more difficult to banish. It also repelled me: I was pushed backwards as if by a great wind, struggling to stand my ground.

I gritted my teeth and fought on, and as I gathered my own strength and rallied, the ruby eyes in both sword and dagger began to drip blood that was far redder than that which now streaked the blades. I regained control; my retreat was once again slow and steady, as I had planned, even though more and more witches came hurrying out above me.

Soon there were fewer than twenty steps remaining before I reached the ground and passed beyond my staff, at which point the boggart would attack. But then I heard a noise from above – the click that I remembered from the previous night. And out onto that high balcony came Alice and the tall moustached stranger whom I took to be Lukrasta, the dark mage of the *Doomdryte*.

At that moment the witch to my left thrust her blade towards my shoulder with such speed that I could not avoid it completely. The distraction from above almost cost me dear, but just in time I twisted away, and the stinging cut I received was shallow. I swung with the sword and toppled the witch from the steps.

After that I dared not glance upwards again, but I could feel the eyes of Alice and the mage on me. I continued down, growing more tired with every step. My arms felt heavy, my breathing ragged as I struggled against the press of witches. I was aware of other cuts; two to my forearms and one to my left shoulder. If I stumbled and fell, it would be all over – though at least I'd have the small satisfaction of knowing that the boggart would attack immediately; there were enough witches out in the open now to make that devastating. But nevertheless I would have failed. My pact with the boggart would end, the Spook's Chipenden house would be once more unprotected . . . and at Halloween servants of the dark would converge from every direction to join the head of the Fiend to his body and return him to power.

I was struck by a sudden blow, and for a second was blinded. I swayed but did not fall. The attack had not been mounted by one of the witches. In a flash of fear I knew that it came from the balcony above. Some kind of magical force had been deployed against me. It had to be the mage – for surely it couldn't have been Alice . . . she wouldn't try to hurt me, I thought. But perhaps she was not in her right mind . . . In that case I would be in danger.

Despite the risk, I glanced upwards and saw an orb of orange fire hurtling towards me from the balcony. I ducked – just in time! Had I not done so it would have taken off my head.

Faced with this new threat, I decided to turn and run down the final steps. As I passed beyond my staff, I looked back at the steps. Instantly I heard a low purr and felt the invisible boggart rub itself against my left ankle. Then it spoke to me right inside my head, as before.

You fought well and executed a perfect plan. Most of them are out in the open. I thank you for this feast of blood!

A TIDE OF BLOOD

The boggart suddenly made itself visible.

It no longer took the shape it sometimes showed to us back in Chipenden – that of a small domestic ginger tom-cat; the creature that had just rubbed itself against my ankle. Earlier I had thought it scary when I felt its large body lying across my legs, but now it was fearsome indeed.

It was *huge*; even on all fours its muscular shoulders were at least two feet taller than my head. It was still cat-like in shape, but now its face was daemonic, its canine teeth protruding from both upper and lower jaws; its stripy ginger fur stood up on end like the quills of a hedgehog; and its right eye was a glowing orb of fire.

All at once it gave a terrible howl that halted the witches in mid-stride. No words were articulated either out loud or within my head, but the message was clear:

The hour of your death has arrived! it seemed to say. *I will crunch your bones and drink your blood and there is nothing you can do to prevent it!*

Then the boggart attacked. As it sprang towards the steps, the witches turned and fled, shrieking in their terror. Their frantic retreat was uncoordinated; the ones nearest to the open door did not turn fast enough. Witch collided with witch, and some fell onto the rocks below.

I saw the boggart swipe one with its paw then bite her head from her body. But it was already losing definition; the monstrous cat was changing into a vortex of orange energy that spiralled upwards into the mass of witches, filling the air with a mist of blood and tiny fragments of bone.

It took less than three seconds for the boggart to kill all those on the steps and enter the tower through the open door. Then there was an eerie silence – for there were no witches left to scream. There were no bodies to be seen, either. A tide of blood was flowing down the steps, carrying with it dozens of pairs of pointy shoes.

I ran up towards the door, twice almost slipping in the blood. At the top I paused before entering very cautiously, for I could now hear shouts and screams from within.

In a second, inner doorway lay a severed head, twice the size of a human one; it belonged to an abhuman – I saw the horns jutting from its forehead, the open mouth crammed with teeth. Its eyes were open and they stared up at me with a puzzled expression, as if the creature was wondering what had happened to its body.

I stepped over it and went through the doorway. The vast space ahead of me was flagged and devoid of furniture, but for two items. The first was the huge coffin, which had been placed on the floor beneath a wide mullioned window. It was empty.

The second was a long wooden table. Lying upon it was the huge body of the Fiend. For a moment I thought that the head had already been attached and I ran forward in alarm, my sword at the ready, but I soon saw that this wasn't the case.

It was positioned precisely, the two stumps in perfect alignment. And I could see evidence of new growth: tendrils of fleshy roots were reaching out, as if to link together, binding head to neck. It was the slow beginning of a process that would be completed at Halloween.

One of the Fiend's eyes was a ruin, thanks to Grimalkin's blade, but the other was intact, and the lid slowly opened and that remaining eye stared out at me. And then the mouth opened to reveal the yellow stumps of broken teeth – another blow from Grimalkin.

'You cannot win!' The Fiend's voice was hardly more than a croak. 'My servants are too many. Hundreds of them are even now converging upon this place. Any small triumph you achieve here will be short-lived. Flee while you can!'

There was no point in replying; so, wasting no time, I grabbed the head and attempted to tug it away from the body. I pulled hard, but something was holding it in place. Then I noticed that some of the tendrils behind the ears had advanced further than the ones I'd first noticed. They had formed bonds between head and neck. I would need to cut them away. So I drew the dagger called Bone Cutter and readied its blade.

'*You have lost Alice to the dark,*' continued the Fiend.

I knew he was trying to distract me, maybe to buy time so that someone else could intervene on his behalf – perhaps Lukrasta – and I knew I should ignore the bait, but I replied before I could stop myself.

'I will end the life of the mage, and with it the enchantment that gives him power over her,' I snapped back angrily.

'*He uses no enchantment!*' cried the Fiend, his voice filled with triumph and growing in strength. '*By her choice she is his. By his choice he is hers. He is a dark mage and she a malevolent witch. They are a perfect pair and delight in each other's company! She met him for the first time when she attempted the ritual. From the moment their eyes beheld each other they were bound together for all time.*'

Fear and dismay filled me. The Fiend was sometimes called the Father of Lies; I knew that, but I could not get his words out of my mind. What if he was speaking the truth for once? What if Alice's trip into the dark, followed soon afterwards by her willingness to attempt the *Doomdryte* ritual, had finally turned her into a malevolent witch?

Savagely I cut away the fleshy strands that held the head to the body and snatched it aloft. Then, carrying it by the hair, I ran through another door and came to a spiral staircase. As I climbed, I passed door after door, all of them open.

I could tell which rooms had been occupied. The flagged floors were slick with blood. At last I reached the one where Alice and Lukrasta had been: an inner door was open, revealing the balcony beyond. There was no blood on the flags. Had Kratch been thwarted here – halted or even destroyed by the power of the mage?

I entered the room cautiously, my heart beating quickly. It was empty, but there was evidence that it had been occupied. On a dressing table lay a small mirror, a comb and a hairbrush. In the very centre of the room stood a large double bed; it was clear that it had been slept in. And then I noticed something on one of the pillows: a folded piece of paper. I placed the Fiend's head on the dressing table, walked across to the bed and snatched up the paper.

I recognized Alice's handwriting immediately, and began to read. It was a note to me.

Dear Tom,
We now belong to different worlds. We were friends once, but now that friendship must come to an end: we can never see each other again. I bear you no malice, but I cannot help you again because now I belong to the dark.

Alice

As I read it again, my hands began to shake. I couldn't believe what I was reading. Perhaps it was a forgery? I thought. It certainly looked like Alice's handwriting, but Alice would never have written such a letter.

The truth was staring me in the face: the Alice I had known no longer existed.

It was something that I had always feared, and now it had finally happened. I felt the bile rise into my throat as my insides twisted.

Alice had gone to the dark.

I stuffed the letter into my breeches pocket, picked up the Fiend's head and ran up the remainder of the stairs, checking in every room. I soon reached the top. There was no sign of Lukrasta or Alice, but I saw blood in two more of the rooms. The boggart might have slain the mage, but it was a creature of its word, bound by the pact between us, so I felt confident that it would have spared Alice.

I had not seen her leave the tower. So what had happened? Was she somewhere close by, cloaked by dark magic, watching me?

Slowly I turned and began to descend the steps. All was silent. Nothing moved. There was no sign of the boggart, either. Having feasted well, it had no doubt returned to Chipenden. I owed it my life.

Then I remembered the Fiend's words – that hundreds more of his servants would be converging on this place. I knew this was more than likely, so I hurried out of the main door. My eyes swept the horizon, but I could see no one. I continued down the steps, snatched up my staff and ran east, clutching the huge head.

I had it in my possession, but only half of my task was completed; now I had to get it back to Chipenden.

CHAPTER
17
THE DARK RIDER

I stopped briefly to quench my thirst at a stream that crossed my path, scooping the water up into my mouth. I looked round, continually fearful of attack from behind. I'd been travelling for more than two days now and had barely slept or eaten. The wounds I'd suffered were slight and I'd lost little blood, but I was sore and very close to exhaustion.

My enemies were following me, some walking parallel to me, hidden amongst the trees. When I halted, I heard the crunch of their feet and the frequent snapping of twigs.

They made no attempt to conceal their presence; I assumed they were certain of ultimate victory. They might decide to rush me at any time, but perhaps they felt they didn't need to. I was still many miles from the relative safety of Chipenden; soon I would be too weak to take another step.

The Fiend's head, which I held by its hair, seemed to be getting heavier by the minute. I stumbled out of the trees onto a vast, featureless, grassy plain, and in the moonlight saw perhaps a hundred servants of the Fiend ahead of me in the far distance. They were waiting in groups of five or six, and as they caught sight of me, they began to advance. They walked slowly. They were still in no rush, but they had evidently decided to finish it now.

Mostly they were witches in long tattered gowns, but amongst them were larger, bulkier creatures. At this distance I could not be sure, but I assumed they were abhumans, creatures born of witches and fathered by the Fiend. They were strong and ferocious, and I remembered my first encounter with such a creature. His name had been Tusk and he had finally been slain by my master.

How I wished my master were standing beside me; not the man with failing health whom I had left behind in Chipenden, but the strong, formidable Spook who had first collected me from my family's farm to train as his apprentice. I felt absolutely alone. I had come so far only to fail.

Then I thought of Alice; the image of her kissing the mage came unbidden into my mind. All the previous memories I had of her – the dangers we'd faced, the adventures we'd shared; our conversations and feelings of warmth and friendship – were eclipsed by that. I felt bitter and angry.

I could now hear footsteps closing in behind me. More figures emerged from the trees on each side. I was surrounded.

I would die here, but I resolved to take as many of these creatures with me as possible. A cold rage began to fill me as I reflected that not only had Alice betrayed me; after all those years of training to be a spook, I would never become one. It seemed so unfair.

But I took a deep breath and thrust those thoughts of injustice, betrayal and despair out of my mind, for they threatened to overwhelm me. I was a spook's apprentice and here, facing my last battle, I would leave the sword and dagger in their scabbards. I would take up my staff, as John Gregory had first taught me.

As I glanced about me, attempting to judge which of these denizens of the dark would reach me first, out of the corner of my eye I saw a figure on horseback approaching at a canter; a dark rider, clothes black like the horse.

I turned to face my first opponent, wondering who it could be, mounted like that. Witches didn't usually ride horses. But then I remembered how Wurmalde had led a horde of Pendle witches to loot the farm, capture my brother and his family and steal Mam's boxes; she had come on horseback. So, although unlikely, it could be a witch.

Perhaps it was the mage Lukrasta. Maybe this was my chance to save Alice from his dominance. If I could kill him before the others reached me, I might somehow be able to reclaim her from the dark.

It was then that I noticed something strange. The figure sat very upright, with legs that gripped the horse oddly. There was no saddle; the rider was tied to the horse with a number of leather straps that passed underneath its belly.

At that moment I realized who it was.

Grimalkin!

She brought her mount to a halt at my side and smiled at me without showing her teeth. My heart soared, filling with sudden hope. Perhaps I could escape after all.

'You have done well!' she cried, pointing to the Fiend's head.

She took it by the hair and tied it to the leather straps before bidding me to mount up behind her. I handed her my staff while I struggled onto its back. I glanced round as I did so, hearing cries of anger and seeing that some of the witches were now running towards us.

Once I was in position, Grimalkin gave me back my staff and drew two of her blades. Then, without further ado, she rode straight for our advancing enemies.

As we galloped through the line, her blades flashed in the moonlight. Howls of anger and pain filled the night sky. The only horses I had ever ridden had been heavy shire ones used for ploughing, so with one hand I clung to Grimalkin, fearful of falling. Nevertheless I managed to stab my staff downwards with the other, helping to fend off the witches.

Soon we were through, and riding north towards Chipenden. As we rode a strong stench of urine filled my nostrils. That was little wonder. No doubt Grimalkin had ridden for over a day to reach me and she would have been unable to dismount. I thought of her broken leg and remembered the terrible sight of the bone jutting through the flesh. I knew that she must be in terrible pain.

At dawn we halted at the edge of a dense wood; saplings fought for space and light below the mature trees. We could hear the roar of water nearby.

I dismounted and, using my blades, cut a path down to a fast-flowing stream. It took a long time because I was so weak; all I really wanted to do was sleep. From the bank I looked up and saw, high above, a waterfall crashing down into the torrent. There was also a rocky ledge beside it, where a few of the saplings had been able to take root. I decided to make camp there.

First Grimalkin used her magic to cloak our hiding place. Then I untied her legs and helped her down from the horse. To my surprise she was able to stand, but walked with a bad limp. The Fiend's head was still was attached to the horse, along with a bag of oats, which she fed to the animal. Meanwhile I went off to find sustenance for us. It would have to be rabbits again.

Wearily, struggling to stay awake, I set traps on the edge of the thickets; within an hour I had snared two plump rabbits. When I carried them back to our hiding place, I halted in surprise and confusion. Grimalkin was standing naked beneath the waterfall, scrubbing the dirt from her body.

'I'm sorry,' I muttered, turning my back in embarrassment.

I heard her step out of the cascading water and take two steps towards me, squeezing the water out of her hair. Then there was a rustling sound and I knew that she was pulling on her dress again.

'There is nothing wrong with nakedness,' she said softly. 'But this body has been badly damaged and must be healed if I am ever to fight again as I once did. Turn and look at my leg.'

I did as she asked. It was twisted and withered, the muscle wasted away. I could see why she limped.

'I healed the flesh and bone with my magic so that I could ride to your assistance. Your master did his best to set it, but he is not a bone surgeon. It will be necessary to break the leg again and begin the process anew. Once we are back at Chipenden, will you help me to do that?'

'Of course I will,' I promised, wondering what my part would be. I shuddered at the thought of helping to break her leg again, but how could I refuse?

'Good – now you wash the dirt from your own body. You needn't be shy. I will be busy cooking our breakfast.'

I waded in under the cascade, the cold water making me gasp and reviving me. Afterwards we sat before the embers of the fire and ate the succulent rabbits. I didn't have much appetite after all that had happened, but I forced the food down. I needed to keep up my strength; it was still many miles back to Chipenden and I didn't know when I'd next get a chance to eat.

I told Grimalkin about the tower. 'That's where I found the head. Alice was inside too; she was with Lukrasta.'

'My magic told me something of what occurred, but I would like the details, and from your own lips. Afterwards I will tell you what I know.'

I nodded and began my tale, starting with my pursuit of the witches. When I told her of the team of horses drawing the long coffin that contained the Fiend's body, her eyes widened in surprise.

'I did not see that!' she exclaimed. 'I should have been aware of the danger the moment they withdrew the silver spears from his body. I cast a spell upon them – I should have been alerted the moment they were touched. Very powerful magic has been used here. It must indeed be Lukrasta.'

I continued my story, describing how I had summoned the boggart to assist me; how I had retreated down the tower steps, and how Kratch had attacked, killing all in sight as well as those inside. Yet I did not tell Grimalkin the boggart's name. I held that back, for it was knowledge that only the boggart and I should share.

Finally I described how I'd seen Alice on the balcony with Lukrasta but had later found their room empty.

'They had shared a bed.' I was bitter, hearing the wobble in my voice. 'She wants to be with him . . .' It hurt me to say that aloud, but in a strange way it eased my pain to have it out in the open.

I passed Alice's note to Grimalkin. She read it quickly, then handed it back.

'Do you think she's in her right mind?' I asked her.

'Does Lukrasta control her by the use of dark magic?'

It was a long time before Grimalkin replied. At last she shook her head sadly. 'I am sorry, Tom. What has happened is my fault. I made a mistake – the second most important mistake of my life.'

Her greatest mistake was no doubt sleeping with the Fiend and having to suffer the consequences. He had slain her new-born baby, dashing his brains out against a rock.

'I meant well,' she continued. 'I wanted to avoid a ritual that demanded the sacrifice of Alice, whom I have always liked and respected. She is brave and has great potential, so I tried to find another way. Then, by chance, when I was in Todmorden, despatching the last of the vampiric entities there, I found the *Doomdryte*. I promised you that I would follow John Gregory's wishes and destroy it, but when it came into my hands, I lied and said I could not find it.

'You see, I believed that Alice was powerful enough to use that grimoire to complete the ritual. The power gained from it, when added to her own innate ability, would have been enough to destroy the Fiend. I waited for her to return from the dark, and then we hid in the cottage near Chipenden while we readied ourselves for what had to be done. But as I said, I made a big mistake. Lukrasta was supposed to have died when he failed to complete the ritual. That was a lie he spread around so that others would not seek to do the same and gain power equal to his own. No sooner had Alice opened the book than Lukrasta appeared in the room beside us. I think he must have touched it with his magic so that he could be warned of any such attempt.'

'Did the other witches attack at the same moment?'

'Yes – within minutes of his appearance. When Lukrasta first materialized, I attempted to use my blades against him, but his magic was so powerful that I could not even move. I told you previously that I did not know what happened to Alice . . . forgive me . . . that was a white lie to save your feelings. Now I must tell you the truth. I thought that Alice would try to use her own magic to defend us, but she just stared at him, an expression of wonder on her face. Then they smiled at each other and embraced.'

My heart plummeted and emotion constricted my throat.

Grimalkin stared at me and shook her head. 'I am sorry, but you needed to know. It was as if Alice and Lukrasta had found one another after a long search. It seemed that they were soul mates who recognized each other in an instant; who had always been meant to be together. Take my advice, Tom, and put Alice from your mind.'

I could not speak, and tears welled in my eyes. If Grimalkin noted that, she did not show it but simply continued with her tale.

'I was paralysed and in a trance, completely in thrall to the mage. Lukrasta wanted to kill me – I cannot remember what was said because my mind was befuddled, but I think Alice pleaded for my life. He also wanted to take the Fiend's head with him, but again Alice opposed him. She said it was better to let the other witches collect it. There were already many on their way and I would be unable to fight them all off. She was eager to get away and he seemed to be of a similar mind. And then they both simply vanished into thin air. I finally found the strength to climb to my feet, but before I could get away from the cottage the Fiend's servants attacked.

'Three times I fought them off; I almost broke through their lines and escaped. But I was still suffering from the effects of Lukrasta's magic and I was not at my best. At last I was forced to retreat into the cottage. An abhuman wielding a heavy club struck me a terrible blow, breaking my leg. I fought on from my knees, but then they managed to snatch the leather sack and it was all over. They had what they wanted – the Fiend's head – and thought that I was dying anyway. So they left me kneeling in a pool of my own blood and fled.

'I thought that my time on earth had finally come to an end, but then you and your master found me. So I live to fight again. You have done well to retrieve the head.'

'But what chance do we have against Lukrasta? What powers does he have that make him so strong?'

'The power gained by one who has completed the ritual successfully is no doubt great. But I do not believe that it makes you a god. When Lukrasta attacked, I could do nothing against him, but that was partly because I was taken completely by surprise. Next time I will be ready, and I already know one way in which his magic might be neutralized. I need time to think about all this – time to prepare so that we may yet prove victorious.'

'We will win!' I exclaimed. 'We *have* to win!'

Yes, I thought to myself, we might still triumph over the Fiend and his servants. We might win.

But I had lost Alice.

A s we set off for Chipenden again, Grimalkin no longer needed to be tied to the horse. But although she said nothing, I could see that she was in pain.

We completed the journey without having to engage any of our enemies. Once, we saw a large party of witches in the distance, heading in the same direction as us, but we soon left them behind.

Eventually the grey roofs of Chipenden were visible, and shortly afterwards we arrived at the boundary of the Spook's garden. I heard a low growl from the shrubs that bordered the first of the trees. Kratch was safely back and was challenging Grimalkin.

After calling out to the boggart that I was bringing Grimalkin with me, we rode up to the front door. My master came out to greet us, an expression of relief on his face; he nodded with satisfaction at the sight of the Fiend's head once more in Grimalkin's possession.

'You've both done well!' he exclaimed. 'I hardly dared hope that you'd succeed!'

'It is your apprentice who deserves the credit,' Grimalkin replied. 'Tom Ward retrieved the head in the face of great odds. I merely escorted him back. However, our enemies are out there in force and heading this way.'

'Glad to see you back safely, lad,' said the Spook, turning to me. 'I must say I've been worried. But I kept myself busy. I was called to sort out a boggart south of Scorton. Managed to persuade it to move on from the cottage it had been plaguing.'

I smiled at my master. It was good to see him engaging in spook's business again.

After I had dismounted, Grimalkin slid down too and walked back and forth, her limp pronounced.

'You've healed rapidly,' said the Spook. 'It's only days since I tied you onto your horse.'

'The fast healing was necessary, but now the leg needs to be broken and reset. I would like to build a small forge in the garden,' the witch assassin told him.

'By all means do what you think necessary. Will you be forging new weapons?' he asked her.

'Yes, that too – but my other need is more urgent.

I must repair my leg and restore it to full strength.'

The Spook glanced at me with a puzzled expression. Neither of us saw the connection between the forge and healing her leg, but as Grimalkin offered no further explanation, we did not pursue it. As she limped away, leading her horse to graze upon the lush grass of the western garden, my master placed his arm round my shoulders in a fatherly way and smiled.

'We need to talk, lad. Let's go up to the library.'

The shelves were still mostly empty, but there were a few recent additions. I went across and examined one at random. It was entitled: *The Flora and Fauna of the North County.*

'That's one of Bill Arkwright's books, isn't it?' I asked, tapping its spine. I remembered seeing it in his library when I'd spent six months training with him. Of course, Bill had died in Greece, and Judd Brinscall was now operating north of Caster.

'Aye, lad, it is. I've got his notebooks here as well – apart from a couple which deal exclusively with water witches, which will be needed at the water mill. Judd brought them. He thought they were suffering from damp and mildew, so they would do better here.'

'Well, we've another book to talk about . . .' I began, my heart sinking.

'The *Doomdryte* – aye, Grimalkin told me what she did. That book should have been burned. Now it will do untold harm. She mentioned Lukrasta too. It seems as if the girl Alice has finally gone to the dark.'

I nodded, trying to control my emotions, not knowing what to say.

'Sit yourself down, lad,' my master said, pointing to a chair. 'Tell me how you managed to get the Fiend's head back from all those witches. That was quite some feat. Start at the beginning and don't miss anything out.'

So I sat down opposite him and told my tale for the second time, explaining about the dream I'd had and the latest of the gifts I'd inherited from Mam. When I came to the part about summoning Kratch, my master raised his eyes in astonishment. I knew that I would now have to tell him about my pact with the boggart. I was sick to death of all the lies and deceits; I truly wished that I had always been honest with my master. Although painful, it was a relief to get everything off my chest.

'I never even knew that it had left,' he said. 'I didn't ask you the details of the new pact you made with it, lad. Do you know why?'

I shook my head.

'Because I suspected that it would have made the agreement with *you* rather than me. You have a future ahead and long years to work together, whereas my life is almost done. I wasn't ready to face it: I didn't want to hear the words that confirmed my suspicions, so I kept quiet. But now I'm more settled in my mind and prepared to bow to the inevitable. So come on, lad. Spit it out. Tell me the details.'

So I told him how Kratch had agreed to come to my aid if summoned and in return could drink the blood of my enemies.

Then I described how it had killed the witches below the tower, and how the waterfall of blood had brought dozens of pointy shoes to the foot of the steps.

But I left some things out. I didn't tell him I'd stroked the creature; nor that I'd given it some of my blood. I knew he wouldn't approve of that. So for all my new resolutions, I still found it impossible to be completely honest with him.

I went on to tell him about Alice and Lukrasta, and chose that moment to hand Alice's note over. I paused while he read it. He handed it back without a word, and I continued my tale, finishing with my rescue by Grimalkin.

'What do you think will happen now?' the Spook asked, getting to his feet and pacing up and down in front of me.

'I'll never see Alice again,' I replied. 'Or if I do, she'll be a stranger to me – maybe even an enemy.'

'Forget the girl!' he said, his voice full of anger. 'I meant the larger, more important, picture. What will the witches do?'

I shrugged. 'They might try to enter the garden and seize their master's head again. We took them by surprise last time, but now they've seen what the boggart can do. No doubt they'll join together and use their magic collectively. That could be a threat. The boggart's power is not unlimited.'

'Aye, that's true enough, lad – we saw that for ourselves when it fought off the Bane. Not only that, Lukrasta himself might come here – and who knows what he's capable of! They say that completing the ritual from that grimoire gives you unlimited power. Well, I find that difficult to believe, but if it achieves just a fraction of that, then we'll be hard-pressed. We know how formidable Grimalkin is, and even she was helpless when confronted by him.'

It was then that I remembered something about my fight with the witches on the tower steps.

'When I was trying to lure as many witches as possible out into the open, Lukrasta came out onto the balcony with Alice and stared down at me. Then he hurled some sort of magical energy at me. I felt the blow and it hurt me. But why, if he's so powerful, wasn't I slain on the spot?'

It was something that I'd been thinking about on the way home. Was it because I was a seventh son of a seventh son and had lamia blood in me? Then it struck me that it might have been Alice rather than Lukrasta who had launched the attack. I didn't want to even think about that, and thrust it from my mind.

The Spook scratched at his beard – a few white flakes of dandruff speckled his black gown. 'My guess is that what *you* are is significant. It might well be that you have some resistance to his kind of dark magecraft.'

I nodded. My master and I agreed. It was a possibility. There were many things that I'd inherited from Mam: the ability to slow or stop time; the knowledge that someone was close to death; and, most recently, locating a threat from a distance, which had enabled me to follow the witches and find the Fiend's head.

'There's something else the witches might do,' I added after a moment's reflection. 'They're heading this way, drawn towards the head. I think they'll bring his body too so that it'll be close at hand at Halloween: midnight on that witches' sabbath – the most powerful feast of all for creatures of the dark – that's when they'll hope to join the two pieces of his flesh together and return him to power.'

'Aye, lad, you're correct about the day. It was at midnight on the witches' Lammas sabbath, high on Pendle, that they summoned him to our world. It's likely that they'll use Halloween, the most important and propitious dark feast of them all, to repair the damage we've done and attempt to ensure his victory over the light. But it may not be at midnight. Sunset is another time when dark spells have increased power – the moment when daylight prepares to give way to darkness.'

After dark I carried a candle upstairs to my old room. Grimalkin was happy to sleep in the garden, by the forge she was building.

Everything in the room had been replaced: the floorboards, the bed, the dressing table and the curtains. There was just one thing that remained; something that I had first examined on the very first night I'd spent in the Spook's house.

Three walls had been newly plastered, but the fourth had not, despite the fact that it was slightly blackened by smoke. My master had left it intact because upon that wall were thirty names, including my own. They were the names of the apprentices he had trained or, in most cases, begun to train.

Over a third of them, including my predecessor, Billy Bradley, had died violent deaths while learning the trade. One at least had gone to the dark, while many others had simply not completed their time. I had met three who had: Father Stocks, Bill Arkwright and, most recently, Judd Brinscall.

I examined my own name and remembered how, on that first night, it had seemed presumptuous to write on the wall. Only later had I screwed up enough courage to do so. I'd searched for a space before adding my name to the preceding ones. It seemed so long ago now; so much had happened since that time.

As I thought of my master again, I sensed that things really were coming to an end. Ever since he'd made his will with the solicitor, Mr Potts, I'd become more and more sure that I would be his last apprentice.

After all, as my master had recently reminded me, Mam had made that prophecy in a letter soon after I was born . . .

Thoughts of Mam brought Alice to mind again. Mam had had a lot of time for Alice, but even she had been uncertain how she'd end up. Her words stuck in my mind.

That girl could be the bane of your life, a blight, a poison on everything you do. Or she might turn out to be the best and strongest friend you'll ever have. Someone who'll make all the difference in the world. I just don't know which way it will go. I can't see it, no matter how hard I try.

Well, now I knew which way it had gone. All false hope had left me. Alice had indeed gone to the dark.

I set my candle down on the dressing table and then started to undress, starting with my shirt. Suddenly my gaze was drawn to my left forearm.

The mark of Alice's fingernails had vanished. Years ago, on the night Mother Malkin had been destroyed, she had dug them into my skin and drawn blood. She'd called it her 'brand'. It had served me well when Mab Mouldheel had tried her magic on me; it had kept me safe.

Alice had told me that it would never fade . . . But now, suddenly, it was gone!

Did this mean that the bond between me and Alice was finally broken?

During one of our first conversations, the Spook had said something to me that I had found both annoying and offensive:

Never trust a woman!

I learned afterwards why he had given me that strange advice. The love of his life had been Meg, a lamia witch, and she had caused him all sorts of problems. And now history had repeated itself.

When I first met her, Alice was already being trained in witchcraft by Bony Lizzie. She'd used magic to protect us both against the Fiend – that was true enough. But from the start she had driven a wedge between me and my master: I had lied or withheld information from him on numerous occasions.

Yes, he had been right all along. I should have listened to his advice.

I should never have trusted Alice Deane.

CHAPTER 19
A PRICE TO BE PAID

I blew out the candle and crawled into bed, feeling miserable and lonely. Sleep proved impossible, and a couple of hours before dawn I got up, stretched my limbs, yawned, and then restlessly paced back and forth across the floorboards of my small bedroom.

After a while I heard a noise outside and peered through the sash window. The eight thick panes of glass obscured my view out into the darkness, so I raised the bottom half of the window. It glided up easily; the carpenter had done a good job. Instantly, cold October air wafted in, making me shiver. I couldn't see much, but I could certainly hear something: I recognized it as the sound of a hammer on metal.

It had to be Grimalkin. She was nowhere in sight, but I decided to go and talk to her and find out more about how she intended to fix her leg, so I got dressed, pulled on my boots and went downstairs.

I went out through the back door and headed towards the noise, which came from the eastern garden, where the dead witches were buried. It was not a place to venture after dark: anyone else would have worked closer to the house or in the pleasant western garden where I sometimes sat for my lessons; they'd have worked during daylight too. However, I doubted whether a few dead witches would bother a powerful witch like Grimalkin. Though the moon was gibbous and the main garden was well-illuminated with its silver light, it was very dark beneath the trees, and I moved forward cautiously. I passed a gravestone; below it was a patch of earth edged with stones linked by thirteen iron bars. It was the grave of a dead witch – the bars were to stop her crawling out.

I saw a light ahead and realized that it came from a small forge: the anvil was set upon a bed of stones; leaning against it were a number of smith's hammers. The forge itself was also constructed of stones, and the witch assassin was crouched before it, holding the hilt of a blade with a pair of tongs.

Close by her side was a hessian sack, the lower half stained with blood – no doubt the Fiend's head lay within it.

I watched as Grimalkin quickly withdrew the blade, then thrust it back, sending up a shower of sparks from the mouth of the forge.

I knew that she made different sorts of blade. The short ones were throwing daggers; the others were for fighting at close quarters. But I had never seen one this long. It looked more like a sword.

Suddenly she spun round and rose to her feet, walking towards me purposefully. She didn't seem surprised to see me; I realized she'd known I was there, watching her work, all along. I felt nervous – until she smiled, her lips covering her pointy teeth.

'I'll leave the blade to heat up for while,' she said. 'Let's walk. I have a few things to tell you.'

Snatching up the sack, Grimalkin headed out of the trees and away from the dead witches. I followed her across the central lawn towards the western garden. Here, by the bench, she paused and stared at me, her eyes glittering in the moonlight.

I was about to ask about her leg, but she pre-empted my question.

'Tomorrow night I want you to assist me. I intend to break my leg and reset it. I will then drill two holes in the bone and join the sections together with a silver pin.'

'You're going to use silver?' I exclaimed in astonishment. Witches could be bound with silver; it was the most potent weapon against them. It caused them intense pain.

'It is a necessary part of the magic,' the witch assassin replied. 'With a powerful spell of healing, the silver will join the bone and hasten the new growth of flesh and muscle. It will return my leg to its former state. But there is always a price to be paid:

sometimes the bill does not come for years; in this case it will arrive immediately. The embedding of the silver pin in my leg will cause me agony.'

'Will the pain fade in time? How long will you have to endure it?' I asked.

'It will last until the moment of my death,' Grimalkin murmured.

'But then how will you manage to function?' I asked.

'There are disciplines of the mind that I have long practised. For example, by a concentrated effort of will, I am able to cross running water – something that is impossible for most witches. The pain is still there, but I can push it into the background. Eventually I will learn to cope with a silver pin.'

'I can't imagine doing that . . .' I told her.

'It is difficult, but if I wish to continue to be a witch assassin, it must be done. Come to the southern garden tomorrow night, an hour after sunset. I will have already done the preparatory work – but to insert the pin into my own leg will be beyond me. It is for this, the final stage of the task, that I need your help.'

I agreed to do what she asked, but I wondered why she had chosen the southern garden, which was where the Spook had bound a number of boggarts.

The following day was uneventful. In the afternoon I circled the village and then walked up onto the fells. I wanted to see if any of the witches were approaching the Spook's house. We didn't want to be taken by surprise and wake up one morning to find the garden surrounded. I also wanted to clear my head and think. It was very hard to put Alice out of my mind. Halloween was now less than two weeks away. I realized that we couldn't just drift into the situation and react, always on the back foot. We needed a plan of action. I would have to work something out with the Spook.

I could see no threat to the house, but in the far distance, on the lower slopes, I spotted a small group of women heading north; they were dressed in black and walked in single file – almost certainly witches. Were they heading for the Wardstone, ready for Halloween? It seemed likely. I wondered how many more had taken or would take that same route?

My master had told me that I was the first of his apprentices ever to be taken to the Wardstone, so it was something of a secret. Mab Mouldheel and her sisters had known about it, but that was because she was the most powerful scryer in Pendle. However, it seemed that half the denizens of the dark now knew of the Wardstone and were travelling towards it. Perhaps they had been summoned there by the Fiend . . . Even though his head was detached from his body and his spirit bound within it, he could still sometimes communicate with his servants.

An hour after sunset, dreading the task that faced me, I set off for the southern garden. Once again it was a bright moonlit night.

The witch assassin was already waiting for me. She was lying on her left side, her leg stretched across a flat slab of rock that

had been positioned over a pit to bind a boggart. I now understood why Grimalkin had chosen this place: the stone would
provide a firm base for her leg when the pin was driven into it.
The flesh had been peeled back and tacked with stitches to keep
it in place. The bone beneath shone in the moonlight. There was
little blood in evidence – no doubt she had kept it at bay using
magic – and I could see the hole that she had already drilled in
the bone. The silver pin lay on the stone beside her leg, and next
to it was a small light hammer.

As I stared at her leg, my mouth went dry and I shuddered.
This was going to be hard, but I couldn't afford to be
squeamish. If Grimalkin could tolerate this, I must force myself
to help her.

'The silver pin is slightly tapered,' Grimalkin explained.
'Insert the narrow end and then drive it home with the
hammer. Three light taps should do it. After that, leave me, and
I will do the rest.'

I noted that the bulging, dripping hessian sack was still close
by. Even now, facing terrible pain, she had to remain vigilant.

I picked up the pin with my left hand, the hammer with my
right. Then I turned, approached Grimalkin and knelt down.
After checking the taper, I held the pin above the dark hole in
the bone. Glancing at her, I noticed a film of sweat upon her
brow and upper lip.

She had already suffered much pain to reach this point;
now it would suddenly become far worse – and it would never
go away.

151

'Don't waver! Do it now!' she commanded. 'The anticipation is worse than the act.'

Wasting no more time, I positioned the pin very carefully and gave it a light tap. Then a second. It was almost fully home, but I felt a little resistance. It was tightening, binding the shattered bones together.

Then I gave a harder third tap, and the pin went in, flush with the surface of the bone.

I had never seen Grimalkin react to pain – beyond the sweat that had stood out on her brow. I had certainly never heard her cry out.

But now, as the pin went home, she let out a scream of agony; her whole body shivered and went into convulsions.

Then she stopped breathing.

CHAPTER 20
TENDRILS OF GREEN MIST

W as she dead? I wondered in horror. Had the shock of the silver pin killed her?

After all, what could be worse for a witch than to have a piece of silver, that most deadly of metals, inside her own body?

Grimalkin lay perfectly still; it was as if her soul had fled. I touched her forehead and found it ice-cold. But there was nothing I could do. She was beyond the help of doctors.

What if I were to remove the pin . . . ? First I would have to turn her onto her other side. There were surely various tools in Grimalkin's forge. Maybe amongst them I could find a pointed piece of metal and strike the pin out from the opposite side?

But as I came to my feet, I shook my head. It was not that it could not be done – it *should* not be done! Even if Grimalkin started breathing again and eventually recovered her strength, that leg would never heal properly without the silver pin. She would never again be the deadly witch assassin of old. She would never be able to perform the dance of death. I felt certain that she would rather die.

I started to walk away, intending to tell the Spook what had happened. But at that moment Grimalkin sucked in a huge breath. When I turned round, I saw that her eyes were open, her face twisted with pain.

'Leave me now!' Her voice was hardly more than a whisper. 'I will do the rest alone.' Then she reached for the sack and clutched it to her.

So I went back into the house and climbed the stairs to my room. It took me a long time to fall asleep. I kept thinking of what I'd just done and the agony that Grimalkin must be enduring. She was prepared to suffer in order to continue her work as a witch assassin.

The following day was bright and mild for October. During breakfast, I told the Spook what I had done to help Grimalkin. 'She must truly be in agony.' He shook his head sadly. Then he fell silent, apparently deep in thought.

After breakfast I headed for the southern garden to see how Grimalkin was doing. She was lying on her back on one of the boggart stones, her eyes closed again. With her left hand she still grasped the neck of the sack. I thought she was asleep.

I was wrong.

She spoke to me without opening her eyes. 'Leave me! Go away! Leave me alone!' she hissed.

I turned on my heel without a word and did as she commanded. Would she learn to live with the pain? I wondered. Would she ever regain her former strength?

Later my master sent me down to collect the week's provisions from the village.

At the grocer's I got a surprise. A letter from my eldest brother, Jack, was waiting for me. I went back out into the street and leaned back against the wall to read it:

Dear Tom,

I have some good news at last. Our brother James has turned up safely after all. He was attacked by robbers, beaten and then held captive for many weeks – no doubt with ransom in mind. He managed to escape after killing two of his captors with his bare hands.

I hope you are strong and healthy. If you are ever close to the farm, by all means call in – we would love to see you again. But please don't visit after dark because I have my wife and child to think about.

Ellie and little Mary send their love.

My best regards,
Jack

It was good to know that James had survived – though I did not believe that he had simply been captured by opportunistic thugs. On our final journey to Todmorden, Grimalkin had told me that the Fiend wished to speak to me: she had opened the sack and allowed me to talk to him. He had used the opportunity to tell me that my brother was to be killed. I already knew that James's captors were servants of the dark and that his life was in danger. I was very glad to hear that he was safely back at the farm.

I suspected that he would have been used to bring pressure upon me. Or perhaps, knowing how the Fiend operated, my brother's head would have been delivered to me in a sack. Mercifully, all that had been averted by James's strength and determination – a blacksmith can prove a dangerous foe.

But while the Fiend still existed, the threat to all my family remained. He had predicted that I would be the last of my mam's sons; that they would all die violent deaths before me.

I was a little saddened by the final lines of Jack's letter. They didn't want me to stay at the farm overnight because they were scared that something from the dark might be following. Ellie was scared for their daughter Mary. I could hardly blame her. After all, years earlier, the powerful malevolent witch Mother Malkin had indeed pursued me back to the farm and threatened them.

I understood now why it was impossible for a spook to marry; I must keep my distance from any family who were still living. How had I ever imagined that Alice and I could be together? My job would have placed her in permanent danger.

Then I laughed grimly at my foolish thoughts. Alice was powerful in her own right, well able to take care of herself; and now she had found another to share her life with.

I collected the rest of the provisions and carried them back to the Spook's house. I found him in the library and showed him Jack's letter.

He was pleased to hear that James was safe and well. 'Once this is over, you should visit your family. You've not seen them for a while.'

'I'd better make sure I go while the sun's shining then,' I said, pulling a face. 'My home is not to be visited after dark!'

'I'm sorry, lad, but you can't blame folks for being afraid of what we deal with. All my life I've made people nervous, sometimes scaring them half out of their skins. It's just something that goes with the job – we have to accept it.'

I slept badly that night, drifting in and out of sleep. Then, in the early hours of the morning, I had a sense that something was wrong. Something bad had happened.

I felt dizzy and sluggish, hardly able to think coherently. I dragged myself out of bed, my heart thudding with the effort, and struggled to raise the sash window. Previously I had lifted it with ease, but now it seemed stiff and my arms felt heavy. At last I was able to look down at the garden. Once again the sky was clear and, by the light of the moon, I saw a mist drifting out of the trees to cover the lawn.

There were two strange things about that mist.

First of all it moved in an unnatural way, stretching out tendrils like long slender fingers feeling their way towards the house. Moonlight neutralizes or changes colours, but I realized there was something strange about this mist; rather than being white or grey, it had a weird green tinge to it. I felt certain that dark magic was being used.

The Spook's back had been better lately, so rather than sleeping in a chair in the kitchen he'd come up to bed. I dressed quickly, went to his bedroom and rapped hard upon the door. There was no response, so I knocked again. Finally I eased open the door and went inside. I needed to alert the Spook to the fact that we were under some sort of magical attack. He was lying on his back, mouth slightly open, and appeared to be in a deep sleep. Then, in the sliver of moonlight that came through the window, I saw a tendril of green mist on the floor; it completely encircled his bed.

I shook his shoulder gently. He groaned; that was all. I called his name and shook him again, more roughly, but I still couldn't get him to wake up.

I suddenly realized there could be witches in the garden! I ran back into my bedroom, snatched my silver chain from my bag and thrust it into my breeches pocket. Then I went down the stairs, three at a time, grabbed my staff from where it leaned beside the back door, and sprinted out into the garden. Here, the mist was now much more than serpentine tendrils. It came up almost to my waist, rising like a tide, as if intent on drowning the house and trees.

So far I had simply felt befuddled, as if moving in a dream, but alarm bells suddenly went off inside my head. I was alert to the danger.

Grimalkin!

The Fiend's head!

I ran towards the southern garden and reached the boggart slab where I had last seen the witch assassin. She was still there, sleeping deeply, surrounded by the green mist, which writhed and coiled like a living snake about to crush its prey.

But the sack was gone.

Someone had entered the garden, using magic to make sure that we were all in a deep sleep. Even the boggart had succumbed.

I had awoken in spite of the dark magic. Somehow I had been able to resist it. And now one of the other gifts I had inherited from Mam came to my aid once more.

There was that flash of light inside my head and the pain in my forehead. And instantly I knew the precise location of the Fiend's head.

It was being carried towards the western garden.

I didn't bother trying to awaken the witch assassin; she was probably still in no fit condition to help, anyway. I released the blade of my staff and ran off through the trees in pursuit of whoever had seized the sack.

Not a moment too soon! Ahead of me I saw a figure carrying it. It was a woman and she was wearing pointy shoes. I lifted my staff like a spear. There was no room for mercy here ... Soon this witch, whoever she was, would have crossed the boundary, where others would be waiting to assist her: I had to strike now. I ran at her full pelt, aiming to drive the blade straight into her back and through her heart. But at the last moment she whirled round to face me.

It was Alice.

CHAPTER 21
A SCRAWNY BOY

'I might have known you'd come after me,' Alice said. 'You're the only one I feared might be strong enough to resist my magic.'

She carried the hessian sack in her left hand. Dark liquid dripped from it, spotting the grass. The stump of the Fiend's head never stopped bleeding for long.

Alice held her head high and met my eyes; there was no trace of shame or guilt in her demeanour; not the slightest acknowledgement of her betrayal. I couldn't help noticing how beautiful she looked. Her face was radiant, her hair held up by a wooden clip. Her dress of dark silk hugged her body.

More than ever now she resembled Bony Lizzie – though she lacked the habitual sneer and shifty eyes of her dead mother; she had only her dark beauty. Would the rest follow along eventually?

'Why, Alice?' I cried, lowering my staff. 'Why are you doing this? I thought the Fiend was your enemy! I thought you'd do anything to destroy him.'

'It ain't worth the effort trying to explain it to you, Tom. You'd never understand so it's best that I save my breath.'

She turned and began to walk away, but I ran forward, grabbed her by the shoulder and spun her round to face me once more.

'No!' I shouted. 'I deserve to know *why* you're doing this. You're going to tell me.'

'You ain't going to like it,' Alice said. 'It's simple, Tom. I went too far. I practised my dark magic too many times, just as Agnes Sowerbutts warned me years ago. And now I've changed – I'm a malevolent witch. It don't matter, because that's what I was always doomed to become. I'd no chance of being any different because I was born bad – bad inside. Don't bother to feel sorry for me.'

'I don't feel the tiniest bit sorry for you,' I said bitterly. 'I just want to know why you'd want to help the Fiend and restore him to power.'

'There are things that you don't know, Tom. Just ask Grimalkin – she travelled far to the north and discovered a threat to us humans far greater than that posed by the Fiend.

If we destroy him now, it will start something that will finish us all, one way or the other. It's best that *he* rules, because the alternative is far worse, believe me.'

I wondered why Grimalkin hadn't told me that. When she was feeling better I would ask her.

'What could be worse than a new age of darkness, Alice? There'll be daemons roaming the land. The Old God Golgoth could bring perpetual winter. People would freeze to death – and starve, because it'd be too cold for crops to grow. We're not just talking about men and women. What about all the children who'd die – don't you care about them?'

'People can endure an age of darkness – it's happened before. But they won't survive the new dark god who'd replace the Fiend. He's worshipped by creatures called the Kobalos, who ain't human. He and his servants plan to wipe half the human race – the men – off the face of the earth. There'd be no mercy for male children, either. Only the women would live on in slavery – they'd be better off dead! So it's better to put up with the Fiend.'

'You say that Grimalkin detected this threat from the north. If so, why is she still fighting the Fiend? You both have the same information, so why is she behaving differently?'

'You can guess the answer to that, Tom. Don't need to think too hard, do you? Grimalkin is a law unto herself. She does what she pleases, whether it makes sense or not. The Fiend murdered her baby, and for most of her life she's been driven by revenge. She doesn't care what nightmare replaces the

Fiend. She don't care what horrors befall the human race. All
that matters to her is destroying the Fiend and paying him back
for what he did. Nothing else counts.'

Alice's words troubled me. Suddenly I remembered that I
had heard of the Kobalos before. I'd read of them in the Spook's
Bestiary. What she said had a ring of truth, but I couldn't accept
that justification for what she was doing.

'You're just doing it for Lukrasta, aren't you, Alice?' I jibed.
'You no longer have a mind of your own – you're in thrall to his
power! Leave him, I beg you. It's still not too late.'

'I ain't in thrall to anybody. Lukrasta and me are partners –
we're equals. We look after each other.'

'How can you say that, when you've only just met him?
We've known each other for years and been through so much.
Isn't our bond stronger?'

'Sorry to have to tell you this, Tom, but the moment I met
Lukrasta, something changed inside me. I'd been gathering my
power and getting ready to attempt the *Doomdryte* ritual, and
that tipped me over the edge so that I joined the dark.
And when I opened the book, there he was – my other half, the
mage I was always destined to be with. It happened in an instant,
and now there's no going back! Look at this!' Alice cried.

She lifted her dress with her free hand and pointed to a
circular mark on the outside of her left thigh.

'Know what that is, Tom?'

I shook my head, staring at it in dismay and knowing that
what she was about to tell me would be bad.

'When I was young, it was just a thin crescent, but each time I used dark magic, it grew. First it turned into a half-moon and then a gibbous moon; the moment I met Lukrasta it became full – it's the sign that I belong to the dark. Note it well – it shows the truth about me!'

'Leave him, Alice,' I begged, tears coming into my eyes. 'We've always been close friends. Come back to me.'

Alice's face twisted with fury and she allowed her dress to fall below her knees once more. Now it really was as if Bony Lizzie were looking out of her eyes.

'Why should I leave Lukrasta for you? Why should I leave a strong man for a scrawny boy!' she cried.

'We are meant to be together, Alice,' I told her, my throat tightening with emotion so that my voice wobbled. Why did she have to be so hurtful?

But I no longer believed what I'd just said. I could hear the pleading note in my voice and I didn't like it. As Alice replied, anger began to fill me.

'You and me together? That ain't possible!' she mocked. 'Don't make me laugh! What woman in her right mind would want to spend her life with a spook? Stop begging, Tom, it don't suit you. But now I'm going to ask something of you. Spent a lot of time together, we have. You're not my enemy, Tom, and you never will be. So please, just accept things.'

'I'll do whatever I have to do in order to stop you!' I shouted. 'And as soon as I see the mage, he's as good as dead!'

'You're little better than a child, with a child's simple

thoughts and needs. Keep away from Lukrasta, or it's you that'll die – or suffer an even worse fate. He's not a man to meddle with. He don't know the meaning of the word "mercy". That's why I came for the Fiend's head instead of him. I didn't want any of you hurt. Lukrasta wouldn't have cared!'

'Give me the sack, Alice. Just put it down on the grass and I'll let you go.'

Alice laughed long and loud at that, the ugly sound echoing through the trees. 'You can't hurt me. One twitch of my little finger and you'd be burned to a frazzle – nothing left but ashes. No, I don't even need to make a sign. Don't need to speak spells either. Just have to think it, I do. If I wish it, you'll be dead and gone.'

'Do you think it'll be that easy, Alice?' My voice was hardly more than a whisper. 'Lukrasta tried to kill me on the steps, didn't he? He tried and failed. I've Mam's power inside me. I won't die that easily, and you know it. And now it's your turn . . .'

With those words I plunged my staff into the ground at my side and swiftly reached into my breeches pocket for my silver chain. Within a second it was coiled about my left hand, ready for throwing.

Under the Spook's guidance I'd spent many long hours practising with my chain. I'd begun by casting against a post in the garden until I could encircle it over and over again, never once missing. Then I'd progressed to throwing the chain on the run, and then against other people I was chasing. Mostly my target had been John Gregory, but I'd also practised with Alice.

I took a a deep breath, held it and cast my chain at her now. She wasn't moving. It was an easy shot. The silver chain whirled aloft, then descended, lit by a shaft of moonlight into a gleaming spiral.

The result was excellent. It dropped down on target to enclose Alice perfectly. The lower section of chain pinned her arms to her sides, while the upper part tightened against her teeth to prevent her from speaking spells of dark magic.

Alice gave a soft little cry before she was silenced by the chain, and she fell to her knees, staring up at me with wide eyes.

My own eyes brimmed over with tears that trickled down my cheeks and I gave a sob of anguish. How had it finally come to this? Never in my wildest and darkest nightmares had I envisioned binding Alice. Yes, I had practised, but this was for real.

And what would happen now? Must I put her in a pit? Must I do what I had often struggled to persuade my master not to do?

I stared down at Alice, my vision blurred. Then I noticed that, despite the chain, her left hand was still holding the hessian sack. I reached forward to snatch it from her . . . and then it happened.

Alice vanished.

CHAPTER 22
A FIERCE, WARLIKE RACE

The silver chain fell in a coil on the grass. Alice had disappeared, taking the Fiend's head with her.

I stared at the place where she had been kneeling, apparently vanquished. How had she done that? Once bound with a silver chain, a witch was helpless. That was what my master had taught me, and all my experience told me the same.

For Alice to escape in this way – to vanish – was an incredible display of dark magic. I wondered for a moment if it was simply some spell of illusion. But when I reached down and retrieved my chain, I was forced to accept what had happened.

When casting a chain, I had to position it perfectly, so that it lay across a witch's mouth, thus preventing her from hurling some spell against her captor. I had done that, but it had been useless against such a powerful witch. I remembered now what Alice had said about not even needing to utter spells.

But maybe it still wasn't over. I could use the most recent gift I'd received from Mam: the ability to locate people and objects. Could I find Alice? If so, I could surely follow the Fiend's head.

On my journey into Cymru I'd known exactly where it was at any one time. But when I tried now, concentrating on the image of the gory head in the hessian sack, nothing happened. I had no sense of it at all. Either the gift didn't work all the time, or Alice was using some powerful cloaking spell. I suspected the latter.

She had won; I had lost. Once again the Fiend's head was in the possession of his servants.

Thrusting the chain into my breeches pocket, I set off for the southern garden. The green mist had gone, the magic dispersed with it. Perhaps Grimalkin would now be awake.

As I approached the boggart stone where I'd left her, I saw that she was on her feet. She limped towards me.

I was amazed to see that she was able to put weight on that leg so soon. And it was an expression of alarm on her face rather than pain.

'It was Alice,' I told her. 'She has the Fiend's head. She used magic to put you into a deep sleep.'

'But not you?' asked Grimalkin. 'Her magic didn't work on you?'

'It made me groggy, but I recovered and went after her. I caught up with her at the edge of the garden. Not that it did me any good. I bound her with a silver chain, and she simply vanished. She has the head and I haven't a clue where she's gone.'

'She's powerful. In Lukrasta and Alice we couldn't have two more dangerous and powerful enemies ranged against us,' Grimalkin observed.

'We talked for a little before I cast the chain. She claims she's doing this for a good reason – she's chosen to help the Fiend because if he's destroyed, something worse will come about. She said you'd gone north and discovered a terrible threat. Why didn't you tell me about it?'

Grimalkin nodded. 'I always intended to, but there were other, more immediate threats that claimed priority. What she said is true, though. We should go and talk to Old Gregory and then decide what to do now.'

I followed her through the trees towards the house. She was limping badly now.

'How's the pain?' I asked. 'Is it more manageable?'

'The pin hurts. It's like a needle of fire boring into me. But I can keep it at bay, and the leg is healing fast. Soon I should be as before. Then it will be time to make our enemies pay.'

I said nothing. We now had to number Alice amongst those enemies. I didn't want to think of Grimalkin and Alice fighting to the death, but this is what it had come to.

* * *

The Spook was already downstairs when we entered the kitchen. We sat at the table and talked there, two candles illuminating the room and casting our flickering shadows into the corners.

I explained to my master what had happened. I left nothing out because he was a stickler for detail. Finally I gave him a quick summary of what Alice had said, as far as I could remember.

'Do you take this threat from the north seriously?' said the Spook, directing his question at Grimalkin.

'Alice is right. Part of it she heard from my own lips. There is indeed a warlike race of creatures who have built a great city in the frozen wastes,' Grimalkin began. 'In ancient times they went forth and waged war on the humans to the south. They enslaved the women and killed all the males. They are barbaric: they murdered their own females long ago. That much is certainly true.'

'They killed all their women!' exclaimed the Spook. 'Is that true as well? That's insane! How do they continue their race?'

'They enslave human women, breed with them and also drink their blood. They have powerful magic too.'

'They're called the Kobalos,' I interrupted. 'There's something about them in your Bestiary.'

'Aye, lad, that there is. It's something I once scoffed at, but now I've been proved wrong. Go and get it from the library!'

I ran upstairs to fetch the Bestiary, then returned and handed it to my master. He quickly found the right page and began to read silently. After a few moments he looked up.

'I got this information from a few notebooks that once came into my hands, supposedly from an ancient spook called Nicholas Browne. It seemed incredible; I wasn't really convinced of their authenticity, but, just in case there was some smidgeon of truth, I entered the information in the Bestiary with a comment that it couldn't be verified. I'd have liked a closer look at those notebooks in the light of what you've told me, but unfortunately they were lost in the fire. Here, lad,' he said, handing me the book, 'read the final paragraph aloud.'

I did as he bade me:

'The Kobalos are a fierce, warlike race who, with the exception of their mages, inhabit Valkarky, a city deep within the arctic circle.

'The name Valkarky means the City of the Petrified Tree; it is filled with all types of abominations that have been created by dark magic. Its walls are constructed and renewed by creatures that never sleep; creatures that spit soft stone from their mouths. The Kobalos believe that their city will not stop growing until it covers the entire world.'

'Remember what else Alice said,' Grimalkin reminded us. 'They worship a god called Talkus who has yet to come into existence. Because of that, they occasionally refer to him as the God Who Is Yet to Be Born. The Kobalos are convinced that he is all-powerful and will lead them in a war against humanity that will never cease until all our males are dead and our females enslaved.'

'Do they predict when this will happen?' asked the Spook.

'They believe it will be very soon,' she replied.

'Alice thinks she's doing the right thing in preserving the Fiend. She thinks that destroying him will make way for the Kobalos god . . . Doesn't that worry *you*?' I asked Grimalkin. 'She claimed it was only your hatred of the Fiend and desire for revenge that stopped you from joining her.'

Grimalkin shook her head. 'I don't necessarily think that finishing the Fiend will lead to the birth of Talkus. Alice's thinking is shaped by the will of the mage, Lukrasta, who certainly wants to preserve his master. I think we must deal with the Fiend first and then turn our attention to the Kobalos threat.'

The Spook nodded. 'Of course, the first part's easier said than done. They have the head once more.'

But by this time I was hardly listening. I had grasped the witch assassin's words as fiercely as a drowning man would the hand that pulls him from the torrent.

'Do you think that Alice is really in thrall to Lukrasta?' I asked.

'In a way, yes,' she replied.

My hopes soared at this confirmation. But Grimalkin hadn't finished yet, and she made herself clear.

'I think that Alice has also changed. I was there: I saw their meeting. It was as if their eyes sent forth coils of mutual attraction that bound each to the other. Such things are rare, but it does happen between thinking beings. Alice is strongly influenced by Lukrasta, yes. But if she is in thrall to him, he is also in thrall to her. Alice is a malevolent witch and has found a place where she feels at home – beside a dark mage. You had a bond between you when you were children, but now you have both grown up. Must I repeat what I told you? I will say it again: forget Alice, Tom, because she is not for you.'

I thought my master would seize upon Grimalkin's words as confirmation of what he had always believed. But he looked sad, and there was pity in his eyes when he turned to me. I was sure he was about to say something, but he just patted me on the shoulder like a father offering unspoken consolation.

He did speak later, soon after Grimalkin had left the house.

'Getting attached to somebody like Alice is hard, lad,' he told me. 'I should know because I was in love with Meg; the truth is, I still miss her. But it's for the best that you're apart – a witch has no business in a spook's life.'

He and Meg, a lamia witch, had spent winters together in his house up on Anglezarke Moor. But now she had gone back to Greece with her sister Marcia; the parting had been hard for him.

I nodded – he was trying to help, but it didn't ease the hurt that I felt inside.

The following morning there was no breakfast waiting. The Spook was sitting there alone, staring at the bare tabletop.

'It doesn't look good. I think something has happened to the boggart,' he told me.

'Alice wouldn't harm it!' I retorted. 'She made you and Grimalkin sleep. She'd have done the same to the boggart, I'm sure of it.'

After all my efforts summoning the boggart to my aid and forming a bond with it, I certainly hoped it was all right.

'Don't be so quick to defend her, lad,' said the Spook. 'She's gone to the dark, so who can tell what she might be capable of? But I'm not accusing Alice. I think it's more likely that Lukrasta did it out of revenge – he didn't enter the garden, but he might well have been nearby. Don't forget that the boggart slew a lot of witches. Lukrasta was in that tower, unable to stop you getting away with the Fiend's head. I've heard it said that he's motivated by a terrible pride. It was something you couldn't have achieved without the boggart, so now he's taken his revenge.'

'Do you think he's destroyed it?'

'I fear the worst, lad. Aye, I fear the worst. And now the house and garden are undefended.'

We sat there in silence for a while, and then the Spook suddenly seemed to cheer up a bit; there was a twinkle in his eye. 'Well, lad, I suppose you'd better go and burn the bacon, as usual!'

And, despite my best efforts, I *did* burn it. But we both finished every singed bit of it – and soft bread smeared with butter helped to make it a little more palatable.

After breakfast I went out into the garden to talk to Grimalkin and told her about the missing boggart.

'Lukrasta may have tried to destroy it, but boggarts are very resilient,' she observed. 'It may eventually recover – though maybe not in time to help us again.'

Grimalkin was leaning against a tree, seemingly deep in thought. Then I noticed something different about her. Across her body she was wearing her usual diagonal leather straps bristling with her snippy scissors and other weapons. But at her waist hung a new scabbard with an exceptionally long blade.

'That's new,' I said, pointing towards the sword. 'Is it the one you were forging the other night?'

'It is indeed,' she replied. 'As you know, I like to try new methods of combat. A witch assassin must always stretch herself.'

I thought she would draw the sword and show it to me, but she made no move to do so. I didn't like to ask – maybe she didn't like anybody else to touch it. Perhaps it was magical in some way, and easily contaminated. So instead I asked about her leg.

'I'm now confident that it will heal fully, but I need to rest it for a couple more days. One of us needs to go in search of our enemies. I would like to know when they bring the Fiend's body north.'

CHAPTER
23
THE ABHUMANS

There is a place in the County known locally as Beacon Fell because, generations earlier, during the civil war, it had been used for signalling purposes; from horizon to horizon fires were lit on the line of hilltops, warning of the approach of enemy troops.

It was heavily wooded, but one section, near the summit, was cleared of trees and made a good vantage point. From here I could look west and south – the two directions from which I expected the Fiend's servants to convey his body.

I settled myself down and kept watch. I expected to be there for at least a couple of days; as usual, I set traps for rabbits to augment the chicken legs and strips of salted ham I'd brought with me. And, of course, I had my usual supply of cheese. The waiting was tedious, and sometimes I studied my most recent notebook, adding to observations and making corrections where necessary.

Memories of my dad drifted into my mind. For a man who'd had little schooling and had gone to sea at an early age, he had been wise. Later he'd become a farmer – which involved hard physical labour from dawn to dusk. But Dad knew his letters and could read and write well. He'd once told me that the best way to think through a problem was to commit all the possible solutions to paper, jotting down anything that came into your head, no matter how crazy it seemed at the time. Then, later, you could read through them, scrapping the daftest ideas and concentrating on the ones that seemed most likely to be effective – although he'd added that sometimes, what at first glance appeared daft would turn out to have real possibilities.

And I really did have a big problem. So I moved to a new page and, on impulse, wrote a heading:

Other Ways to Deal with the Fiend

I hardly thought it likely that I really could just pluck the answer out of my head and find an alternative, but there was no harm in trying. And it would keep the boredom at bay. So I jotted things down quickly as they popped into my head.

(1) Burn the Fiend's head.

(2) Burn the Fiend's body.

(3) Burn both.

All these options were very risky. My master thought destroying the Fiend's flesh on earth would free him to return to the dark to gather his power. So the third was definitely out of the question, but what about the first two? Still risky, no doubt, but burn either head or body and he certainly couldn't be put back together again; his spirit might still be trapped in the remaining part. It reminded me of the old rhyme told to children:

All the king's horses and all the king's men
Couldn't put Humpty together again.

That brought a third solution into my head.

(4) Cut the Fiend into many small pieces – too many to be found.

Now, that was a possibility. At present he was in two pieces, but if, like Humpty Dumpty, he was cut up into many, which were hidden, it would be almost impossible to retrieve and reassemble them all.

I carried on jotting down ideas – some dafter than others. By the end I had quite a list, and I resolved to show them to my master when I got back to Chipenden.

* * *

Just before noon on the second day of my vigil, the weather, which had been chilly but bright for almost a week, began to change for the worse. I'd had a good view of the distant Irish Sea sparkling in the October sunshine, but now the water slowly darkened and low clouds drifted inland.

There was hardly more than a breeze, although the first cloud was overhead within the hour, and then a light drizzle began to fall. It was a lot warmer than before, but the drizzle turned to rain and I was soon wet and uncomfortable. The visibility deteriorated steadily, with a mist rolling in from the west. I was just about to return to Chipenden when I heard a chanting in the distance, getting louder as it approached the fell. I'd been expecting witches, but these voices were male and very deep.

At first I couldn't make out any words, but gradually the sound drew nearer and they became clear:

'Turn wheels! Push cart! Heave it up! Burst your heart!' boomed the voices.

Then, out of the mist, moving up the grassy incline, something astonishing emerged. It was the long eight-wheeled cart bearing the brass-handled coffin containing the body of the Fiend. But in the place of the six strong dray horses were four incredibly large abhumans.

'Turn wheels! Push cart! Heave it up! Burst your heart!'

My heart filled with dismay at the sight of those daunting creatures. How could we hope to fight them?

Two pulled the coffin by means of thick ropes harnessed to

their shoulders. Two more were pushing it from the rear. All four were stripped to the waist, their thick-set, muscular bodies glistening with rain; their trousers were saturated and splattered with mud, their feet bare. However, their most distinctive features were the ram-like horns that sprouted from their heads. They were huge – far bigger than Tusk: each must have been at least nine feet tall.

I could attack them on my own, but had little hope of victory against such monstrous brutes. No sooner had I rejected the idea of trying to hinder their progress than other figures emerged from the mist, following the big cart.

I noticed a tall, fierce woman in the lead. Dressed in the manner of Grimalkin, she had leather straps crisscrossing her body, from which the hilts of weapons were visible in their sheaths. I saw that she also had yellow orbs dangling from each ear-lobe. Was she the leader of this throng? I wondered. Was she a witch assassin?

And it was indeed a throng. More and more figures emerged from the mist, all armed to the teeth. The majority were witches, with black gowns, matted hair and pointy shoes. Amongst them were a few more abhumans, though none as big as the four monsters with the cart. There were other witches carrying blades like Grimalkin, and I wondered if they were the assassins of clans who dwelt far beyond the County. Some witches carried long poles with blades lashed to the end. But it wasn't their weapons that filled my heart with foreboding: it was the sheer number of them. After ten minutes the column was still emerging from the mist. This was an army! What hope had we against so many?

I realized that instead of taking one of the possible routes to the Wardstone or coming towards Chipenden, they were heading northeast. Perhaps they intended to meet up with more of their kind in Pendle?

I left Beacon Fell and headed back towards the Spook's house.

We talked in the kitchen as we ate our supper, the rain pattering against the windowpanes.

My master had cooked the meal, and it was delicious, but he was in a sombre mood and just picked at his plate of ham and potatoes. Grimalkin, on the other hand, cleared her own dish quickly and helped herself to more.

'How many do you think there were?' she asked.

'More than a thousand – they were still coming when I left. Where have so many witches and abhumans come from?' I asked. 'Is the tall woman who led them an assassin like you? She had yellow earrings in the shape of spheres.'

Grimalkin knew her immediately. 'Her name is Katrina – she is the witch assassin of the Peverel clan, who dwell far to the southeast in a county known as Essex. The orbs are shrunken human skulls in which she has stored power; as you know, I prefer to use the thumb-bones of my dead enemies. The quantity of bones means that a greater variety of magic is available to me – but each to her own method. They say she is formidable. We have never met, but no doubt we will cross blades soon. The Fiend's followers will have gathered from all over this land, from clans that dwell far beyond the County, all banding together to help their master in his hour of need.'

'Aye, and there are so few of us!' exclaimed my master.

'We will be outnumbered, certainly, but we are more than you might think,' said Grimalkin. 'As you know, Pendle is divided against itself, and in some cases so are the clans. There are many witches who oppose the Fiend. Tomorrow I will use a mirror to summon those who dwell in more remote locations, but I will also ride to Pendle to rally our local allies.'

At Grimalkin's mention of the use of the mirror, I saw the Spook grimace and stare down at the tabletop. He had accepted the need to form such alliances, but still couldn't condone the use of any form of dark magic.

'Mab Mouldheel and her sisters have already been to the Wardstone. I spoke to her when they passed through Chipenden over two weeks ago. They promised to help us at Halloween,' I told Grimalkin. 'But I wouldn't trust her as far as I could throw her,' I added.

'You never bothered to tell *me* that, lad,' the Spook complained. 'You've been a good, brave, diligent apprentice – I've never had a better. But there's something that you've lacked. You've kept too many secrets from your master. And for that you should be sorry!'

'I am sorry for what happened in the past,' I said, 'but this is different. It just slipped my mind.'

'Slipped your mind!' he said angrily. 'You meet a witch who's the leader of the Mouldheels and don't think *that* worth passing on to me? That's not to mention all the other things you've kept from me!'

'I was going to tell you, I swear it, but the day after, we found Grimalkin injured, and then I had to follow the witches. Since then it's been one thing after another.'

The Spook nodded but didn't meet my eyes. My omissions were piling up in his mind. He was clearly hurt by my lapse.

'I agree that Mab Mouldheel is not entirely to be trusted,' Grimalkin added after what seemed an uncomfortable silence, 'but she helped us in Greece and I know she is opposed to the Fiend. Very few of her clan support him. They should come to us in numbers. Against such vast opposition we need all the help we can get.'

Recent events had exhausted me, and no sooner had my head touched the pillow that night than I fell into a deep and dreamless sleep.

I awoke in the early hours. It was absolutely dark. I was finding it difficult to breathe.

There was a weight on my chest.

I felt a moment of terror, for the thing on my chest was moving.

Was this a nightmare? Was I still asleep? I wondered.

A moment later I was assured that I was wide awake by a voice whispering right inside my head.

Help me. I am desperate. Give me some of your blood or I will die.

It was the boggart, Kratch! The voice sounded weak and wobbly.

Without hesitation I spoke into the darkness. 'Where have you been?' I asked. 'I thought that you'd been destroyed.'

I fell away from this world towards the dark and lacked the strength to get back. I flickered like a candle in a storm on the edge of oblivion. I struggled long and hard; now I am finally here, but fear to fall again. It is as if I am on the edge of a cliff above a dark abyss. Help me or I will fall, never to rise again!

I was afraid to offer more of my blood, afraid that I might die in the process; afraid of what the consequences might be. But if I wished to have the boggart as an ally – how could I refuse?

'You can have some of my blood. Take it!' I commanded.

There was the lightest of touches on the back of my left hand as the boggart's claw scratched my skin. There was no pain. But then I felt the lapping of a very small rough tongue.

It seemed to go on for a long time; after a while I felt my heart thundering in my ears. It was a slow, heavy beat and it seemed to be labouring.

'Enough! Enough!' I cried. 'If you take too much, my heart will stop and I'll die!'

The lapping ceased and there was a new sound – the low,

light purring of a cat. And then, but for the thudding within my head, there was silence. Kratch had gone.

I sat up, fumbled in the dark for my tinderbox and lit a candle. And there I stayed for a while, feeling weak and nauseous, the room spinning around me.

When I felt strong enough to stand, I walked unsteadily down to the kitchen to get a cup of water. I sat slumped at the table and began to sip it, enjoying the feeling of the cold water slipping down my throat, thinking over what had happened.

Of course, there was no certainty that the boggart would be able to regain its strength and help us in the approaching battle. But it had not been destroyed – that was the good news. However, the thought of what I had done still filled me with unease.

The first time the boggart had taken my blood I'd had no choice in the matter; this time I'd given it freely. Should I have done otherwise? To deny it what it asked might have been fatal, and we needed its help more than ever.

But the process reminded me of what some Pendle witches did – they had a familiar and fed it their blood; in return, it became almost a part of them, like extra hands or a pair of eyes, able to do their bidding at a distance. In the first year of my apprenticeship Alice had done something similar, giving her blood to the daemonic creature called the Bane. But the Bane was nothing like a rat, a toad or a bird – the small creatures used by most witches; he had threatened to dominate and control her.

That might happen to me – for Kratch was a powerful boggart.

What if it came to me again asking for blood?

What should I do?

A PLAGUE OF SKELTS

The following morning I woke up late and was the last one down to breakfast.

My master and Grimalkin were already at the table, engaged in conversation. They were tucking into big plates of bacon and eggs.

'Good news, lad!' the Spook greeted me cheerfully. 'The boggart's back and it's cooked us a hearty breakfast. My compliments to the cook!' He looked towards the fireplace, where a fire was blazing, filling the room with warmth.

The invisible boggart responded to his words with a faint purr.

I took my place at the table with a barely perceptible nod to each of them. Then I reached across and heaped up my plate with eggs and bacon, cutting myself a thick slice of bread and butter. I ate in silence, barely listening to the conversation between the witch assassin and my master. The food was cooked to perfection, though not as piping hot as I liked it; I wished I'd come down earlier.

'So are you in agreement with that, lad?' asked the Spook.

I looked up. I'd been concentrating on eating. 'Am I in agreement with what?'

'Aren't you listening? Keep your mind on things!' His voice was sharp. 'You look a bit peaky. Did you sleep badly?'

I nodded. 'I was awake half the night.'

'Sleep is important, lad. But there's nothing better for combating insomnia than being physically exhausted when you go to bed. So what I'd like you to do is get yourself to the mill north of Caster and ask Judd Brinscall to join us in the coming fight. He's a handy lad with a staff, and those three big dogs will be more than welcome too. And what about that blacksmith brother of yours – James? You said he's safe and well now. He's a strong lad and gave a good account of himself up on Pendle Hill when we fought those witches. Maybe you should go out to the farm afterwards and ask him to join us.'

I shook my head. 'My family is in enough danger already. Remember what the Fiend warned about James? He was doubtless attacked by creatures of the dark, not robbers as he thought. I'd rather not bring him into more danger.'

'I'll leave it up to you, lad. But remember: the odds are against us and we need every good soul we can get. All the County families will be in danger if we lose this battle and the Fiend is restored. Anyway, contact Judd first. I'll expect you back tomorrow. Don't forget that time is short – it's only six days till Halloween.'

In order to do as he asked I'd have to run part of the way – the mill was at least a full day's journey each way. But he was right. Time was running out.

'I'll set off as soon as I've eaten,' I told him.

'Good lad! And while you're doing that, Grimalkin will travel to Pendle to see how many allies she can gather for us there.'

I prepared to set off. I didn't bother with my bag because I'd be travelling fast. But I had my silver chain tied around my waist under my shirt and I was carrying my staff. I brought the two daggers, but had left the Destiny Blade behind.

Grimalkin was leaning against her horse, apparently whispering into its left ear. She wore the leather scabbards across her body, and they bristled with blades. Her lips were painted black. She looked formidable, and ready for combat.

'You're going to ride?' I called out to her.

She nodded and led her mount to where I was standing.

'My leg is getting stronger every day but is still not ready for the walk to Pendle and back . . . You fed the boggart last night, didn't you?' she asked.

190

'Yes,' I admitted. 'It came and asked for my blood so I agreed. Otherwise it would have died. That's what it told me.'

'You probably saved its life. But your face was so pale this morning – it's a wonder your master didn't suspect as much.'

'I never told him about the previous time, so the thought would never have entered his head. He was too busy enjoying his breakfast to notice.'

'Beware, Tom – the danger is that such a creature might take too much and kill you.'

'That's what worries me,' I told Grimalkin. 'And there's something else . . . What if it starts to dominate and control me like the Bane did with Alice? That's the second time I've given it my blood.'

'That is another danger,' she agreed. 'But if it works out well, you could establish a good partnership with the boggart. Remember what happened with Alice?'

I thought back to those dark days in Priestown, when Alice had released the Bane from its prison in the labyrinth behind the silver gate. 'The third time she gave it her blood . . . that was to be the crucial moment when she became completely dominated by it.'

'Yes,' said Grimalkin, 'and that's the moment of risk for you too. But the Bane was a dark daemonic entity – far more powerful than this boggart – and Alice was always being tugged towards the dark. You are strong. If you are careful, you could form a more equal partnership.'

I nodded; what she said was interesting.

Grimalkin rode southeast towards Pendle while I headed in the opposite direction, taking the high route over the fells. As I walked, I thought about the boggart – both the threat and the promise of greater united strength. And I remembered what it had said to me:

You are brave! You are worthy to walk with me.

Those words suggested that it was indeed offering me an equal relationship rather than seeking to control me. But could you trust a creature of the dark? It had little of the human about it.

I strode up onto Parlick. Halfway up I came to some narrow sheep trails cutting across the rough grass, and I followed one round; it brought me onto the western flank of a sequence of fells, with the sea visible to my left.

It was another bright sunny day with little cloud. I couldn't help thinking that we'd soon pay for the fact that, apart from the downpour on Beacon Fell, we'd had little rain lately. The County is mostly wet and windy, and nature would probably redress the balance by giving everything a long hard soaking.

I set a fast pace but soon got winded and had to rest. It was all right the Spook telling me to complete the journey quickly so that I'd sleep, but losing so much blood to the boggart had weakened me; it was unlikely I'd reach the mill before dark.

While I nibbled at my cheese I realized that I hadn't yet talked to the Spook about the ideas that I'd jotted down in my notebook.

I thought about the list again and contemplated the battle

ahead. We would be outnumbered, but the aim was not to defeat our opponents but to somehow ensure that the head and body of the Fiend were kept apart. This had to be done either before sunset or midnight on Halloween, when their dark magic would restore his power.

I knew from studying my master's maps – now unfortunately lost in the fire – that several ley lines passed through the Wardstone. If I could get myself into the right position, I could summon the boggart to my side again. Of course, this time our enemies would be well aware of the potential threat. No doubt Lukrasta would try to destroy Kratch. And Alice might be by his side, joining her strength to his.

I pushed the hurtful thought aside and continued on my way, passing east of Caster as the sun sank below the horizon. Here I crossed a ley line that ran east towards the Wardstone; the invisible line of power was also one of the old tracks that led from the coast towards the hill. But there was no sight of any witches nor any indication that they had been in the area.

By the time I started to follow the west bank of the canal, the sun had set. This place held many memories. Here I'd been pushed into the cold mucky water by Bill Arkwright and taught to swim the hard way! He'd been a tough master, but I'd grown to like him; I recalled sadly how in Greece he had fallen when holding off some fire elementals while the Spook, Alice and I escaped.

My most scary memory of that time took place here on the

canal bank. I'd climbed down into the hold of a black barge and come face to face with the Fiend himself, sitting on a huge throne and surrounded by black candles. It was from his lips that I first learned that Alice was his daughter; and that Bony Lizzie was her true mother . . .

The mill was hidden behind a row of trees and the moon was obscured by clouds, so it was difficult to find the place where I needed to leave the canal. But then I came to the bridge and heard a stream rushing below in the darkness, so I scrambled down the bank and followed this west. Soon I was ducking beneath the branches of weeping willows to reach the six-foot-tall iron fence that bordered the mill garden.

It was then that I heard a noise in the darkness somewhere to my left. I turned just as the moon emerged to illuminate a fearsome insect-like creature with a flat head and a long snout. I recognized it immediately – that long bone-tube put its identity beyond doubt. I raised my staff, but it scuttled away and I lost sight of it when the moon went behind a cloud again.

It was a skelt! They were rare, and to find one so close to the mill was disturbing. What was it doing here? I wondered.

After that I proceeded more cautiously, following the fence through soggy ground to find the narrow gap that was the only entrance to the mill. I waded through the salt-water moat to the inner garden. All this – fence and salt water – formed part of the defences against water witches; the whole area teemed with them. But there was another deterrent – the dogs!

As I headed towards the mill, they began to bark. I heard a

door open, and then the three big wolfhounds were racing through the darkness towards me. A tremor of fear moment-arily knotted my stomach. Claw and her two fully-grown pups, Blood and Bone, were used to hunt down water witches. I knew them well; they were savage. They should have recog-nized me by my scent, but they were bounding towards me and I was still nervous.

At the last moment the furious barking ceased, and then I was down on my knees, patting them, and being licked in return.

'It's Tom Ward!' I called out before continuing, the dogs running around me in circles.

I wished it was Bill Arkwright stepping out to greet me, but things changed and you had to live with it. Instead it was Judd Brinscall who came to shake my hand and give me a warm, welcoming smile before leading me inside.

Soon I was seated at Judd's table tucking into a large plate of lamb's liver and onions. Judging by this, Judd was an excellent cook. I was starving so, aside from the first pleasantries we'd exchanged on meeting, I hadn't yet told him the reason for my visit.

He waited patiently, watching me eat, and I suddenly remembered his betrayal of the Spook at Todmorden. He had helped to lure my master into a situation where he almost lost his life. Of course, Judd's family had been targeted by dark forces and he'd been acting under duress. At the time I'd found it difficult to forgive him for his betrayal, but now I realized that I had to let bygones be bygones.

'How are things here, Judd?' I asked, swallowing the last tasty mouthful. 'Do you know, I saw a skelt not too far from your fence.'

I expected him to be surprised, but he just nodded. 'The water witches are under control at last. I must have killed a dozen of them, and I've another three in pits; now I have another infestation on my hands – this time it's skelts.'

My blood ran cold at that. I remembered what Grimalkin and Alice had told me about the Kobalos to the north: they awaited the birth of their god in the form of a skelt. Skelts formed the hilts of the hero swords too. Why should there be so many skelts around – especially at this critical time as we approached Halloween?

'But they're rare, surely,' I said. 'Bill Arkwright once told me that you could go for years without seeing even one.'

'That's true,' Judd agreed. 'He told me exactly the same thing. But they're anything but rare now. They're killing a lot of sheep. Every morning there's a dozen or so lying drained and dead along the canal. Farmers no longer put their animals in fields anywhere near water or bog. I could do with a bit of help – I don't suppose your master would loan you to me for a couple of months?'

'In other circumstances, Judd, I'm sure he'd have been glad to offer you my help, but I'm afraid we're facing a crisis and we need *your* help. That's why I'm here. Mr Gregory has asked me to bring you to Chipenden – the three dogs too, if you don't mind.'

The Spook had written to Judd informing him of what had happened, but now I explained in detail. Judd listened in silence, his face grave.

'It sounds like the odds are against us,' he said at last, looking glum.

'It's likely to go hard with us,' I agreed. 'Not all of us will live to tell the tale.'

For a moment I thought he was going to refuse his help, but then he leaned forward and patted my shoulder. 'Well, get a good night's sleep, Tom. We'll set off for Chipenden at first light.'

It was late when we reached the Spook's house. After eating supper and discussing matters with my master, Judd went to bed in the spare room that had once belonged to Alice. I sat with the Spook for a while, watching a big fire roaring in the grate. The nights were starting to get colder. Winter was approaching.

'Well, lad, thanks for bringing Judd and the dogs to our aid. Tomorrow morning you can set off for the farm to collect that big blacksmith brother of yours. No doubt you'll enjoy meeting up with your family again.'

I felt annoyed – I'd already told him that I didn't want to involve James again. Hadn't he listened to what I'd said? My master was certainly persistent, but he meant well, so I tried to keep the anger from my reply.

'No,' I told him firmly. 'As I said, I've caused enough trouble for my family. Jack and Ellie and Mary could have died when they were taken prisoner by the witches. They'll always be in some danger because of the job I do – but no, not this time. I'm sorry, but I can't do it. Not when the risk is so great.'

I thought back to those dark days when I'd helped to rescue my family from a cell in Malkin Tower. The experience had almost killed Jack and driven him to the edge of insanity. And then James had risked his life in the battle on Pendle Hill.

'I understand, lad.' The Spook looked grave. 'But I would still like you to think again. Sleep on it overnight. If you change your mind, let me know in the morning. After that, I won't mention it again unless you do. Now, there is something else we need to talk over. What about the boggart? You know that several ley lines run through the Wardstone . . . you could summon it again. But *should* we use it in the battle ahead?'

'It'll be weaker after what's happened,' I said. 'Even at its full strength it would have been no match for Lukrasta and all those witches, had they been prepared. This time they'll be ready for it.'

'That may be so, but it would destroy some of them and help us to achieve our aims. You aren't willing to put the life of James on the line – I understand that well enough— Sorry!' The Spook held up his hand. 'I promised I wouldn't mention that again. But this is a boggart we're talking about – a fearsome creature of the dark that would take your life and mine but for the bargains we made with it. Surely you can see that?'

I nodded. 'I won't squander its life, but I'll summon it if our need is great; if we face defeat . . .'

The Spook nodded. 'That's good to hear, lad. Now for the most important thing of all – how are we to deal with the Fiend? I've been thinking about that lately. The ritual's out of the question – we agree on that – and the girl's foolish experiment with the *Doomdryte* came to nothing. Is there another way?'

'I've been thinking about that myself,' I told him. 'I've jotted some ideas down in my notebook . . .'

'Then read them out to me, lad.'

I did as he asked, but I suspected that he already had some ideas of his own.

I had nine: some sounded really stupid to me now, but I read them out anyway.

'The fourth one seems the most promising,' said the Spook. 'Cutting the Fiend into small pieces is gruesome, but it could work. Hiding them might not put an end to the Fiend, but it would certainly make it difficult for his supporters to locate and reassemble each one. In Ireland we should have thought more carefully about simply separating the head from the body.'

'So you think that's a good idea?' I asked.

'It's as good as anything I've been able to come up with, lad. It will be very difficult to implement, but we can do it . . .' He sighed, and then added, 'We'll be greatly outnumbered; we must prepare to fight to the bitter end. And we've got to believe

that we'll succeed. Maybe a few of us will get through to the
Fiend. In that case we should just take pieces of him and
scatter . . . You have those three blades – the hero swords which
were to be used to sacrifice Alice . . . what if we use them
against the Fiend in a similar way?'

'What, cut off his thumb-bones?'

'Aye, lad, why not? They have great significance to witches.
They're a source of magical power. That's why Grimalkin
wears them as a necklace. For one witch to lose them to another
is a source of shame; some believe that it means that after death
they'll be trapped in the dark for ever, never able to return to
this world. So my advice to you is to take his thumbs and carry
them away with you if you can. Do to him what you were
supposed to do to Alice!'

'Cut out his heart?'

'I doubt you'll get chance to do that, but sever the head from
the body if it's already reconnected, then take the thumbs and
run. That might buy us some time. If more of us get through,
we'll each take another piece of him.'

We sat in silence for a moment, thinking about the huge
challenge that awaited us. I did feel better now that we had a
plan in place.

The Spook stirred. 'Now get yourself off to bed, lad. You
must be tired after your journey. Grimalkin agrees with me that
they will probably attempt to restore the Fiend at sunset. So
gather your strength – Halloween is only four days away.'

I went up to my room and crawled into bed. The journey to

and from the mill had indeed tired me out. I was exhausted and my eyes closed the moment my head touched the pillow.

I woke up just as swiftly.

The boggart was lying across my legs again. I could hear it purring loudly.

I need more of your blood. Give it to me now! Kratch demanded in a rasping voice.

'Why do you need my blood so urgently,' I asked. 'Won't your strength return without more? Haven't you taken enough already?'

I need more for the coming battle! the boggart cried.

'Why does it have to be *my* blood? Can't you take the blood of an animal? Or I could walk with you down a line until we reach one of the many enemies who seek our lives. Why not take the blood of a witch?'

Your blood is special to me. It is the blood of a brother.

'We are brothers?'

Yes, we are brothers in spirit. And without me you will be defeated.

'But if you fight alongside us, you may be destroyed,' I pointed out.

'Nothing lives for ever. I have dwelt in this world too long already!'

The boggart seemed prepared to sacrifice itself. Was it really tired of existing? But what it said changed nothing. I would still be cautious and avoid using it if at all possible.

'I will not summon you to certain destruction unless we face defeat.'

Then give me more blood and I will await your call.

'I am afraid to give you more,' I admitted. 'You might take too much and stop my heart.'

It is good that you say that. Only the truly brave can admit that they are afraid. I look forward to fighting alongside you again. Fear not – you will not die in this bed. I will take what I need – not one jot more. Trust me, I will leave you your life, and within a day you will completely recover your strength.

But I remembered the threat to Alice from the Bane. The third time blood was given was truly dangerous. Who knew what the consequences might be? I had to weigh Grimalkin's advice against that. She saw the dangers, but had argued that the boggart wasn't as powerful as the Bane. One day, because I was strong, I might achieve a very useful partnership with it. But then another thought struck me . . .

'But will giving you more of my blood change me? There is a significance attached to the third gift of blood.'

Yes, it will change you. All exchanges between conscious beings result in change. I will become more human and you will become more boggart. Isn't that fair?

I didn't know what that would mean for me, but my instincts told me to go ahead. My master had always taught me to follow my gut feelings. And it had proven good advice: that inner sense of what was right had rarely let me down.

'Then take my blood,' I said softly.

I felt the scratch on the back of my left hand, and then the rough tongue of the cat-boggart began to lap. Soon the metallic smell of my blood filled my nostrils. It seemed to go on for a long time, and eventually my heart began to labour and the pulse in my temple turned into a throbbing headache.

I fell into a deep, dark, dreamless sleep, aware that the boggart was still lapping.

Would I ever wake up? I was too weak and weary to be truly afraid. At that moment I didn't care what happened to me.

The next thing I remember, morning light was streaming in through the window. I felt the boggart lying across my legs again, but it was invisible.

Can you hear that? it asked.

'What?' I asked. 'What do you mean?'

I can hear the birds singing!

'The birds sing every morning,' I said.

I took little notice of them until this moment. I thought no more of them than I did insects buzzing around a stagnant pool. But their singing is like music. I would rather listen to them than eat them.

And then the weight of the boggart left my legs and it was gone. When I got out of bed, I felt weak and dizzy. I hoped that I'd recover quickly. I was going to need all my strength for the coming battle.

After breakfast the Spook went up to his library. I headed into the garden for a stroll. Grimalkin was turning her horse out to graze. She had evidently just returned from a ride.

'I have been out to scout the movements of our enemies,' she reported. 'There is a large encampment on the lower slopes of Beacon Fell. They seem to be preparing to head north.'

'Did you manage to enlist more allies for the battle?' I asked.

'Yes, but some I had counted on are afraid to join our cause. Still, we will have enough to carry the fight to our enemies.'

She pointed towards the eastern garden and gave me a strange smile. She was wearing her many blades, but I noticed that the long one that she had recently forged was no longer at her hip.

'Walk with me,' she commanded.

So I followed her among the trees to her forge. It was cold now, filled with ashes. The sword lay on the grass beside it. She picked it up and held it towards me, hilt first.

'I forged this for you,' she said. 'It is a gift. Take it!'

I looked down at the sword in astonishment. The first thing that struck me was that it was ugly. It was nothing like the ornate, carefully crafted hero swords, supposedly fashioned by the Old God Hephaestus. This one looked unfinished, and lacked any embellishment. Rather than glinting in the sunlight, the blade was dull and rusty.

Grimalkin smiled as if reading my mind. 'Never look a gift horse in the mouth,' she warned. 'This blade may not look pretty, but combat is not about that. Embellishments are often an affectation that pleases the creator. I prefer functionality. The sword I have crafted is a formidable weapon. It is designed to win. It is designed to kill your opponent. Take it!'

So I accepted the blade. As soon as I held it in my right hand – the one I used for wielding the Destiny Blade – I knew that the balance was perfect. The skelt sword had not been made for me, and I had only slowly learned to adjust to its feel and weight. This was much lighter, and instantly felt perfect in my hand. I would fight more easily with such a blade.

'I made it from a meteorite that fell to earth far to the north,' Grimalkin explained. 'The ore is very rare. This starblade retains its edge without the need for sharpening. And it will never break – it is exceptionally strong.

'That ore has an additional quality,' she continued. 'It readily absorbs the magic of the person who crafts it. After that it will accept changes from no one else. Thus I have built into it a powerful shield against any dark magic that is intended to harm you. While you wield it or wear it on your person, you will be impervious to such threats. With that blade in your hand, you may face the strongest witch or mage and be in no fear of them. But it will not make you invulnerable. My own magic would fail if I directed it at you, but that would not daunt me. I would use my blades and kill you anyway. So beware. Another may do the same. Many mages are also warriors.'

I nodded and then remembered my recent conversation with my master.

'I was talking to the Spook about the best way to deal with the Fiend. We think we should firstly sever the head from the body again and then take the thumbs. After that, we could cut away as many pieces of him as possible and scatter them to the winds. I think I should make the main cuts with the hero swords. After all, they were to have been part of the ritual that involved Alice. What do you think?'

'I agree. It will at least make the task of his servants more difficult next time they attempt to restore him,' she replied. 'But I doubt whether that alone will prove sufficient to destroy him completely . . .' She stared at the ground, frowning.

'I thank you for the blade.' I smiled at the witch assassin. 'But why give it to me now? Have you scryed that I'll have need of it soon?'

'Use the hero swords against the Fiend, but take the starblade along as an additional weapon. Sooner or later you will need it . . .'

I resolved to do as she advised. Magic would be used against us and this blade would help to protect me.

CHAPTER 25
BREWER'S FARM

Late in the morning I was in the library with my master. I was jotting down information about the new sword in my notebook; he was updating his Bestiary.

I'd told him about Grimalkin's gift, but he had made no comment. I knew why. It might ward off dark magic, but magic had also been used to create it. He would never fully come to terms with that.

He caught my eye and gave me a sad smile. And in that second I changed my mind.

Sometimes we don't make decisions as a result of careful reflection and a step-by-step process of logical thought. It is as if something deep within the mind has been considering a problem, and suddenly makes a decision which we accept.

I'd said I wouldn't risk my brother James, but suddenly I realized that something far greater than an individual life was at stake here. I was willing to lay my own life on the line. Shouldn't I at least go and give James that option? After all, he had been a formidable figure, leading the charge against the witches during the battle on Pendle Hill.

'I'll visit the farm and ask James if he'll join us,' I said to the Spook.

'Thanks, lad. I know it's hard for you to involve your family, but I believe you've made the right decision. I could send word to my only remaining brother, Andrew the locksmith, but he isn't a fighter, whereas James will be a real asset.'

'If James is killed in the battle, I'll have made the wrong decision,' I muttered.

'The odds against us are great; we could all die,' replied the Spook, weariness and resignation in his voice. 'Many of us surely will. But if we succeed, then the sacrifice will have been worthwhile. I am not a vengeful person, but I've seen a good deal of evil in my life: I've seen families brought to their knees by war; I've seen brother fight brother and son turn against father – and all those things were the result of the Fiend's influence in this world. Not to mention the direct attacks by servants of the dark – which I've tried to thwart all my life. Aye – as I've said, I'm not a person who would ordinarily seek revenge, but it's time to pay them back for what's been inflicted, not only upon the County but on the wider world beyond.'

I nodded. I knew that he was right.

Within the hour I had set off for the farm that was once my home – where I was raised alongside my six brothers, four of whom were now dispersed across the County with families of their own. Jack still ran the farm, but he now had the help of James, who was also working as a blacksmith there. I certainly wasn't going to ask Jack to help us in the coming battle – he had a family, as did my other brothers.

I had mixed feelings about going home: so much had changed. Mam was no longer there; both she and Dad were dead. I remembered I had been happy there as a child. But I could never go back to that; it had changed into something else.

I halted and made camp overnight, still some miles from the farm. It was best to arrive in the light, as Jack had requested.

Early the next morning I came down through the wood on Hangman's Hill, crunching through the fallen leaves. Here, on a cold winter's night, a select few could doubtless still hear the ghasts of the dead soldiers executed during the civil war swinging from their ropes. But now the trees were full of morning birdsong and the sun was shining through the chilly air, casting twig-patterns on the grass.

There was no hint of a ghast, but to one side I could see the huge swathe of trees felled by the Fiend when he'd come for me. I'd taken shelter in the special room where Mam had once kept her boxes; the Fiend had been unable to prevail against the magic she'd used to defend it.

At last I could see the familiar shape of Brewer's Farm below me – the locals called it that because it had once been the only source of locally brewed beer. Dad had never bothered with brewing, though, and we had just called it 'the farm' or 'home'.

The farm dogs warned of my arrival, and Jack came out of the barn and strode towards me. He was a big man whose bushy eyebrows often met in a scowl. But today he was smiling.

'Tom! Tom! What a surprise! It's good to see you!' he cried.

He grasped me in a bear-hug, but without his usual trick of trying to crush my ribs. As we broke apart I saw that he didn't tower over me as he'd done formerly. I would never be as tall as Jack, but in a couple more years I might come close.

'How's the family – Ellie and little Mary?' I asked.

'Oh, they're just fine. You won't recognize Mary. She's bright as a button and a right little tomboy, full of mischief. She's always climbing things and getting into trouble.'

'And James?'

'He would never admit it, but he was more than a little shaken by his ordeal at the hands of those thugs. He's back to his usual self, though. His forge makes more than the farm now – he's very generous and does more than just pay his way. He's been a good brother to me.'

This was going to make things even harder. If James came with me, I would be depriving my other brother of his help and financial support.

'So what brings you out this way, Tom?' Jack continued. 'No doubt you're here to sort out a few of the problems we've been having locally.'

'What problems?' I asked.

'Nothing's happened near the farm – apart from the usual,' Jack said, gesturing towards Hangman's Hill. 'But on the far side of Topley village all Hell's broken loose. It's been like that for weeks. Ghosts, boggarts, witches – you name it. There've been sightings of ghosts just outside the churchyard, and a boggart has taken up residence at Beck Cottage. The owners stayed on less than a week after it took over. Now it's becoming dangerous – it keeps throwing stones at passers-by. We've seen a lot of witches too: small groups have passed through, heading north, stealing and threatening folk as they go.'

No doubt the witches were heading for the Wardstone to join other supporters of the Fiend. But this increased level of activity from the dark made me wonder. Was it because of the coming crisis at Halloween? Were dark powers gathering everywhere?

'I've actually come to ask for James's help with a big problem we've got to the north,' I said, 'but I'll certainly find time to sort that boggart before we leave.' I reckoned I could spare a hour or two to deal with it before I returned to Chipenden.

'You said "we" . . . do you intend to take James with you?'

I nodded. 'That's if he'll agree to help.'

'You'll be taking him into danger? You expect him to help you fight the dark in some way?' The smile was gone from Jack's face, to be replaced by a growing anger. 'Don't you think he's suffered enough recently?'

'Yes, he's suffered; we've all suffered in one way or another. But the whole County and beyond is facing something much worse. And don't think that'll you'll be safe here, Jack,' I warned. 'There's danger ahead, and it's got to be faced, even if it takes the lives of both James and me.'

The anger faded from Jack's face; I saw instead a mixture of fear and sadness as he stared at the ground.

'Ellie's having another baby,' he said at last. 'After what happened at Pendle, I thought we'd never add to our family. But she's nervous, Tom, so play down the danger, won't you?'

Ellie had been pregnant when she and Jack and Mary were captured by the witches. The trauma of their abduction had caused her to lose what would have been her second child.

'Of course I will, Jack – and congratulations!'

He beamed at me and clapped me on the shoulder before leading me towards the house. The forge lay just beyond the barn, but I couldn't see James at work there.

'James is repairing farm machinery on the other side of Topley,' Jack said, reading my thoughts. 'He'll be back before dark – most likely in time for the evening meal. I'd be grateful if you didn't tell him what's needed while we're dining – it will only upset Ellie. She gets tired and we go to bed early most nights, so you'll get your chance to talk then, out of her earshot. I'll break it to her gently once we've gone to bed. Will you be all right sleeping on the couch downstairs?'

'Of course I will, but are you sure? Will Ellie be happy with that? I know having a spook's apprentice around makes you all nervous. I had planned to be away by dusk.'

'Ellie will be fine, and so will I, Tom. We'll manage this time. Besides, James will be more ready for bed than a long journey. We'll survive until morning, don't you worry.'

I wondered why Jack had changed his mind about me staying in the farmhouse after dark. Was it because of the danger we all faced? Maybe it was because he thought he might never see me or James again and didn't want to turn me out on what might be our last meeting?

I turned to see that Ellie had come out to greet me. I noticed that her corn-coloured hair was lighter now; the recent years had leached something of the glow from it. There were also faint lines at the corners of her eyes and mouth. But when she smiled, you realized how lucky Jack was to have a wife like her. I had a sudden tightness in my throat at the thought of losing Alice, but with a surge of anger I thrust it away from me.

'Oh, Tom! It's so good to see you!' Ellie gave me a warm hug. 'Mary! Mary! Tom's here! Come and see your uncle!' she shouted.

A little girl came running through the doorway to stare up at me with big round eyes. She bore no resemblance to the dirty, terrified child I'd seen clutching her mother in Malkin Tower two years earlier.

'Hello, Mary,' I said with a smile.

'Hello, Uncle Tom. Have you come to kill the bog?'

'She means the boggart that's been throwing stones,' Ellie explained. 'She can't stop talking about it.'

'Hopefully I won't have to kill it,' I told the child. 'Sometimes you can talk a boggart into moving on.'

'Can I come and watch? I want to hear it speak.'

'I'm not allowed to take other people with me when I go to deal with boggarts,' I told her. 'Most don't talk, but if this one does I'll remember every word and repeat it back to you. Will that do?'

Mary smiled and nodded.

I smiled back, then glanced quickly at my brother and his wife. They were a happy family. I'd almost forgotten how pleasant it was to spend time in their company. Then a wave of sadness washed over me. I might die in the coming battle. I might never see them again.

James came back just in time for supper, just as Jack had predicted, and he shook my hand warmly. He looked strong and fit – his job no doubt kept him that way. He was as tall as Jack, but much more muscular. His nose had been broken at one time and not properly reset, so that it was squashed against his face. But despite this he was still handsome in a roguish way, and smiles came to his face very easily.

I did as Jack asked and didn't mention the real reason for my visit even when James asked me outright.

'What brings you home, Tom? Anything special, or are you just passing through?'

I swallowed a mouthful of hotpot to give me time to think. 'I hear you've been having some local problems with the dark,' I told him. 'Tomorrow I'm going to try and sort out that boggart the other side of Topley.'

Jack gave me a grateful smile.

'Tom's going to talk to it!' Mary announced.

'Of course he is, love,' Ellie told her with a warm smile. 'Most things in this world can be solved by talking. It just takes a little patience, that's all – something which most men lack.'

I smiled at Ellie, wishing that were really true. Could we talk the servants of the Fiend out of supporting their master come Halloween? It would be easier to hold back the tide.

NOBODY WILL BE SAFE

When Jack and Ellie went upstairs, James rose from the table. 'Come and look at the forge, Tom,' he suggested. 'It's changed a bit since the last time you saw it.'

It gave me the perfect excuse to talk to him alone. He lit a lantern and led me across the yard, then proudly showed off his new equipment: two big new vices, an anvil, and rows and rows of specialist tools hanging from hooks on the wall.

'I love this job,' he told me. 'There's a lot of satisfaction to be had in doing a job well and providing a service at a reasonable price. People appreciate that. The other local smith has retired now, and I've almost more work than I can handle.'

I nodded. 'You've done well, James. But I didn't give you the whole story because Jack doesn't want to upset Ellie. I'm here to ask you a favour. Remember when you led the charge against the witches on Pendle Hill? Well, something similar is afoot and we need your help again.'

I explained what had been going on and how there would be a violent struggle at Halloween between us and the forces of the dark. Jack's face became grim as he listened; twice he shook his head.

'It sounds bad, Tom, but I'm not sure that I can help. I did it last time because my family were in danger, but this is different. The crops haven't been too good these last few years – the yield's been low – and some of the cattle had to be put down recently because of foot-rot. Things are tough. Jack and Ellie need me to keep the wolf from the door. Can't you get the military involved?'

I shook my head. 'Soldiers don't think much of spooks,' I told him. 'I don't think they'd help, and they certainly wouldn't be prepared to fight alongside our witch allies. They would probably consider both sides to be their enemies. Early this year a large patrol of soldiers was killed by servants of the Fiend near Todmorden. Soldiers aren't suited to that sort of battle.' I had already discussed this idea with the Spook, and we had decided it wouldn't help to get the military involved. 'Whether you help us or not is up to you, James.'

'I'm just not sure, Tom . . .'

'There is one thing you should consider. Those thugs who kidnapped you – they weren't just robbers. They were under orders from the dark – no doubt from the Fiend himself; the intention was to hurt you to put pressure on me. I'm sorry, James,' I added guiltily, 'but that could happen again. Not just to you, but to Jack, Ellie and little Mary. If we do not prevail at Halloween, nobody will be safe. I promised my master that I'd ask you, and now I have. I must confess that at first I was reluctant to drag you into this; I didn't want to put you in danger again – but it's desperate times . . . Anyway, as I said, it's your decision, James, and I will respect that.'

'When are you going back?'

'Tomorrow morning. I'm off to deal with that boggart now – it's a thing more easily done in the dark.'

Despite the coming battle, routine spook's business still had to go on. The boggart would eventually kill somebody if I didn't sort it out. It was my duty to do so.

'Right, Tom,' James said with a sigh. 'Let me think it over. I'll give you my decision tomorrow.'

The boggart proved uncooperative.

Talking it through didn't seem to work. You *can* sometimes persuade such a creature to leave the area, but this one was stubborn.

Like most other types of boggart, stone-chuckers spend most of their time invisible – just as well, because they are very ugly, and have six arms. In the first year of my apprenticeship my master was almost killed by one that had taken up residence in a farmhouse near Adlington.

I could have tried to intimidate it by laying lines of salt and iron around the farm. But that doesn't always work, and anyway I had no time to spare. So although it was risky, I went up against it head to head; it was armed with rocks – while I had salt in my left hand and iron filings in my right.

My aim was good. The two clouds of salt and iron came together perfectly to slay the boggart. All that was left of it was a stinky puddle of slime on the floor. I came away with a lump the size of an egg on my forehead, but I'd got the better of it and was still alive.

I was settled on the couch back at the farm soon after midnight. And, despite a thumping headache, I eventually got to sleep.

I was woken early by Jack setting off to do his chores and Ellie cooking breakfast. I sat down to a big plateful of toast and scrambled eggs. Mary was already at the table, spooning porridge into her mouth.

'What did the bog say?' she asked.

'Not a word.' I smiled at her. 'We fought and I won. The bog's gone.'

'Uncle Tom won!' Mary cried to her mother.

'Of course he did, love. I never doubted that he would. That's his job and he's good at it.'

Ellie was smiling, but as James came in, the smile slipped from her face. One glance told us both what his decision was.

In one hand he had his big blacksmith's hammer; in the other was a travelling bag.

'I'm coming with you, Tom,' he said, confirming what we'd already guessed.

Within the hour James and I were saying our farewells. Jack shook my hand and patted me on the shoulder. 'Take care, Tom. Take care. Come back safely, you two.'

Ellie gave James a big hug, and when they broke apart, tears were streaming down her face.

As we set off, leaving the farm behind, I wondered if I'd ever see it again.

And I wondered if I was taking my brother to his death.

Two days before Halloween we met at dusk in the kitchen of the Spook's house; I had escorted the members of our small gathering through the garden so that they would not be ripped to shreds by the boggart.

I suspect that even in his wildest dreams my master had not foreseen a situation where such a mixed company would be seated around his table, their eyes shining in the candlelight.

The Spook and I had grown used to Grimalkin's presence, and Judd and James were no problem. It was Mab, the young leader of the Mouldheels, and a sullen witch with dirty finger-nails called 'Fancy', who probably taxed my master the most.

'The first thing to decide is where we should gather our forces,' he said.

'Need we gather at all?' asked Fancy. 'Best to attack at once from many directions!'

I could smell her foul breath all the way across the big table, and I began to suspect that it was dried blood rather than dirt under her long fingernails. But she was the leader of a large group from the Deane witch clan and she had to be tolerated. We needed every ally we could get.

'No!' said Grimalkin emphatically. 'We need to *combine* our strength and focus it. We should be like a spear-point. We need to penetrate to wherever our enemies are holding the body of the Fiend. John Gregory and Tom Ward have put forward an idea that seems sound to me. We will cut the Fiend into as many pieces as possible, and scatter, each of us taking one; we can hide them or, even better, do as I have done: keep each part with us and defend it to the death. If it does not put an end to him, at least it will delay any attempt to restore him to the power he once was. Have you attempted to scry the outcome?' She had turned her gaze upon Mab Mouldheel, who was seated on her left.

Mab delighted in being the best scryer in the whole of Pendle, and her pretty face broke into a smile at that tacit acknowledgement of her status by Grimalkin, who had good scrying abilities of her own. One downside of having Mab with us, though, was the stink of her unwashed bare feet, which was even worse than Fancy's foul breath.

'I have.' She beamed. 'But things are unclear. I know that there will be many deaths on both sides: it is highly likely that at least one of us seated at this table will be slain. Would you like to know the names so you can prepare yourselves?'

'Keep your dark thoughts to yourself,' growled the Spook angrily. 'Speak not of such things while you're under my roof.'

Mab smiled at him sweetly. 'As you wish, John Gregory, but I would add this – the decisions we take around this table will further shape the outcome of the battle. Once those decisions have been made I will scry again. I will then reveal to all the likely outcome of the battle. If anyone sitting here wishes to know if they will or will not be numbered amongst the dead, let them come to me privately and I will tell them.'

'So, it's agreed,' my master went on. 'We assemble in one place, concentrate our forces and strike at our enemy's flank like a sharp spear driving towards its heart, which is the Fiend.'

For a moment Fancy opened her mouth as if to protest, but Grimalkin gave her such a savage glare that she immediately closed it again. Everyone around the table, including Fancy, then nodded in agreement.

'Where's the best place to assemble?' I asked. It seemed to me that wherever we chose, our enemies would either spy us with ease or use dark magic to find us.

'Just south of Clough Pike?' suggested the Spook.

'It's as good a place as any,' replied Grimalkin. 'Wherever we meet, you can be sure that our enemies will discover it and set ambushes for us. So I will take a small party of Malkins with me to clear the way.'

'I'd like to say something about the timing.' James spoke for the first time, his deep voice rumbling across the table. 'Before, on Pendle Hill, we failed to stop the summoning of the Fiend into the world because we arrived too late. It had already been done. We *must* get the timing right.'

It was a very good point. With the help of Mam's sisters, the flying lamia witches, we had eventually won the battle and disrupted the gathering of the witch clans on Pendle. But we had certainly arrived too late.

'I'll attempt to scry it,' Mab muttered.

'You sound doubtful,' Grimalkin said, raising her eyebrows.

'If Alice and Lukrasta try to cloak the information, it may prove difficult,' she replied.

'You're the only one who can do it – I believe you will be successful!'

Mab almost glowed at more praise from the witch assassin. I realized that Grimalkin had achieved her purpose – given something for Mab to live up to. The witch would now push herself to the limits to get that vital information.

Soon after that the witches took their leave. I escorted them to the edge of the garden while Grimalkin headed for her usual place near the boggart stones.

'Take great care in the battle, Tom,' Mab warned. 'For you, life and death are in the balance. And if you manage to survive, even greater risks await you soon afterwards. There are three times when you are likely to die: during the battle; immediately following it; and finally facing a powerful adversary.'

'Thanks for those cheery thoughts, Mab,' I told her

sarcastically. None of that filled me with confidence, so I quickly banished her words from my mind.

'No offence, Tom – you know I like you. Wouldn't want anything to happen to you, would I? I wouldn't rely too much on that rusty sword that Grimalkin gave you, either.'

I stood watching the two witches as they headed away from Chipenden. I was seething with anger. I knew that Grimalkin wouldn't have told Mab about the sword – she had scryed it for herself. Could nothing be kept from her?

However, she had already admitted that Alice and Lukrasta could deny her: this might pose a problem. We needed to know the time of the ritual.

As for her warnings about my death, I knew that the enemy outnumbered us many times over. There was no guarantee that we would win, so it was no use worrying about it.

What would be would be . . .

When I got back to the kitchen, my master, James and Judd were still sitting around the table. I could sense an atmosphere.

'Sit down, lad!' the Spook snapped, an edge of irritation in his voice.

'What's wrong?' I asked.

'It goes against the grain to ally myself with witches. Grimalkin I have respect for, despite what she is, but the other two – especially that sly woman with blood under her fingernails and the stink of it on her breath – well, I never thought it would come to this!'

'We have no choice,' I said, trying to calm him. 'If we're

to have any chance, we need them and those they lead.'

'Yes, *lead*! That's another thing that rankles.' He raised his voice in anger now. 'James spoke up, but you were quiet, lad – and *you* didn't utter a single word, Judd. They'll make all the decisions if we let them.'

'I'm sorry, John,' Judd replied. 'I'm not good at speaking out in company. I've only just arrived, still learning about the situation. I thought it best to just sit and listen.'

The Spook looked at him and nodded wearily.

'I know you're not going to like this,' I told my master, looking him right in the eye, 'but it has to be said. We face a big battle. This is not one or two of us against some single threatening entity from the dark. So we need a leader who is strong in combat skills; someone who can unite us. It can't be James – he's mostly unknown to our allies. It can't be a spook or an apprentice, because witches barely trust us at best. It has to be Grimalkin. They'll all follow her – either through fear or respect. She knows what she's doing in this situation. So we have to accept that and live with it.'

'Live with it or die with it!' snapped the Spook. 'If we deal with the Fiend, it'll be worth it, I suppose – at last we'll have paid him back for all the suffering he's inflicted. Well, I'm off to bed now. We'll be travelling tomorrow, and sleeping on hard ground. So take your last bit of comfort while you can.'

I nodded and smiled, but his words struck home. It might be the last time either of us ever slept in a bed again.

CHAPTER 27

THE CLASH OF WITCH ASSASSINS

Mab returned at noon the following day with the results of her latest scrying, beaming at her success. She had learned that the ritual would take place at sunset, rather than just before midnight, which had seemed most likely.

Soon after that Grimalkin took her leave. 'We will meet just south of Clough Pike, as agreed,' she said. 'I go to clear the way. Then it will be time for the battle that will decide everything.'

She was taking a few hand-picked witches with her to search for and kill those who might lie in wait for us.

'Aye.' The Spook nodded. 'That time is fast approaching.'

Grimalkin walked away from us without even a trace of a

limp. No doubt she still felt pain from the silver pin, but she was disguising it well. Suddenly she turned and looked back.

'Remember to carry both swords with you,' she told me.

Within the hour we had set off for the appointed place. The Spook, James, Judd and I travelled together, along with the three dogs, Claw, Blood and Bone. The bands of witches went separately; they would meet us at midday tomorrow. We spoke little on the journey, even when we made camp far to the west of the Wardstone. We sat around the fire, deep in thought, staring into the embers.

Later, James regaled me with stories about life on the farm during the past year. Little Mary had evidently got up to all sorts of mischief. But I had little to say in reply. Most of my news concerned struggles against the dark, which disturbed most people. I didn't mention Alice either – I couldn't bear to talk about her any more.

Halloween began with rain; we ate a late breakfast of cold chicken, miserable and shivering in the partial shelter of a wood, with big drops dripping from the branches.

We were the last to arrive at Clough Pike, and my heart sank to my boots as I gazed around. How few we had managed to gather to our cause, in the end: the Spook, my brother James, Judd Brinscall with the three wolfhounds, Grimalkin and perhaps a hundred and fifty Pendle witches, the majority of them from the Mouldheel clan, led by Mab and her two sisters. There were also about a dozen witches whom Grimalkin had summoned from the far north; they had crossed the sea to fight alongside us. We were silent, driven to inner reflection by the task that faced us, in the course of which many of us would surely lose our lives.

The wind whistled across the fell-tops, and somewhere in the distance I heard the call of a lapwing, but the dogs were as silent as we were. Animals are sensitive – perhaps they had an inkling of what lay ahead.

Then, as we prepared to head towards the Wardstone, there was a surprise addition to our group. The sky had cleared, and now, as the sun dipped towards the horizon, I glimpsed something dark flit across it. Moments later, a winged figure was falling towards us.

Once seen, never forgotten. It was Slake, the vaengir; Mam's lamia sister, whom I'd last seen in Malkin Tower. She'd told me she would stay there until the Fiend was destroyed, and only then be free to fly away.

The witches scattered, some shrieking in fear, as she dropped towards where the Spook and I were standing. Some of our present allies would have fought against us on Pendle two years earlier. They had reason to fear the winged lamia who, together with her sister, had played a decisive part in the battle.

Slake landed in front of me and my master. I studied her in awe. Black feathered wings were folded across her back, covering the more delicate inner ones; her powerful lower body was scaly; and her four limbs ended in razor-sharp talons. It was not comfortable standing so close to her, gazing into her cruel, unblinking eyes.

'Zenobia's plan is not being carried out!' she hissed in accusation. 'I scryed your disobedience and came here to see for myself!'

Zenobia was Mam's lamia name. I had been asked to sacrifice Alice, and that was what Slake expected to happen. She had not come to join our cause; she had arrived to challenge me.

'The victim is no longer "willing",' I told her. 'She's formed an alliance with the mage Lukrasta. She thinks it better that the Fiend should survive, lest another god take his place – one who'd lead his people in a war to annihilate humanity. Whether I wish it or not, the sacrifice would be useless.'

'The Fiend has already been bound to the Wardstone for the ritual,' said the lamia. 'I flew over the stone and saw what was being done. His head and body are joined. Time is short. Have you a better plan? What do you propose to do?'

'We'll do what we can,' said the Spook, answering for me. 'We've gathered as many as we can here. We'll disrupt the ritual, then try to separate the head from the body again and carry it away. This time we'll carve him up before we scatter, each with a small piece, and attempt to keep them out of the clutches of his supporters.'

'You are few and they are many – perhaps five of them for each one of you. And they will have Lukrasta and the girl Alice on their side. The outlook is bleak.'

I thought back to the battle on Pendle Hill. With the help of

Slake and her sister lamia we had won – though our main objective had not been realized. We had failed to prevent the witches from summoning the Fiend. Slake was right – the outlook was indeed bleak. It seemed likely that we would fail again.

'We can but try,' I said.

'Aye! It's better to die fighting than stand by and do nothing,' agreed the Spook.

'I agree wholeheartedly with that,' said Grimalkin, coming to face the winged lamia. 'A great battle awaits us, the odds against us are overwhelming, and the price of defeat is terrible. All my life has led up to this point. What could be better than to die in such a battle? I tell you this – I am Grimalkin, and if I die, then I will take many of our enemies with me. So will you join us, sister?'

By now the other witches had moved closer and were listening with rapt attention to the witch assassin's every word.

Slake stared at her for a long time. Then, slowly, she nodded her fierce head. 'Yes, I will join my strength with yours. Remember that each one of us gathered here needs to take the lives of at least five of those who oppose us. Do that and we might win, despite the great odds.'

Moments later, we were heading for the Wardstone, Grimalkin leading the way. We made slow progress. The ground was soggy underfoot, with pools of deep, stagnant water to trap the unwary. The wind was growing in force, but it was no longer a prevailing westerly, gusting instead in our faces. The sky was still clear, the setting sun illuminating the landscape clearly; as yet, there was no threat of rain.

But then, suddenly, I saw a flash on the horizon directly ahead. Was it lightning? I wondered. There was no answering rumble of thunder. Soon afterwards there was another flash of blue.

'Magic is being used,' said Grimalkin. 'You can smell it!'

There was a faint stink of brimstone being carried towards us on the air and I knew that she was right.

As we drew nearer to our goal, the dark mass of the Wardstone slowly reared up before us like some malevolent beast ready to pounce. In the setting sun it looked as if it had been painted with blood. Then we spotted our enemies encircling the rock; as we approached, they turned to face us, weapons at the ready. The sight was daunting. It was one thing to know the numerical odds we faced; much worse to see their massed ranks in the flesh. How could we win through to the Wardstone against such opposition?

I looked for Alice or Lukrasta but could see no sign of them. That was a relief. To find Alice among the opposing forces would have sickened me.

Behind them I could make out the huge form of the Fiend bound to the Wardstone. Ropes encircled his body; these were fastened to pegs that had been driven into the rock. It seemed that he had to be in contact with the rock in order for the dark magic to work. Why else would they have bound him in such a way? Without the ropes he would have slid off onto the flat boggy ground below.

Never had he looked more terrifying. I feared that at any moment he might open his eyes, see me and tear himself free to come for me. I knew that the ritual had not yet been completed, but the terror did not leave me.

As we advanced, the ground became a little firmer, and we picked up our pace. We would not halt now. At any moment I expected to be setting off in a wild charge. The Spook had accepted Grimalkin's leadership, as I always knew he would: she would make the decisions regarding the coming battle, giving the all-important order to attack.

She walked ahead, in complete command of our small army. Who would challenge her right to lead us? In this type of battle, there was no question that she was the right person.

I looked up as lightning targeted the Wardstone. This time it wasn't a sheet of light; this was a blue zigzag that came out of a cloudless sky. It struck the massive body of the Fiend, who began to writhe, twisting his head from side to side. The ritual had started, and dread filled me once more.

My mind went back to the tower, and I remembered the tendrils that had grown from the base of the head to intertwine with those from the stump of the neck. Here the process seemed far more advanced. Was the head already fully attached to the body, as Slake had indicated? I wondered fearfully.

Suddenly I felt a pressure against my face and body. It wasn't just the wind, which seemed to be blustering at us straight from the Wardstone. This was a strange cold force, immediately chilling me to the bone and causing my body to tremble uncontrollably. I glanced left and right and saw that others were feeling something too. One witch began to shriek and pull handfuls of hair from her scalp. Another fell to her knees and began to beat her forehead against the ground.

Others were still moving forward, but much more slowly now. Even Grimalkin and my master seemed to be struggling. I was finding it an effort just to lift my feet. Powerful dark magic was being used to halt our advance – no doubt through the collective will of the mass of witches who opposed us. Lukrasta and Alice might also be contributing.

Seventh sons of seventh sons are usually able to defy the spell called *Dread*, which induces a terrible fear in its victims. But the Spook and I both came to a complete halt. I felt rooted to the spot, befuddled, all my will power drained from me.

What about the starblade? I thought. Wasn't that supposed to protect me from any attack of dark magic? Could it be that the force being used against us was even stronger than what Grimalkin had forged? Maybe Lukrasta was just too powerful?

The witches around the Wardstone began to taunt us, pointing and shrieking with wild laughter. Then the tall witch assassin, Katrina, stepped forward and began to mock Grimalkin, calling out to her in a loud voice. As she shouted, the shrunken skulls in which she stored her magic spun and danced.

'I see you shiver and shake with fear, Grimalkin! Your knees tremble, and terror dries the stinking spittle in your fetid mouth. Fools have whispered your name in the dark and trumpeted forth lies about your vaunted reputation. But all is falsehood! I am Katrina, the *greatest* of all the witch assassins – the most formidable who has ever walked the earth! In the face of my strength you are weak; I am brave and you are cowardly. I can hear your knees knocking together. You dare not step forward to fight!'

I expected Grimalkin to answer, but she remained silent and, to my dismay, I saw that her whole body was trembling. But surely it was not fear that caused her to shake; it must be the enemy magic.

'This night you will die, Grimalkin!' Katrina continued. 'You face a stronger assassin than you have ever met before. When dawn comes, our master will be lord of the earth and your shrunken skull will adorn my body to mark my victory!'

Still Grimalkin did not reply, but I could see that she was moving now, forcing herself forward defiantly, taking one slow painful step after the other to where the grinning Katrina was waiting, sharp blades at the ready.

Had Grimalkin's magic failed her? I wondered. Where were her usual grace and strength? And what chance did she have against such an opponent backed by the powerful magic of Lukrasta?

Then, suddenly, in one fluid movement, Grimalkin cast off the spell completely, drew two blades and ran directly towards her enemy, accelerating with every stride. It was as if she had used her own magic to throw off the yoke that held her back.

Or was it simply her iron will – the determination and self-belief that had served her so well in the past?

There was no trace now of the injury that had caused her to limp so badly. If she felt pain, as surely she must, it did not affect her in the slightest.

When she reached her opponent, there was no wary circling, no tentative exchange of blows; caution was thrown to the winds by both antagonists. Grimalkin was performing her usual dance of death, spinning and whirling, her blades reflecting the red from the setting sun. But Katrina seemed to be matching her, meeting each cut and thrust with her own blades.

I had a sudden moment of doubt, and feared for Grimalkin. She had always seemed so formidable, so totally in control whenever it came to combat. What if her leg wasn't back to full strength and she had finally met her match?

The loss of Grimalkin now would be a devastating blow to us all – but particularly the witches. If, in addition to their numerical superiority, our enemies proved to have the deadlier assassin, we might lose the battle before it had even begun.

With the odds against us so great, it required an act of faith; you had to *believe* that you would win. The defeat of Grimalkin might shatter our self-belief.

The opposing sides had begun by shouting encouragement to their own champion or hurling insults at her opponent; but that didn't last. Gradually they fell silent, concentrating all their attention upon the spectacle of two well-matched witch assassins, each at the height of her power and skill.

At one point they came together, blade against blade, in close combat. Muscles straining, they both tried to win the ascendancy. Grimalkin gained ground, only to be thrust steadily back again. To and fro they struggled – I could hardly bear to watch. I kept thinking about the shattered bone held by that silver pin. Surely Grimalkin's leg would give way.

But suddenly, to my relief, they broke apart again, and now speed and timing became more important than brute strength.

For a while they seemed evenly matched, but then the tide of battle seemed to change. Grimalkin's power now ebbed, as Katrina pushed her back like some unstoppable wave. Blood sprayed upwards, and a huge groan went up from our side as Katrina drew first blood.

Grimalkin had received a cut above her left eye, and she staggered backwards, for a moment apparently overwhelmed by her opponent's furious onslaught. Things were going badly for her. Blood was pouring down, partially obscuring her vision, and she now seemed less agile, barely managing to defend herself against each stab or thrust of a blade.

Then, to my dismay, Grimalkin turned her back on Katrina and ran towards our lines. My heart sank. I'd never thought to see such a day.

'See – she flees! She flees!' Katrina cried in exultation, while behind her the enemy witches whooped and cheered with glee.

It was then that Grimalkin halted her flight to turn and face her enemy once more. She wiped the back of her hand across her forehead to divert the flow of blood and muttered under her breath. She was panting hard but made no response to Katrina.

I noticed then that the blood was no longer dripping from the wound. She had used her magic to stem its flow.

Now she began to run towards her opponent again, accelerating with every step.

Three things happened almost simultaneously.

A red spray of blood plumed up above the place where they came together – but this time it was not Grimalkin's.

Katrina slumped to the ground.

The victorious witch assassin ran on, still not checking her pace.

She headed straight for the waiting ranks of our enemies.

CHAPTER 28
THE BATTLE OF THE WARDSTONE

Grimalkin had slain Katrina almost casually, like an upstart pawn swept from a chessboard by the advance of a black queen. She looked black indeed. Although in alliance with the light, for this struggle against the Fiend and his supporters, she was Grimalkin, the darkest and most dangerous of all the witch assassins; Grimalkin who loved to fight; Grimalkin who would do anything to win – and would willingly die here if it proved necessary.

The truth was that we all faced death here. For my part I was somewhat fatalistic – if it happened, then so be it. But I wanted to survive. The future – even a future without

Alice – called to me, and I didn't want that taken away.

Ahead, the massed ranks of the Fiend's supporters waited for us, weapons at the ready. No longer were they making catcalls and baying for blood; they had already been given blood, which lay red and slick upon the grass around the dead body of their champion, Katrina. Now they looked on in silent astonishment as Grimalkin ran on.

She feared nothing. It was as if she truly believed she could defeat that multitude single-handed. Her blades flashed and flashed again, reflecting the amber light of the setting sun. She was whirling, doing her deadly dance – but then that horde of enemy witches and abhumans began to surround her, pressing in on every side.

Not one of us moved. We were still paralysed by the power of their dark magic. I was struggling to break free of the spell, but my breathing was laboured, my limbs sluggish and I could not force my left foot to take the first step.

But then someone else finally broke free of that magical binding and began to run forward. It was John Gregory, my master – who was defying that powerful enchantment like a true seventh son of a seventh son.

He ran towards Grimalkin. In addition to freeing himself from the spell that bound him, he seemed to have cast off the years, and I was reminded of the time, very early in my apprenticeship, when he'd sprinted to my rescue, slaying Tusk and binding Bony Lizzie. Then, as now, his hood had fallen back and, lit by the setting sun, his hair streamed out behind him like tongues of amber fire.

The silver-alloy blade at the end of his staff looked like a flame too, and he jabbed forward with it, surprising his opponents; for they were facing away from him, trying desperately to overcome the witch assassin through sheer weight of numbers.

But they soon became aware of the new threat, and turned to face him. It made no difference. My master sliced through them like a heated blade through soft butter, and was almost immediately at the side of the witch assassin.

According to the Malkin curse, he was supposed to die 'in a dark place underground with no friend at his side'.

On the first count, this was wrong. He was fighting on the highest hill in the County, the sun had not yet set and light still filled the heavens.

On the second, it was also wrong – at least, I like to think so. For without either of them realizing it, he and the witch assassin had indeed become friends; or, at the very least, comrades in arms.

The Spook had always believed that the future was not fixed; that we shape it with every action, every decision we make each and every day. And now it seemed to me that he'd been proved correct. What scryer, what prophecy, could ever have foretold that most unlikely of alliances?

As I watched him, I was still struggling to break free of the enchantment. A lump came into my throat at the sight of him fighting back to back with Grimalkin against their common enemy. That image of him is burned into my memory and will remain with me to my dying day.

It was my last glimpse of his part in the battle.

I never saw him alive again.

Now, stirred to action at last, the power of the enemy magic fading, our small band surged as one towards the enemy; towards the place where the Spook and Grimalkin still fought together against overwhelming odds.

This was a battle between the servants of the Fiend and those who opposed him. There were Pendle witches on both sides, but the majority of our enemies came from beyond the County – including those four monstrous abhumans who had moved the cart carrying the Fiend's body to this place.

There were witch clans from Essex and Suffolk; from Cymru too; and from Scotland. From far overseas they also came to fight here; to fight and die. I learned later that Romanian witches had fought alongside a small force of Celtic witches from Ireland.

The strength of those aligned against us was indeed fearsome. But perhaps our will to win was greater. We were spurred on by the thought of what would happen if we lost. And we didn't need to defeat them all. Our aim was simply to disrupt their attempts to restore the Fiend, force our way through to where his body was tied to the rock and sunder it once more. We would become the spear that Grimalkin had envisaged.

Historians have given learned accounts of great battles from the past which have determined the fate of nations and shaped our world. The Spook had some such detailed narratives in his library before it was destroyed by fire. They outlined manoeuvres and deployments prior to engagement; the positioning of ranks; the order of attack. They described such battles from the point of view of 'gods' looking down from a great height upon ant-like combatants marching far below.

There were generals too in such accounts; skilled strategists and tacticians who sat high and proud on their horses behind the line where battle was joined. They noted the ebb and flow and instructed the sections of their army accordingly.

But if Grimalkin was indeed our general, she was too busy in the thick of battle to be concerned with the larger picture. We had only one clear objective – to reach the Wardstone and deal with the Fiend before it was too late.

Did our enemies also have a leader? Or had it been Katrina? If anybody was truly orchestrating the movements of our opponents, surely it would be Lukrasta?

I glanced up towards the Wardstone, thinking that was where he might position himself, wondering if Alice would be at his side. But I saw only the huge body of the Fiend.

I believe that battles are really nothing like those depicted by the histories that I have read – at least not for the individual combatant. There is fear, anger, and a certain sense that forces much larger than you hold you in their grip and decide whether you live or die. Then there is the stench of blood and excrement, and the screams of the wounded and dying.

It was like that for me from the moment we clashed with the enemy. I was not in the lead. Others ran faster than I, so at first I simply followed in their footsteps, and our opponents fell back before us. But gradually our advance towards the Wardstone slowed.

I saw my brother James using his huge blacksmith's hammer to clear our way – and I feared for him. Judd too I saw fighting somewhere to my left, and I wondered how many of my friends would perish this day.

At first I used my staff, reaching down over the shoulders of those in front of me to stab the enemy. Slowly the gap diminished as the allies ahead of me died and I stumbled over their bodies.

There was one moment of terrible grief – for one of the bodies I stepped over was known so well to me. The face of my dead master looked up at me, his unseeing eyes wide open.

But the tide of battle carried me forward and I forced the stinging sorrow away. All that mattered right now was survival, and to make our way through to the Wardstone.

At some point the staff was torn from my grip. There was no space to use my sword, so I used my daggers as I was pressed forward against the witches.

The two short hero swords, Dolorous and Bone Cutter, felt light in my hands, and found the flesh of my enemies. There was blood on their blades – and oozing from the skelt eyes in the hilts.

How long that close bloody fight went on I cannot estimate – my mind was befuddled by the tricks of time. I remember claws and blades striking at my face, arms, shoulders and chest; at one point blood ran down into my eyes and I was temporarily blinded. But I fought on – until eventually something gave. Against the odds we had broken through and were suddenly racing towards the Wardstone, harried on either side while a smaller group of witches waited ahead – their last defence, the rearguard of their army. Amongst them stood the four monstrous abhumans, wielding clubs, and as I watched, one dashed out the brains of a fearsome Deane witch, who was no match for her huge adversary.

Somehow I had to reach the Fiend, but how was I to get past the abhumans? Then, suddenly, Slake swooped down, screeching her hatred, claws extended, wings a blur, and the first of those monsters fell back, blinded, tatters of bloody skin hanging from the ruin of its face.

I saw Grimalkin again: a throwing knife despatched the second of the abhumans. Her blades whirled, and she hamstrung the third, bringing him to his knees, ready to be despatched by a long blade through the left eye.

Next I caught sight of a big man with a hammer running straight at the fourth. I realized it was James – and felt a moment of fear. I never saw who prevailed, because in seconds I was closing on the Wardstone, where the body of the Fiend was surrounded by a coven of thirteen chanting witches.

There was a scream just behind me, and I knew that one of

my allies had fallen; others were running with me, but somehow I was drawing ahead.

I have always had a good sense of time, awaking from a night's sleep at exactly the hour I had appointed. Now I sensed that the moment of the Fiend's restoration had come; I ran faster.

The giant body stirred. The huge eyes opened and glared down at me; eyes full of victory and anticipation; eyes that promised unimaginable eternal torment.

On Pendle we had once failed. Now we had failed here too.

We were already too late.

The Fiend was back in the flesh.

His vengeance would be terrible.

A QUESTION OF TIME
CHAPTER 29

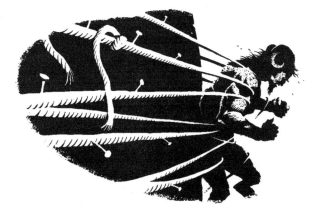

I did not think. I leaped up onto the rock and began to climb towards the Fiend.

I glanced behind me. Nobody else was following me up. Perhaps the Fiend's supporters had prevented them?

I was alone. This was an outcome I hadn't anticipated, and my heart sank into my boots. I'd always thought that Grimalkin and the Spook would be with me – along with perhaps a dozen others – to share what had to be done.

This meant that it would no longer be possible to cut the Fiend into pieces and flee, but I could still play my part. Many had sacrificed their lives to bring me to this place. Their hopes rested on me now; whatever the cost, I couldn't let them down.

The witches around the Fiend had completed their ritual, and now thirteen pairs of malevolent, glittering eyes concentrated their attention on me. As they began to chant again, the air sparked and crackled around me as if about to burst into flame.

I was afraid.

The starblade hadn't protected me against the earlier spell that had halted me in my tracks. Would it help now?

To my relief, Grimalkin had been right about her gift: I found that their magic had no effect on me at all. I could hear the cries and the clash of weapons from the battle still being fought around the Wardstone, but the figures below seemed somehow distant, and were slowly being obscured by a green mist tinged with tendrils of blue. The mist that had filled the Spook's garden, bewitching both Grimalkin and the Spook, had been brought about by Alice's magic. Was she summoning this one too? Was it more dark magic? Magic not intended to harm me, but still effective because it prevented my allies from joining me on the Wardstone?

'Do not kill him!' the deep voice of the Fiend boomed out. 'His soul will be mine for all time, but I wish to torment his flesh before he dies.'

The witches began to advance towards me, no doubt intending to seize me and give me to their master. I tried to remain calm and hold my fear at bay. Everything depended on me now. Even if I failed, I must do my very best. I would fight until the last spark of life remained within me.

247

The gigantic figure of the Fiend loomed above me, his face a grotesque gargoyle, a gloating, cruel smile showing the stumps of his broken yellow teeth. I noticed that his eye was still missing too. Although his head was firmly back upon his shoulders, he had not reverted to his original form as I had expected. Had something gone wrong with the ritual? I wondered.

Suddenly he turned his head and leaned towards me, snapping some of the ropes that bound his left shoulder and arm and pulling a shower of nails out of the rock.

In response, I concentrated my mind, bringing one of Mam's gifts to bear against him.

Concentrate! Squeeze time! Make it stop!

I had used this talent successfully many times, and had gradually become more and more skilled – it had enabled us to subdue the Fiend in Ireland.

But this time it seemed to have no effect. Was the Fiend resisting me with his own ability to control time?

I tried again: *Concentrate! Squeeze time! Make it stop!*

Time continued as normal, ticking me forward towards my destruction. The one power that might have given me a chance against such a formidable opponent was ineffectual. Maybe it was because of the Wardstone . . . That rock had its own power over time.

Terrified, in a moment of panic I called out a name:

'Kratch!'

I did it without thought. I had promised to call on the boggart only if my need was great – if we faced total defeat. Wasn't that the situation now?

I glanced at the Fiend, expecting to see him lumbering to his feet, but the massive head twisted from side to side and he brought his free hand to his face, rubbing it across his forehead.

Was he in pain? He certainly seemed befuddled.

'*Kratch!*' I shouted for the second time.

The witches were almost upon me and I had a moment of doubt. I was summoning the creature to certain destruction – and to achieve what? It could only delay my fate. This powerful coven might be prepared, ready with a spell to fling at the boggart the moment it appeared. Even if it did prevail against the witches, it would have no chance at all against the Fiend.

My master had believed it was merely a creature of the dark; an entity that, but for the pact between us, would consider me its prey. But it had helped me once already, more than fulfilling its part of the deal. It had expressed a willingness to die if necessary. It had also called me 'brother' and wanted to fight alongside me. Alone, I had no chance at all.

I looked down again. The green mist was thickening and spreading out below the Wardstone.

I turned back to the advancing witches and called the name of the boggart for the third time:

'*KRATCH!*'

Then I heard a purring deep inside my head, and the boggart spoke words that only I could hear:

I am here, brother! Now we fight to the death! I thank you for bringing me to a place where there is so much dark blood! I will drink the nectar of the witches first. The big one, the old maimed god, is also ready for the taking! I give him to you, but leave some of his rich powerful blood for me!

And then the boggart attacked the coven.

It began as it had last time. For a moment Kratch was visible as a giant cat-like beast – a fearsome distortion of the ginger tom-cat sometimes glimpsed in the kitchen at Chipenden. Then it morphed into a spiral of orange fire and whirled towards the nearest of the witches. She disintegrated in an explosion of flesh and blood. Tiny fragments of bone fell from the air like hail, but rather than melting on contact with the rock, they hissed like hot cinders falling into water.

Now their number was only twelve; not the thirteen required for a true coven. Their power must surely have been diminished.

I moved again, ready to attack the Fiend, who was now twisting his head from side to side as if in pain, seemingly oblivious to the struggle around him. The green mist completely encircled the Wardstone, and now I could neither see nor hear anything of the battle.

But then the other witches rallied, and joined together in a new chant. I heard Kratch scream; it was a cry torn from him by pain but filled with rage too. There was only one thing I could do: follow the boggart's advice.

I scrambled further up the rock, drawing with my left hand one of the hero swords forged by the Old God, Hephaestus –

the dagger known as Bone Cutter. At the top, I emerged near to the Fiend's left leg, continuing on towards his barrel of a chest. He still seemed preoccupied, so he failed to see the threat that I presented. And then – by luck or fate; call it what you will – I was gifted a chance.

His left hand ceased its rubbing and rested for a moment at his side, palm uppermost. I stabbed down with the blade, right through it. I expected it to come to a stop, but instead it bit deep into the rock and held firm.

The Fiend let out a bellow of rage and attempted to tug his hand free, but Bone Cutter was embedded to the hilt in his bleeding palm, the blade stuck fast.

I scrambled up onto his chest and jumped down the other side. His right wrist was still tied to the rock, so my job was easier. I drew the Dolorous Blade, and thrust that through his right hand. Now that he was immobilized, I drew the third, bigger hero sword – the Destiny Blade. I wondered now if, all along, its true destiny had been to end the power of the Fiend. Was that why it had been forged so long ago? Had this been its ultimate purpose?

At this moment I knew instinctively what must be done: I used the blade to sever the thumbs – of first the left and then the right hand.

I quickly turned my attention to the huge head and, gripping my blade with both hands, swung it down on the neck with all my strength. The Fiend thrashed from side to side, and screamed and howled, making my task difficult. Then, in his agony, he began call out threats.

'Do this and all men will die!' he roared. 'Do this and all women will curse your name!'

I ignored his bluster and continued to strike down with the sword. It took three blows to sever the head from the body. It rolled away down the slope, lodging in a crevice.

I made no attempt to cut out the Fiend's heart, but did the next best thing: once again I lifted the sword with both hands, then plunged it down into his chest. The blade went straight through him and buried itself deep in the Wardstone.

The great roar of agony seemed to come from the very earth itself rather than from the Fiend's mouth. The ground began to shake and the whole rock suddenly surged upwards, so that I was thrown off my feet and cast down onto the ground, winded.

I had done all I could – but would it be enough to destroy the Fiend?

As I came up onto my knees, I saw steam rising from all three blades, and there was a sudden sickening stench of burning flesh. Another scream came from the ground, which trembled and convulsed. Then I got to my feet and gazed in astonishment as the sword hilts glowed red and melted.

The Destiny Blade began to drip molten metal onto the Fiend's chest, while the ruby eyes of the skelt embedded themselves in his flesh. Dolorous and Bone Cutter did likewise, bubbling and dripping, the rubies forming two unnatural eyes in each of the open clutching palms.

I turned away in revulsion, the bile rising in my throat at the smell. But one part of me felt a sense of triumph at what I had accomplished. I wished that Lukrasta and Alice could have witnessed this. Alice had dismissed me as a child; I wanted her to see what this 'scrawny boy' had achieved.

There was nobody here to help me – I still couldn't see what was happening below me. Now I needed to collect the head and thumbs and flee. But before I could do so, the rock shifted again, throwing me to my knees. My head struck something, and I tasted blood in my mouth – and then I fell into blackness.

When I recovered consciousness, I glanced up and saw the headless body of the Fiend still lying on the Wardstone. The air was very warm; far too hot for the end of October in the dank, chilly County.

I looked about me. There were pieces of the dead witches scattered across the rock, though I could see no sign of Kratch. He had defeated the witches and no doubt drained their blood, but had he been destroyed in the process?

I could hear no sounds of the battle. Had the two sides ceased fighting and dispersed? The green mist had finally gone, but when I looked below the Wardstone, I got a shock. The country around seemed to be somewhere quite different – a large flat plain ringed by walls of sheer rock. I saw mountains in the distance, some snow-capped, others smoking. Were these volcanoes? I wondered. I had visited Greece, but had never seen a fire mountain – though my master had told me about them. In the distance was what looked like a lake; it boiled and bubbled, with steam rising from its surface.

The sky was clear, but no sun, stars or clouds were visible; yet there was enough light to see by. This was nothing like the world I knew. So where was I?

Had the Wardstone travelled through time, carrying me with it? The Spook had suggested that this might be possible. If so, I'd surely been transported to a very early era in the earth's history. According to my master, the ancients believed that it began as a molten sphere and cooled down very slowly.

Then I remembered what Alice had said would happen to our world after the Fiend was gone. Was this the future . . . the earth shaped by a new dark god?

This place was surely too inhospitable to support any kind of life – though no sooner had that thought entered my head than I spotted something moving by the shore of that boiling lake. I tried to make some sense of what I was seeing. What could possibly live here? Then I saw that there was not one but many of these things, and they seemed to be moving towards me.

They looked like small insects, though I soon saw that it was only distance that made them appear small. When I realized what they were, I was afraid. They were skelts – a host of them, all heading towards the Wardstone.

One part of me wanted to run. But if I left the Wardstone, it might move on through time again and leave me behind to die in this inhospitable place.

The skelts were getting closer now – there were too many of them to count. I could see their multi-jointed legs and the long bone-tubes that they plunged into their victims to drink their blood.

Finally, in the face of that advancing horde, my nerve broke and I prepared to flee. I glanced around, planning my escape route, but saw skelts advancing from all directions. Within moments I would be completely surrounded.

CHAPTER 30
A TERRIBLE HUNGER

I put my hand on the hilt of the sword that Grimalkin had given me. Apart from the silver chain tied about my waist, it was the only weapon I had left – the three hero swords, having done their job well, were still impaled in the Fiend's body.

The first of the skelts reached the base of the rock, stepped up onto it with its thin legs and began to climb towards me. I watched it warily but didn't draw my sword. I felt weary, weakened by the heat and my exertions in the battle. The skelt paused less than a yard from me, regarded me with its two red eyes, and gave a little twitch of its head, its long snout quivering slightly. Then it moved on, heading for the Fiend.

It scuttled up onto his chest, settled close to the wound made by the sword and plunged in its bone-tube. Instantly the tube turned red: the skelt was drinking the Fiend's blood. Soon others were passing me to join the first, driven by a terrible hunger. But each one that came close to me paused and gave the same twitch of the head.

What did it mean? Whatever the reason for this behaviour, I was just grateful not to be attacked.

Within minutes, the huge body was hidden by a mass of writhing, twitching, ravenous skelts. Did the Fiend truly feel pain? I wondered. Was he still conscious, his spirit trapped within the flesh of that gigantic body?

It was difficult to judge the passing of time, but at last the feeding frenzy ended. One by one, the skelts left the Fiend's body, passing by me in single file as if I weren't there. As they did so, I stared at each of the creatures in fascination and wonder.

Each carried a small piece of the Fiend in its mouth. Until that moment I had never thought of skelts as having teeth – for they had that terrible bone-tube; but below this I now saw a mouth full of small, needle-sharp teeth. With a combination of teeth and bone-tube, they had ripped away what they wanted.

I suddenly realized that these creatures were carrying out our plan. Each took away a small piece of flesh or a fragment of bone in its mouth. I had maimed and incapacitated the Fiend, making this possible. What I had started, they had finished. It was strange to think that they had become my partners in the final destruction of the Fiend.

* * *

They moved away towards the lake, carrying their prizes. I watched until they had receded into the distance. Then, one by one, they disappeared into the boiling water, taking the remains of the Fiend with them.

I looked at the place where he had been bound to the rock. All that was left was a few stains and damp patches. Could that really be the end of him? Had the combination of the hero swords and the skelts really destroyed him?

It seemed likely. After all, it would be almost impossible for the Fiend's servants to return him to power if all those pieces of his body were hidden.

All at once I remembered the Spook. My master had died to make this possible. I felt very sad, but he had played a large part in this outcome. We had won.

I sat on the rock for what seemed like ages. I was hungry, but even more thirsty; the air was growing warmer and my mouth was parched.

In the distance I saw what appeared to be a waterfall cascading down the rock face. From there, a stream cut across the valley and flowed into the lake. I knew that eventually I would be driven by my thirst to leave the Wardstone.

But what would happen, I wondered fearfully, if the rock moved through time while I was away? I could be trapped here until I died. So I tried to ignore my thirst and thought about the passage of time here. No doubt the Wardstone didn't *appear* to leave its place on the County fells for long. But time might pass differently here. There was no knowing how long I might be trapped in this scary, inhospitable place.

At last, as I watched, a green mist began to cover the landscape; first the lake and then the cliffs were hidden from view. Then the rock lurched and I was thrown forward onto my face. I felt dizzy and nauseous. Once again, I lost consciousness.

I awoke with a headache, lying face-down on the ground. The first thing I was aware of was the change in temperature. It was cold and I lifted my head, hoping to see the County, for the rock below me was now covered in a white frost.

But despite the cold air and whining wind, I had certainly not returned home. The sun sat on the horizon, perhaps five or six times larger than I had ever seen it before, and a dull orange. There were no clouds, but it seemed much dimmer than usual. I found I was able to look directly at it – something I'd never been able to do with the County sun, in one of its rare appearances between rain clouds.

I was thirstier than ever, but I forced myself to stay where I was and look around. The ground below me was flat and grassy but coated with a thick hoar frost. In the distance I saw a hill and, atop that, a dark tower. It looked very similar to the one in Cymru, where I'd found the Fiend's head.

And then I spotted a dark figure approaching from the direction of the tower. Long before she came near, I knew that it was Alice.

At last I stepped down from the rock to meet her, my feet

crunching on the frosty grass. Her face betrayed no emotion at all. I couldn't tell whether she was angry, or even glad to see me – although I thought the latter unlikely. We both came to a halt a little distance away from each other.

Alice was wearing a long black coat trimmed with fur and fastened with a broad leather belt. It looked expensive – something that a titled lady might wear. She appeared so different to the girl I'd first met; then she'd worn a tattered dress tied at the waist with a piece of string.

But there was one thing that hadn't changed. She was still wearing pointy shoes.

'I hope you're satisfied,' she said, her voice colder than the frosty air.

'You mean what I did to the Fiend? I don't regret that one bit.'

'Don't you? That's because you don't know what you've done. We saw it all in a mirror. You stabbed him with the blades – with the skelt blades, mind. Don't forget the skelts! And then that big rock that has your name carried you off into the dark—'

'Into the dark?' I interrupted, astonished at her words.

'Ain't no doubt about it – I been to that bit of the dark myself. It's one of the domains. Lots of different domains, there are, most of 'em controlled by one of the Old Gods. Haven't you thought about what happened after you stabbed him? Doesn't that worry you?'

'The skelts, you mean? The way they cut the body of the Fiend into pieces?'

'Yes, Tom, what else? The way they cut him up into pieces and carried him into that boiling lake. Do you know why they did that?'

I didn't reply. I was remembering what she'd told me about a god shaped like a skelt.

'They fed those bits to their god, Talkus; the bloodthirsty god who's just been born. Newborns are hungry, Tom. Every woman knows that. Talkus is hungry for power. And just as Grimalkin takes the bones of the witches she slays and wears them around her neck to take their power, so the Kobalos god drew the power of the Fiend into his own body! And now Talkus will lead his people in a war to exterminate every male and enslave every female. Are you starting to see what you done? The Fiend, evil as he was, would've stood beside us against that threat. As much as he likes hurting us, he wouldn't have allowed Talkus to carry out his plan and conquer the whole world for his people. Now he's gone and we're no longer protected. Only Lukrasta stands between us and that skelt god. He's the only human mage who has a chance. The Kobalos have lots of mages, and now that this god is born, their strength will be increased tenfold. Even Lukrasta may not be powerful enough to fight them.'

'What about you, Alice? You have power.'

She shook her head. 'What I have belongs to Lukrasta. He'll need most of my strength if we're to fight Talkus and the Kobalos, so I've offered it to him. He'll know how best to use it.'

261

Anger surged through me at the way Alice was completely in thrall to him. I preferred Grimalkin's stance on Talkus. We had removed the Fiend – that had been our most urgent task. Now we would find a way to deal with Talkus and the Kobalos. And as for Lukrasta – why did we need him? I would deal with the mage, and then Alice would help us with her magic.

'Where is Lukrasta now?' I demanded.

'He's in the tower.' She gestured towards it. 'He's waiting to talk to you. Once the Fiend was destroyed, he brought the rock here so that you could meet. But you've made him angry, Tom – I know it. He's got a terrible temper and he's dangerous when he's angry. So don't go. Climb back onto that big stone and I'll send it back to the County.'

'I'll do that, Alice, if you'll come with me.'

She stared at me for a moment, and I saw something flicker in her eyes. This was my last chance to win her back from the dark. I held my breath. But then her expression changed and I knew that I had lost.

'Ain't coming back with you, Tom. Not now. Not ever. I belong here with Lukrasta. He needs my strength. There's nothing for me back in the County. I feel different. I feel cold and I don't care about people any more – not even you.'

'I don't believe that, Alice.'

I listened to words tumble from my mouth, but I didn't really believe what I had just said. I felt only pain and I was desperate, clutching at straws.

'Think what you like. You ain't me – how can you know how I feel inside?'

'Well, even if you do feel that now, you can change. We all change – all the time. Don't you remember saying that to me? With help, you can change back to what you once were. Surely that isn't impossible? I can help you to do that, Alice. Please, let me help you.'

'No, Tom – climb onto that rock and I'll send you back.'

I shook my head and set off towards the tower. Alice stepped into my path, trying to stop me. Our shoulders collided with some force and she went spinning down onto her knees.

'No, Tom! No! Come back! Come back!' she cried.

But I just carried on walking.

Lukrasta wanted to talk to me, did he? And he was easily roused to anger. Well, I would make him very angry and then I would kill him.

I was tired of being walked over. I was going to make him pay for what he had done. I wanted revenge, and I was determined to achieve it.

Only one of us would leave that tower.

CHAPTER 31

THE TOWER OF TIME

The nearer I got, the more certain I was that this tower was identical to the one in Cymru, where the boggart had killed the witches. It was very high, square and constructed from grey stone blocks.

There was the same long narrow flight of steps leading up to the big iron door; the same arrow-slits in the walls; the same high balcony where Lukrasta had stood with Alice, his arm round her shoulders. He had hurled something against me there; some form of dark magic. Would he do so again? This time I did not have the boggart with me. I wondered if it had survived the battle on the Wardstone and returned to Chipenden . . .

But I had something else to aid me. I now carried the star-blade; I hoped I would no longer be vulnerable to his magic.

But I guessed Lukrasta would not want to attack me from afar. He would prefer to look me in the eye as he killed me. Perhaps he wanted me to die in pain. What sort of a man was he? Power changed people; in time it might corrupt those who had started out with the very best of intentions. How might it affect an ambitious mage who had successfully completed the *Doomdryte* ritual?

By now he was probably more god than a man; an amoral god who considered the rights and desires of human beings unimportant. Lukrasta had lived a very long time – at least a thousand years, maybe longer . . . He might have evolved into something terrible.

I was soon approaching the tower, and I began the long climb to the top of the steps. The stones were slippery with ice and I had to be cautious. At one point I paused and glanced back at the surrounding land. It was mostly flat, unlike the mountainous region in Cymru. But the most alien feature was the sun. It still sat on the horizon, large, orange and bloated, and seemed to be in the same position as when I'd arrived. Was it early morning or late evening? I wondered. It had moved neither upwards nor downwards, but had perhaps shifted along a little? Was this another domain within the dark? Or maybe, on this occasion, the Wardstone had carried me through time?

I continued my careful ascent to the iron door. Last time I had hammered upon it with the hilt of my sword until the witches had opened it. I saw that it was now ajar; slowly it began to move, grating on the stone, opening wide as if pulled by some invisible hand. Of course – Lukrasta wanted to trap me inside his tower so that he could put an end to me at his leisure.

I stepped inside; immediately the door slammed shut behind me. I didn't bother to try it – I knew that it would now be locked.

Before taking another step I looked about me. Although the outside of the tower resembled the one in Cymru, the inside was very different.

I found myself in a small circular room with a single wooden door leading from it. This door had a silver handle and, at head height, a strange symbol, also of silver, shaped a little like a horseshoe. I recognized it.

It was *omega*, a letter from the Greek alphabet.

Ω

My mam had taught me Latin and Greek, which had come in useful when learning my trade as a spook. When we bound a boggart, we carved on the stone the Greek letter *beta*. But the letter on the door was one we never used. Omega was the last letter in the Greek alphabet.

Why was it carved here? I wondered. Could it possibly mean ... the end of something?

I was nervous about what I would find on the other side of

that mysterious *omega* door, but to find Lukrasta I had to go forward. Glancing back, I now realized that I couldn't retrace my steps even if I'd wanted to. The metal door behind me had vanished.

I had no choice but to advance further into the tower. It was an early demonstration of the powerful dark magic that Lukrasta had at his disposal. He was deciding and controlling my movements.

I grasped the handle firmly, twisted it and pushed. The door opened without resistance. Beyond was only darkness. I couldn't see a thing.

Apart from the sword that Grimalkin had given to me and my silver chain, I had no weapons; I'd lost my staff on the battlefield.

But I did have two things that might help me – the small tinderbox that my dad had given me, and the candle-stub I always carried in my breeches pocket.

It was the work of moments to light the candle. With that held high in my right hand, and with my left hand on the hilt of my sword, I brought a yellow glow to that dark place.

To my surprise, I found myself in what appeared to be the kitchen at the Spook's Chipenden house. But it was greatly changed. There were cobwebs everywhere; a thick coating of dust and grime lay on the floor and on the table and chairs. Disturbed by the flickering light of the candle and the soft tread of my boots, a rat scampered away into a gloomy corner.

I looked about me. The fire was cold in the grate and the glass of one of the windows was cracked. The house looked as if it had been abandoned for many years. It was as if there were no more spooks to carry on the work of fighting the dark.

The Wardstone could travel through time . . . but were we back in the past or in the future? Perhaps I was correct about the meaning of *omega*. Was I being shown the end of something?

I reflected that in the domain of a powerful mage I could not truly trust my eyes. Dark magic could create powerful illusions – not least the spell *Dread*; I recalled how the daemon's house in Todmorden had changed at nightfall from a warm, comfortable abode into a ruin.

I could trust nothing here. Of course I was not really in the Spook's house. Although it *seemed* real, this was an illusion created by the magic of Lukrasta. I turned to leave, but again the door I'd entered by had vanished. I felt a surge of anger. He was playing games with me; feeding me untruths. I was trapped within his illusory world.

I wondered about the starblade: Grimalkin had said that it would protect me against dark magic that was intended to harm me. But right now I wasn't actually being harmed – just shown what the mage wished me to see.

What now? How long would I have to wander through this maze before Lukrasta finally confronted me?

I had a sudden hunch that I should go upstairs. Was it my instinct, telling me the right thing to do? Or was it Mam's latest gift showing me where to find Lukrasta? If this was indeed the case, there was no flash of light inside my head to confirm it.

Of course, it might simply be more of Lukrasta's magic. I began to climb the stairs anyway.

As I headed for my bedroom, the candle began to flicker violently in the draught from a broken pane of glass and almost went out. I shielded it with my cupped hand. The room was damp; there was mildew on the blankets. The bed hadn't been slept in for a long time.

Only one thing in that room had survived the fire – that wall where each of the Spook's apprentices had scrawled his name. I stared at it. Something was different. I could see my own name almost lost amongst the others. But another name had been added to the original thirty:

Jenny

But Jenny was surely a girl's name. How could a girl be the apprentice to a spook? What madness was this? What game was Lukrasta playing?

Angrily, I turned to leave the bedroom and descended the stairs. I went through the kitchen again and out through the back door. But this was more trickery: instead of the Spook's garden, I found myself in a wood, and darkness had suddenly changed to daylight. Not that there was much of it left. The sun had set and light was rapidly being leached from the sky.

I was being controlled by Lukrasta.

He was showing me what he wished me to see.

Soon, I resolved, there would be a reckoning.

CHAPTER 32
DRAW YOUR SWORD

There was still enough light to make out the shapes of buildings through the trees ahead. A light breeze was blowing towards me and it carried an unpleasant smell – something fetid and unclean – in the air.

I emerged from the wood to find myself on the edge of a ruined village. The roofs had collapsed; some of the houses were just heaps of rubble and blackened beams lay everywhere.

This sight reminded me of the aftermath of the war that had swept through the County. The same enemy patrol that had burned down the Spook's house had attacked the village.

They'd killed, burned and looted. But the devastation here looked much worse.

It was then that I came upon the first of the dead bodies. It was that of a man; he had clearly been dead for a number of days and decomposition was well underway. I soon saw others: some were children; all were male. Had the women escaped? I wondered.

The next person I found lying in the rubble was still alive, though badly injured. He was lying on his back, with a heavy stone lintel lying across his left leg. His trousers were soaked with blood – the leg was badly crushed. To give him any hope of life it should have been amputated, but it was now too late for that. The leg was already gangrenous. I could smell it from ten paces. The poison would have spread through his body.

He groaned, opened his eyes and stared at me.

I suddenly recognized him: it was the village blacksmith.

With a shock, I realized that the ruined village was indeed Chipenden.

But this couldn't be real. It was just a magical illusion, surely?

This man had been the Spook's main contact in the village; the skilled smith who had fashioned the retractable blades in the ends of our staffs; who'd kept him informed of village news and gossip – a necessary contact for a spook who, because of the nature of his job fighting the dark, was isolated from the life of the community.

The blacksmith was clearly dying, but I noticed something else. He looked older. It wasn't just the gaunt face, perhaps a result of lying in pain without food, water or shelter. His hair had greyed at the temples.

'Mr Ward?' he said, his voice hardly more than a croak. 'Is it you? Can that be possible?'

Illusion or not, he had spoken to me, and I replied automatically. 'Yes, it's me,' I said, walking over to kneel beside him.

'But you're dead!' he exclaimed. 'How can this be?'

I shook my head. 'You're mistaken. I'm alive. Who did this?'

'Why ask that? Surely you know. Who else but beast warriors and their mages . . . ?'

He must mean the Kobalos . . . A terrible thought came into my mind. That while I was on the Wardstone, many years had passed back on earth. What if I'd stepped through the second door and had been carried by Lukrasta's magic to a Chipenden far in the future, when the Kobalos had invaded the County?

The smith began to cough and choke. 'Water, please,' he begged. 'My lips are parched. Give me water.'

I was torn. This was surely some magical deceit conjured by Lukrasta, another illusion. That's what I wanted to believe. And yet the plight of the poor smith seemed all too real. How could I refuse him?

He raised a shaking hand and pointed towards the trees. 'The stream,' he said.

At the foot of the slope was a shallow stream that bubbled over rocks. The water was ice-cold and delicious. I'd drunk from it myself many times. But first I needed something to carry it in.

'I'll be back soon,' I told the smith, and then began to search through the ruined houses. In the shell of a kitchen, I found what I was looking for. Pots, pans and other utensils were strewn amongst the rubble. I picked up a large pan and carried it down the slope into the trees.

I knelt beside the stream and angled the pan against the flow of water. It started to fill.

'I wouldn't bother with that,' a deep voice said behind me. 'You're just wasting your time. He died a few moments after you left him.'

I dropped the pan in the water and leaped to my feet, whirling round.

It was my enemy, the mage Lukrasta.

It was the first time I had been close to him; he was even more formidable than he had looked from a distance. I gazed at the long moustache; the feral mouth with sharp white teeth and lips that were unusually pink, as if suffused with blood. But on closer inspection, the eyes were his most striking feature. They were close set, and blazed with a fierce intensity. They were arrogant eyes, mirrors of a soul filled with the knowledge and certainty of its own power. He was almost a head taller than me, and his body was muscular, like that of the dead blacksmith in his prime.

In a scabbard at his hip he carried a sword. That pleased me. I wanted him to defend himself.

'What did you hope to achieve by all these illusions?' I asked. 'Are you trying to play with my mind to give you some sort of advantage?'

'They were not illusions,' said Lukrasta. 'The tower is real, and everything within it has the potential to be real too. This is my home – the very same tower that that you entered in Cymru.'

'That's impossible,' I replied, looking him in the eye. 'Here, the tower stands on a flat plain. If this is Cymru, where are the mountains?'

'Over aeons, mountains can be levelled, seas can evaporate and a landscape can change beyond recognition. This is still Cymru; the place is the same but the time is different. Did you not notice the sun?'

'That is not our sun,' I said, shaking my head. 'I think you're lying. The Wardstone carried me into the dark. We are probably still there, in another of the domains.'

Lukrasta gave me a sardonic smile. 'No,' he said. 'We are still in Cymru, as I told you. But we are close to the end of the world. The earth is almost devoid of life and cools as the dying sun cools. The Wardstone can travel through time and space as well as visit the dark. That enabled me to bring you to this place. But my home, the Tower of Time, can move through that dimension, but not space. It always remains rooted in this same spot.'

Lukrasta had a sincerity about him that was all too convincing. That was why the witches had taken the Fiend's body to his tower. They had wanted him to use his powerful magic to protect it. But with the boggart's help I'd put paid to that.

'Then what about what I saw in that room?' I asked. 'You said that everything in the tower is potentially real. What do you mean by that?'

'Yes, everything you saw is from a time and place on earth, conjured up by my magic. I have shown you what *could* come to pass if things do not change. It is similar to the scrying of a witch. What she foresees *might* come to pass. But things are not fixed, and decisions and acts by others can change the future. When the witch scrys the same thing at a later date, it will have changed – she will find something different. Thus it has always been. The future is never fixed. *You* can help to change it.'

What he was telling me was very close to what my own master had always believed – that each of our actions shapes the future; that it is not fixed. Well, I was about to change the future again.

'Yes, I think I'll do just that!' I told him bitterly, images of Lukrasta and Alice together flickering into my mind. 'I'll start by putting an end to you. Draw your sword!'

'Haven't you listened to a single word I've said?' Lukrasta asked impatiently, an edge of anger in his voice now. 'You have made a great mistake in putting an end to the Fiend. Now the Kobalos god has been born. He will steadily grow in power until none of the Old Gods will be able to resist his will. Through that birth, the mage strength of the Kobalos has already been tripled and will continue to grow. They are breeding new creatures to fight a war of conquest and extermination against mankind. *You* will play a part in our defence. You must do so! That is the least you can do to make up for your foolishness.'

'What I intend to do is go back to Chipenden and continue to fight the dark in the best way I know – as the Spook's apprentice.'

'In that case you will need a new master. John Gregory died in the battle.'

I felt a mixture of grief and anger, but I knew it was true because I'd glimpsed his dead face – though to hear it from Lukrasta's lips was unbearable. So I vented my feelings in the only way I knew.

'Draw your sword!' I commanded him. 'I won't give you another chance.'

'What a fool you are to challenge me! What do you hope to achieve? Who do you think you are?' demanded Lukrasta.

'I am a seventh son of a seventh son,' I told him. As I drew the starblade with my right hand, flakes of rust fell onto the grass at my feet. 'I'm the son of a good man, a farmer who taught me right from wrong; who taught me manners; who taught me what goodness is. But I'm also the son of the first Lamia who, although a loving mother, could be fierce and cruel beyond your imagination. I'm the child of them both. And I've been trained by John Gregory, perhaps the greatest spook the County has ever known. I'm Thomas Ward, your worst nightmare. You've lived too long, Lukrasta, and this is the time of your death. And now I'll say it for the third time: draw your sword!'

Lukrasta muttered under his breath and made a sign in the air.

I tensed. This was the moment of truth. Would the starblade be strong enough to protect me against his magic?

Sparks flickered at his fingertips and a blue light flashed towards me. But I held the sword vertically before my face and the light played around its sharp tip before changing to orange and fading away.

I smiled then, showing my teeth.

Grimalkin had forged a powerful weapon for me. The mage couldn't hurt me with his magic. I was about to have my revenge. I would pay him back for taking Alice from me.

'Where did you get that weapon?' he demanded, his voice cold and imperious.

'It was fashioned by the witch assassin Grimalkin, and she gave it to me,' I told him. 'She calls it the "starblade" because of what it was made from. While I possess it, your magic is powerless against me. So let's see how well you can fight. Let's see how well you can die.'

Lukrasta straightened his back, held his head high and looked down at me. 'The last thing I took you for was a fool!' he growled. 'It looks like I was wrong.'

Then, finally, he drew his sword.

CHAPTER 33
LAMIA BLOOD

L ukrasta drew his sword but did not attack. He waited, his weapon held vertically like my own. His expression was inscrutable but his eyes were fixed upon my blade.

I would have to initiate the fight.

I took a tentative step towards him and thrust the tip of my sword towards his chest. He made no attempt to parry. He just took two rapid steps backwards, taking us further from the stream.

I jabbed again, and he retreated further. There was a tree behind him; soon his back would be against the trunk. So, thinking to force him to retreat, I ran at him, bringing my sword round in an arc towards his head. For the first time he used his own sword. Its blade met mine in mid-air, and the woodland was filled with the sound of clashing metal and the beating of wings as a flock of frightened birds took flight.

I pressed home my attack, getting into the swing of things, seeking an opening in his defence. But he too was moving now, on his toes, his weapon blocking each thrust and swing of my own. Lukrasta certainly knew how to use a sword, but I sensed that he was not fighting to his full ability, and that angered me. He was moving sideways in an arc rather than backwards, and now my own back was to the trees. Even though he was on the defensive, he still managed to manipulate me, choosing his position and manoeuvring me where he wanted me.

So I stepped up the pace and drove him towards the stream.

I was really getting into a rhythm now, using all the tricks that Grimalkin had taught me. The sword felt light, the balance just right. It was the perfect weapon for me. I was getting my second wind, my speed gradually building. It was as if I could predict each of Lukrasta's moves in advance, but that was relatively easy because each was a reaction to what I did. He was still fighting defensively.

I had him at the edge of the water now, and I saw my chance. He seemed to hesitate and glance backwards down at the stream.

Was he like a witch, unable to cross running water?

Seeing his hesitation and temporary loss of concentration, I took my opportunity. The scything stroke of my sword should have sundered his head from his body. But he suddenly stepped back into the water with far more grace than he had so far displayed.

My blade missed.

But his didn't.

Passing within a hair's breadth of my left eye, the tip of his sword cut my cheek to the bone.

I staggered back, my cheek burning, feeling the blood run down my face and onto my neck. Lukrasta was smiling at me arrogantly, standing up to his knees in the fast-flowing stream. It had been a trick. He had been waiting for me to overextend myself.

'Only one side of your face will be handsome now!' he mocked. 'But never fear. I'm sure there is a woman somewhere who will take pity on you!'

He could have said anything but that. He had taken Alice from me; he had ended my dream of being with her someday; he had shattered our friendship as casually as a drunken man hurls an empty glass against a wall.

I fought on, filled with increasing fury, desperate for revenge – although that did not lessen my skill. I was one with the sword, pressing harder and harder against my opponent. But he matched every jab and every swing I made.

All but the last one.

I moved without thinking, repeating the ruse I'd used against Grimalkin when she had hunted me down after the battle on Pendle Hill. Then, I had flicked my staff from my right hand to my left and driven its blade through her left shoulder, pinning her to a tree, never dreaming that we would later become allies.

Grimalkin had taught me how to fight with a sword, but John Gregory had taught me to wield a staff, and it was my master's teaching that now came to my aid.

I flicked the sword, caught it with my left hand and drove it through Lukrasta's shoulder. His eyes widened in surprise and he dropped his own weapon into the water. When I pulled the blade from his flesh, he groaned and fell to his knees.

The water was up to his waist, swirling away the blood that dripped from his shoulder. That was nothing to the blood he was about to lose. I grasped my sword with both hands and held it above my head. Lukrasta looked up at me. He was stupefied; unable to believe what was about to happen.

I gathered my strength, ready to strike his head from his shoulders. A second and it would be done. My enemy would be dead.

But then a voice cried out behind me.

'Don't, Tom! Please, Tom! Please don't kill him!'

It was Alice.

I shifted slightly so that I could see both of them. I watched her out of the corner of my eye, but kept my attention on Lukrasta.

'Why beg, Alice? Why don't you save him? All you have to do is blast me with your magic. That should be easy enough for a witch like you,' I jibed.

'Don't mock me, Tom, it doesn't suit you. I wouldn't hurt you

for anything. You should know that by now. But even if I
wanted to, I couldn't. Ain't possible, is it? Magic can't hurt you
while you have that sword.'

'You know about the sword?' I asked in astonishment.

Alice nodded. 'Grimalkin told me she was going to forge you
a special blade. She said it couldn't be broken and could ward
off dark magic. I suppose that must be what you're holding,
otherwise you wouldn't have beaten Lukrasta.'

'I beat him fair and square, Alice!' I snapped angrily. 'The
sword gave me no special advantage.'

'That's not what I meant. He didn't want to hurt you, Tom.
He didn't want to fight you. He would have knocked you out
with his magic, that's all, and then sent you back to the County.'

'That's not what you told me earlier!' I snapped.

'I didn't want either of you hurt. I knew you would quarrel.
And it's exactly as I feared.'

'You must think me a fool. I would be if I believed that. You
didn't care about me – it was Lukrasta you wanted to protect.
Your *friend* Lukrasta thought me a fool to fight him. Look at
him on his knees. Who's the fool now?'

Tears started to run down Alice's cheeks. I felt a pang of jealousy, and in anger raised the sword a little, ready to strike.

'Please! Please! Listen to me. You're both on the same side.
Don't do it, I beg you,' she pleaded, coming to the bank and
wading in to stand between me and Lukrasta.

For the first time I looked at her directly, still keeping an eye
on Lukrasta. There was something pitiful about the way she

was crying; it was obvious that she cared deeply for him.

Suddenly I was divided. I felt within me a need for vengeance; my urge to kill Lukrasta was strong. No doubt that was the lamia blood coursing through my veins. But as I had told the mage, I was also a seventh son of a seventh son; my father's blood was also in me. And he had taught me right from wrong.

Years ago Dad had been involved in a dispute with a neighbouring farmer. The man had been grazing his cattle on Dad's land for at least a decade, ignoring his protests and claiming the field was his. Finally, fed up with the situation, Dad took his grievance to the local magistrate, and after much deliberation and study of parish records, Dad had won. The magistrate ordered the neighbour to stop grazing his cattle there and to give Dad a dozen animals by way of compensation.

But Dad had refused the cattle, saying he was content just to have the field officially acknowledged as his own. Later I'd asked him why he'd done it. Didn't he deserve to have those cows to make up for the grazing he'd lost over the years?

Dad had smiled. 'Listen, son,' he'd said. 'Never kick a man when he's down. In the long term it'll pay off.'

That farmer eventually turned into a good neighbour: it was Mr Wilkinson who'd helped after the farm had been raided by witches. He'd seen the barn burning and had rushed to help, only to suffer a blow to the head. He had been lucky that the witches hadn't killed him. Later he'd looked after the livestock and dogs until Jack and Ellie returned. So in the end Dad had been proved right. The 'kick' that I was about deliver would be a lot more damaging and permanent than the harm done by a boot. So I listened again to Dad's voice in my head.

Then I lowered my sword and stared at my enemy. It was almost dark now, and Lukrasta's face was in shadow.

'You're welcome to each other,' I said, the edge of bitterness still sharp in my voice. 'Now I want to go home.'

Alice nodded and turned on her heel, saying nothing.

I followed her up onto the muddy bank, leaving Lukrasta still on his knees in the stream. She led me back through the ruins of the village to a wall with a door in it.

'Go through that,' she said, 'and you'll find yourself on the steps outside the tower. You'll be back in Cymru, but in our own time. Sorry, but you'll have to walk back to the County.'

Suddenly a pale moon came out from behind a cloud and cast my shadow onto the wall. It was a giant shadow; an impossible shadow – perhaps three times larger than it should have been. I pointed towards it.

'Do you remember what you told me soon after we first met?' I asked Alice.

'Yes. The moon cast your shadow onto a barn wall, and I said that the moon shows the truth of you.'

'And you've never spoken truer words. That's me, Alice,' I said, pointing to my shadow. 'The scrawny boy is only what you *think* you see. I'm the hunter; the hunter of the dark. So don't make me hunt you! I never want to see you again. Keep well away from Chipenden,' I warned, pointing the sword at her. 'This will protect me from your magic and I'll put you in a pit as soon as look at you. You'd better believe me.'

'There's lots of things you don't know, Tom. I won't waste my time trying to explain now because you're bitter and angry. But I will tell you one thing. We'll meet again, and you won't put me in a pit. Thanks for sparing Lukrasta's life. You don't know how important that was.'

I didn't bother to reply. I opened the door and gazed out at the Cymru of our time. Without looking back at Alice, I slammed it shut and began to hurry down the steps. The ice had gone; the sun was back to normal, about to retreat behind a cloud that threatened rain. It was early morning – the morning after the battle – so I needed to make the most of the daylight hours.

It was a long journey home and my cheek throbbed with every step that I took.

CHAPTER 34
THE LAST LESSON

I t took me nearly three days to walk back to Chipenden. I
arrived at dusk, intending to spend the night there, resting,
before returning to the Wardstone to collect my master's body
and bring it back to the house for burial. But when I reached the
edge of the garden, I found Grimalkin waiting for me under
a tree, her horse grazing on the lush grass beside her.

I had lots of questions for her. Who had died? Who had
survived? I was particularly concerned about James. But what
I saw silenced me.

Beside her, bound within a blanket, lay a body.

She had brought the Spook home.

* * *

We sat by the hearth in the kitchen, with the Spook's body laid out on the table. I had stared at his face for a while, thinking of our time together until tears came into my eyes. When I turned away, Grimalkin had tied the blanket about him for the final time.

'Is James all right?' I asked.

She nodded. 'Yes, he's gone back to the farm.'

'And Judd?'

'He lost a couple of fingers, but what bothered him most was that one of the dogs was killed, the bitch called Claw. He said he should never have taken them to the battle. There were other deaths – the Deanes suffered badly, and the Mouldheels too. One of Mab's sisters was killed – the twin called Jennet. But the lamia, Slake, survived. She intends to return to Greece. Despite their numerical advantage, the enemy suffered far heavier losses than we did. Romanian and Celtic witches fought on their side, and every one of them died. Perhaps less than half the Essex witches escaped the County.'

I nodded, then described all that had happened to me afterwards. Towards the end of my account I asked her about the sword. 'I fought Lukrasta and defeated him. He tried to use his magic against me, but it had no effect. The starblade protected me. So why didn't it keep the dark magic at bay during the battle?' I asked. 'I was paralysed like everybody else.'

'It was a spell that joined the power of all the enemies who faced us,' Grimalkin replied. 'Combined with that was the magic of Lukrasta. Alice also probably added hers too. The star-blade has its limits. I did my best, but nothing is perfect.'

'It must have been Alice!' I exclaimed angrily. 'It protected me against Lukrasta when we fought – she didn't add her magic then.'

'Such bitterness is bad for you,' Grimalkin said. 'It achieves nothing. Put her from your mind.'

For a while I said nothing. Then, as I gradually calmed down, I went on with my account, ending with my decision not to kill Lukrasta.

'Alice thanked me for sparing his life,' I told her. 'She was crying. I think she loves him very much.'

'Maybe she does and maybe she doesn't,' replied the witch assassin. 'But for now their fates are bound together. You did the right thing, of that I am certain. We must deal with the Kobalos now, or at least begin the process. Despite her grief at the loss of her sister, Mab scryed for me to see what she could about our new enemies. Their god, Talkus, has been born, but it will take him time to reach his full strength and gain dominion over the other gods, daemons and entities from the dark. The Kobalos are preparing for war, but that will also take time. We must use this interval to ready ourselves. And Lukrasta will be important in helping to deal with their mages. I intend to begin by finding out more about their strengths and weaknesses. Will you join me? I am travelling north tomorrow.'

I shook my head. 'No, I've had enough of killing. I plan to follow in my master's footsteps and become the Chipenden

Spook, protecting folk in the County from the dark. It's what John Gregory trained me for – it's what he'd have wanted.'

'Whether you help me now or later is your decision,' Grimalkin replied. 'But eventually you will be forced to do so because the Kobalos will come here. Then they will kill all the people you seek to protect – but not the women. For the women and girls they will have other uses.'

'If that happens, I'll have to help, but it's a long way to the land of the Kobalos. There are many kingdoms between us and them. If those human kingdoms unite, the Kobalos may lose. They may not venture this far. Here . . .' I said, drawing the starblade and holding it out towards her, hilt first. 'Thanks for the loan of this blade, but I won't be needing it any more. I'll use the traditional weapons of my trade.'

Grimalkin shook her head. 'It's a gift, not a loan. It was made for you and nobody else. I won't take it back.'

'In that case I'll hide it in a place where I won't be tempted to use it,' I told her. 'I've seen too much death recently. I've killed again and again until it sickens me. Swords are not for me. I'll go back to using a staff; back to my silver chain, salt and iron. I'll fight the dark in traditional ways. I'm sorry, but I've thought it over on my way back from Cymru. It's what I want to do.'

'It's your decision,' she told me, 'so let's speak of something else. I could improve your face. I cannot get rid of all the scarring, but the disfigurement would be greatly reduced. Would you like me to try?'

I nodded.

'It will hurt,' she warned. 'For that kind of magic there is always a price to be paid. But unlike the pain caused by the silver pin in my leg, it will be of only short duration.'

'Yes, it would be worth it. I've already seen the way people look at it. Being a spook puts people off enough without this scar.'

After we'd talked I walked down to the village and bought a coffin from the village carpenter.

'I'm sorry to hear of your master's death,' he told me, shaking his head sadly. 'He was a good man.'

The Spook was a tall man, and so I was surprised to find that the carpenter already had a coffin big enough to accommodate his body. Otherwise it would have spent another night unburied.

'Mr Gregory ordered and paid for this last month,' the man told me.

The Spook had sensed the imminence of his own death, I realized.

Grimalkin helped me to dig the grave. As we prepared to slide my master's body into the dark hole in the damp earth, I nodded at the sword that I had laid down on the grass to one side.

'I'm going to put it under the coffin,' I said. 'You won't take it back, and this way there is less chance that anyone else will be able to get their hands on it.'

'But what if you change your mind? You would have to disturb his grave to retrieve it.'

'That's another good reason for placing it here,' I answered. 'I would never disturb my master's grave. May his body rest in peace.'

Grimalkin said nothing, but she stared at me for a moment, then shook her head. I shivered at the expression in her eyes. She was not only a powerful witch, but also an excellent scryer, and you never knew what she glimpsed in the future. Whatever it was, she didn't tell me. Even if she had, I would have disregarded it because the future is not fixed.

So I put the sword in the grave and we lowered the coffin on top of it. Then we stood there in silence for a few moments. What Grimalkin thought I do not know, but her eyes were downcast.

I do not make a habit of praying, but I remembered what I had said at Dad's grave; now I repeated the words to myself.

Please, God, give him peace. It's what he deserves. He was a good hard-working man and I loved him.

For in truth he had been a teacher, a friend and also a father to me.

Then, together, without speaking, Grimalkin and I filled in the grave. The only sounds to be heard were the thrust and lift of our spades, and the soil falling upon the wooden casket. The air was very still; even the birds had fallen silent.

Immediately afterwards, Grimalkin attended to the scar on my face. For some reason known only to herself, it had to be done in the dark. I sat in a chair in a storeroom adjacent to the house.

'Keep still!' she hissed. 'However severe the pain, you must not move.'

I felt her finger touch my face, tracing the line of the scar that began just below my eye. She muttered three words under her breath, and then I felt a strange sensation in my left cheek. At first it felt like ice, then like fire. Whether she cut me with a blade or some other instrument I don't know. But the pain was intense and I felt blood running down my face.

Although it was extremely difficult, I did not move – though inside I was crying out in pain.

Later I examined my face in a mirror. She had opened the scar again; in my opinion it looked worse than ever. But I thanked her anyway. I didn't care how I looked any more. I felt flat, my emotions deadened.

At dawn we said a brief goodbye. Grimalkin gave me a nod and headed over to where her horse was grazing. She told me neither where she was bound nor when she would return. I had refused her request to help with the new threat, so we had probably reached the end of our temporary alliance. She would go back to her business of being a witch assassin.

I wondered if I would ever see her again.

That night I dreamed of Alice . . .

Alice looked terrified. She stared up at me and I could see her whole body trembling.

I was shaking too, sick to my stomach.

Alice was tied to a large flat stone on a raised platform.

There was a large mound of stones nearby, but it wasn't a cairn such as was often found at the peak of a high fell. It was hollowed out, and a fierce fire burned within. It was a furnace created for a terrible purpose.

It was Halloween, and I was about to begin the ritual that would destroy the Fiend.

Standing on the other side of Alice, directly opposite me, was Grimalkin. She was balancing Bone Cutter and the Blade of Sorrow in the palm of her hand. The first would be used to slice the thumb-bones from Alice's hands; the other to cut her beating heart from her chest.

If Alice cried out while I sliced the first bones, the ritual would fail. Her silence and bravery were essential to a successful outcome.

'I'm ready, Tom,' she said softly.

'It is time to begin,' added Grimalkin.

I loved Alice.

And Alice loved me.

But now I was about to kill her.

'Goodbye, Tom,' she said. 'You were the best thing that ever happened to me. I have no regrets.'

I tried to reply, but my throat seemed to swell and I couldn't get the words out. My eyes brimmed with tears.

'Do it now! Quickly!' Grimalkin commanded.

I blinked the tears out of my eyes and, very gently, took Alice's left hand. Next I held it firmly against the stone. Now I had to position the knife. I took it from Grimalkin and readied myself for what must be done. It was difficult because my hand was shaking violently, my palms sweating, making it difficult to grip the blade.

I took a deep breath and forced the blade through the base of Alice's thumb. I was screaming as I did so, but Alice was brave. Not one cry escaped her lips.

I awoke suddenly, my heart racing. It had been a nightmare of what might have been. That terrible dream had seemed real, but we had taken a different path and the future had changed.

Then I became aware of a weight resting on my legs and heard the sound of purring.

So the boggart had survived, after all.

It did not speak to me; it did not demand my blood. Had it done so, I would have given it willingly. John Gregory had begun the process by doing a deal with the boggart to guard the house and garden. My own partnership with the boggart was far closer and I knew not where it would take me. I knew that I was very unusual, but the dark was changing; the battle would perhaps demand different tactics.

We keep notebooks so that we may learn from the past; but now I know that a spook must look to the future, and adapt and change. A wise man continues to learn until the day he dies. John Gregory was wise, and he realized that sometimes a compromise with the dark is necessary. That was perhaps the last lesson that he learned.

CHAPTER 35
THE CHIPENDEN SPOOK

Late in the afternoon the day after we laid the Spook to rest, the bell rang at the withy trees.

I found a red-faced farmer in muddy boots waiting for me there, nervous and frightened and badly needing help.

'My name's Morris – Brian Morris from Ruff Lane Farm just south of Grimsargh. There's a boggart made its home in my barn,' he told me. 'It's throwing great big rocks at the house. One went right through the kitchen window. Luckily my wife had moved away from the sink to tend to the baby. Had she been standing there, she'd have been killed for sure.'

It was routine spook's business, so I nodded and answered in what I hoped was a reassuring tone. 'It sounds like you're under attack from a stone-chucker. Get back home as quickly as possible – you and your family should leave the house. Stay with a neighbour. I'll follow as soon as I collect my things. With luck, I'll sort it out tonight. Otherwise two nights at the most and it'll be gone.'

'No disrespect, lad, but I'd prefer it if your master attended to my problem.'

'That won't be possible,' I told him firmly. 'Unfortunately John Gregory is dead. My name is Master Ward, and I'm the Chipenden Spook now. I'm offering you my help.' I stared hard at him until he lowered his eyes.

'I won't be able to pay you right away,' he said. 'Times are hard.'

'After the next harvest will do,' I replied. 'Now be on your way. Get your family out and leave the rest to me. I'll deal with it – don't worry.'

He turned and, with a barely perceptible nod of acceptance, trudged off into the distance.

I went back to the house to collect my bag – not forgetting a small parcel of cheese for the journey.

My life as the Chipenden Spook had begun.

Once again, I've written most of this from memory, just using my notebook when necessary.

I am no longer John Gregory's apprentice. Now I am the Chipenden Spook, and I must do my best to keep the County safe from ghosts, ghasts, boggarts, witches and all manner of creatures from the dark – some, perhaps, as yet unknown. For, as my master taught me, life as a spook is one long process of learning.

Out there in the County, many incidents are, as yet, un-explained. We can learn from the past by using the legacy of knowledge left to us by former spooks; but the dark is always throwing up new challenges and surprises, and we must adapt and learn to counter any new threat.

Although I am no longer an apprentice, there is one local spook who will still be able to contribute to my learning. Judd Brinscall has offered his aid and experience should I require it. I am practising regularly to enhance my skills with staff and chain, the main weapons of a spook. As for the scar on my face, it is greatly improved. There is now just a faint white diagonal line running down from my eye. So Grimalkin's magic did its work.

That is the difference between me and previous generations of spooks. I am prepared to accept the use of magic, but only if the ends justify it and there is no cost to others. No doubt that is because of the lamia blood coursing through my veins. And I have another potent ally to help me should I require it – the boggart.

It had been the Spook's boggart; now it is mine.

But the sword will remain under my master's coffin. I am sick of killing. Now I will concentrate on dealing with the dark in the County.

As for my master, John Gregory, I will never forget what he did for me. In the eyes of most priests, spooks are no better than witches and cannot be interred in holy ground. Some are buried as close as possible to the boundary of a churchyard. But I didn't want that for my master.

We buried the Spook in what I guessed must be one of his favourite locations, next to the seat in the western garden – the place where we had often sat for my lessons. It was full of happy memories, with a view of the fells in the distance and the sound of birdsong filling the air. I was the thirtieth and last of his apprentices, and he must have spent many satisfying years here as he trained boys to fight the dark.

One day, perhaps, I will have an apprentice of my own. Maybe this is the place where I will also be buried.

I had the local mason craft a gravestone, and on it carve the following:

HERE LIETH

JOHN GREGORY OF CHIPENDEN,

THE GREATEST OF THE COUNTY SPOOKS

It was a fitting epitaph. What I had ordered to be written there was true; there was no exaggeration. For over sixty years my master had fought the dark and kept the County safe. He had always done his duty, and done it well, displaying great skill and courage. Finally he had laid down his life in order that the Fiend might be destroyed.

But life goes on. Last week I had good news from Jack. Ellie has given birth to a healthy baby boy. They've called him Matthew, and now Jack has a son to help with the farm when he is older.

My job now is to keep the County safe from the dark.

If I achieve half as much as my master, I will be satisfied.

Thomas J. Ward

THOMAS WARD NOW BATTLES AGAINST THE DARK
ALONE. READ ON FOR A SNEAK PEEK AT JOSEPH
DELANEY'S NEXT BOOK, THE FIRST IN A
BRAND-NEW SERIES . . .

There was a cold draft coming from somewhere; maybe *that* was making the candle flicker to cast strange shadows onto the wall at the foot of the bed. The floor was uneven; perhaps *that* was why the door kept opening by itself as if something invisible was trying to get in.

But those ordinary, commonsensical explanations didn't work here. As soon as I'd walked into the bedroom I'd known that there was something badly wrong. That's what my instincts told me and they've rarely let me down.

Without doubt the room was haunted by somebody or something. And that's why I was there, summoned by the landlord of the inn to sort out his problem.

My name is Tom Ward and I'm the Chipenden Spook. I deal with ghosts, ghasts, boggarts, witches and all manner of things that go bump in the night.

After all, someone has to do it.

I walked over to the window and used the sash to raise the lower half. It was about an hour after sunset and a crescent moon was already visible above the distant hills. I was looking down on a graveyard shrouded by trees. This was the village of Kirkby Lonsdale and it was less than twenty miles northeast of Caster, in an isolated location not being on the most direct route from that city to any sizeable town.

I went downstairs, leaving the inn by walking through the front room where three locals were drinking ale by the fire. They stopped talking and all turned to watch me but not one called out a greeting. No doubt any stranger to the village would have received a similar response – silence, curiosity and the drawing together in common defence against the outsider.

Of course, there would be an additional factor here. I was a spook, and although I was needed to deal with threats from the dark I made people nervous and often afraid. Some folk crossed over to the other side of the street to avoid me just in case something from the dark was hovering close to me.

And it was the way of things in the County that, by now, all in the village would know my business here.

A voice did call me as I walked through the front door and out onto the street. 'Master Ward, a quick word in your ear!'

I turned and watched the landlord approach. He was a big hearty man with a florid face and a loud voice full of forced good-cheer – something that he had, no doubt, cultivated for the benefit of his customers. But although I was spending the night in one of his rooms he had an air of impatience and superiority that I'd noted when he dealt with his staff and also the man who'd delivered fresh casks of ale soon after I'd arrived.

I was counted as the hired help and he obviously expected a lot for his money.

'Well?' He raised his eyebrows. 'What have you found out?'

I shrugged. 'The room's haunted all right, but by what I don't know yet. Maybe you could speed things up a little by telling me everything that you know. How long has this been going on?'

'Well, *young* man, isn't it up to you to find out the situation for yourself? I'm paying you good money so I certainly don't expect to have to do your job for you. I'm sure your former master, John Gregory, God rest his soul, would have had the job done by now.'

With his last sentence the inn-keeper had got to the heart of the problem; and it *was* his problem, not mine. My master was dead. He had died the previous year in a battle near the Wardstone, fighting to destroy the Fiend who'd threatened to bring an age of darkness and fear to the world.

I had inherited John Gregory's role and was functioning as the Chipenden Spook. But, in truth, I hadn't really completed my apprenticeship and was young to be plying my trade alone like this.

I'd met quite a few people over the past few months who shared the attitude of this landlord. I'd learned quickly that it was important to put them right and get off on the right foot.

'Mr Gregory would have asked you the same question that I

just did, make no mistake about it,' I told him. 'And I'll tell you something else – if you'd failed to answer he would have picked up his bag and gone straight home.'

The inn-keeper glared at me, a touch of anger twitching his brows. He clearly wasn't used to being spoken to like that. I stared back without blinking but I kept my expression mild and my tongue still. I waited for him to speak.

'A girl died in that room exactly a month ago tomorrow,' he said at last. 'I employed her in the kitchen and sometimes, when it got busy, she helped out by serving ale. She was fit and strong. One morning she didn't get up and we found her dead in bed with a look of terror on her face and blood all down the front of her nightgown. But there was no sign at all of a wound on her body. Since then her ghost walks and I can't let the room – or any others, for that matter. We can hear her pacing back and forth even down in the ale room. By now there'd have been a dozen people in there with more to come. It's affecting my business badly.'

I nodded and offered him my best sympathetic expression. 'What about the cause of death?' I asked. 'What did the doctor have to say?'

'He seemed as puzzled as everyone else but thought it might have been some sort of internal haemorrhage and that she'd coughed up blood. But it was the look of horror on her face that made us all uneasy. The doctor said seeing all that blood coming out of her mouth might have terrified her and caused her heart to stop. Or she might have carried on bleeding inside. To my way of thinking, he didn't really know why she'd died.'

'Well maybe I'll be able to tell you more tomorrow,' I replied, 'after I've talked to her ghost. What's her name?'

'Her name was Miriam,' he replied.

A special Q&A with Joseph Delaney about *The Spook's Revenge* and his brand new series . . .

How do you feel now that The *Wardstone Chronicles* are finally complete?
I find it incredible that I have managed to write a series that contains thirteen books and two spin-offs. I only thought there would be three! I am happy with this final book and hope I have tied up most of the loose ends.

Was writing the final chapters an emotional experience for you?
Not really. I am the 'pilot' and the readers are the 'passengers'. When turbulence strikes I'm not worried because I have experienced it all before. So I hope the readers feel some emotion because of what happens. I want them to be scared, happy and sad – to experience a whole range of reactions and emotions.

Was it difficult trying to give all of your characters a satisfying ending?
Yes, but at one level I think the story itself decides what has to happen. I know that not everybody will be pleased with the way the book ends. Certain characters come to the end of their story and others may not behave in the way that everybody would like!

You have said before that you 'discover' your plots rather than carry out detailed planning in advance, but are there parts of the final book that have been in your head for a long time?
I always intended to visit the Wardstone at the end of the series. How could I avoid going there when it is mentioned at the beginning of every book and Tom Ward is the hero? But the truth is that I even began this final book of the series still not knowing fully how it would end.

Has it been difficult to keep the ending secret from curious fans? Are you excited to see their reaction to it?
Yes, many readers have tried to find out the ending from me. They were easy to resist because I didn't know myself! I am excited to see how the final book is received.

Of the 13 main books in the *Wardstone Chronicles*, is there one that stands out to you as a favourite?
I have always preferred *The Spook's Battle* to the others. It marked the point when I realised that the *Wardstone Chronicles* would be a long series. Grimalkin comes into the story for the first time and the Fiend is summoned to earth – these are two important elements that help drive the ongoing narrative and generate subsequent books.

What can you tell us about your brand new series?
I don't want to give too much away. I know how the first
book ends and I am happy with it. The new series is
scheduled to be a trilogy but my writing method is still that
of 'discovery'. There could be more than three – but I am
certain that there will not be thirteen!

How will it differ from The *Wardstone Chronicles*?
It will have some of the same elements and is from the
world of spooks and witches. However a new darkness is
rising. Those of you who have read *Slither's Tale* will know
what I mean!

After nine years the story of *Wardstone Chronicles* is finally complete. We asked the fans of the series from Joseph Delaney's Facebook page to tell us what the books have meant to them over the years.

Here is a selection of their answers . . .

'I was in Year 8 when the first book in the *Wardstone Chronicles* was introduced to me by my best friend. Ever since then I have been in love with the series. I know that I will always love these books, the characters and the adventures that they go on. To Joseph Delaney, I am forever thankful for making my teenage years so special.'
Virginia Cole

'I first discovered the *Wardstone Chronicles* when I was about 13 and wandering around WH Smith with my Mam, looking for a new book to read. I then saw an ominous-looking, leather-bound book staring back at me. I was already captivated and bought *The Spook's Apprentice* straight away. On my holiday to Melbourne in 2007 I remember being jet-lagged and (foolishly) ignored the 'do not read after dark' warning, while reading *The Spook's Curse* and I definitely couldn't sleep that night. I'd like to thank Joseph Delaney for the many wonderful and beautiful stories he has left me with, as well as useful information on how to deal with boggarts – always remember the salt, iron and tinderbox!' *Sam Hutchinson*

'I discovered the series on the internet. When I read the book synopsis I realized that I had to have that book. I bought it. It was the best thing I ever did. Thank you for sharing this amazing adventure with all of us.' *Anderson Estevam Lopes*

'The Spook's series pulled me in from the very first book. I have read all the books so far and really could not pick a favourite. The characters are awesome and the plot is original and each book is even better than last if that's even possible!'
Edel Waugh

'I live in the Netherlands and I think I discovered the books in the Netherlands. I was totally creeped out by the first book. I love the series with all my heart, it is amazing and I am a big fan. I really love Joseph Delaney for making this series: it is creepy, exciting and so fun to read.' *Roos Busink*

'The *Wardstone Chronicles* became my favourite series a long time ago, seven years to be precise. I discovered them at my local library and I immediately fell in love with the book covers, which looked like old, leather diaries (needless to say, I borrowed them immediately!). This series means a lot to me, it's actually the great part of my teenage-hood (I'm 21 now!). When I read the *Wardstone Chronicles* I relive all my happy memories and I still discover new details.'
Alexandra Vivarelli

'I have loved the Spook's series for as long as I can remember, eagerly anticipating every new book and then reading them far too quickly but loving every second of them. I am turning 20 this year and these books will always be a favourite of mine, they helped me through a difficult time in my life and knowing I could always escape into them was a great comfort to me. Knowing that the last one is coming out soon makes me very sad, but excited at the same time. It will be the end of a fantastic series!' *Rebecca Rankin*

'As a northern exile with plenty of family buried all over Pendle's churchyards I love the series because it reminds me of home and the places of my childhood. As a teacher I love the Spook's books because I've been able to use them to get so many of my students into reading. If only the series didn't have to end.' *Paul Hargreaves*

'I've grown up with these books and have loved them for years. I feel like when the series ends my childhood finally will with it. Thanks for the memories!' *Sam Ball*

'I love Spook's because it takes a new perspective on horror, medieval and narrative books. I found it on the net and instantly loved it to the core. THANK YOU J.DELANEY!' *Ghayur Haider*

'My favourite series ever. I could hardly put them down. Day by day, page by page, the characters become real to me. I got to know them and followed their journeys like they're my old friends.' *Supakanya, Tennessee, USA*

'I LOVE THE SPOOKS BOOKS! They are by far the most amazing books I've ever read. I love all the different creatures and mythologies! I wish that the series would never end!' *Phoenix Steinfeldt*

'I am 20 years old and I have been following these books since I was 11. I have never missed a release date. The *Wardstone Chronicles* is a series I have always loved to escape to. Following Tom, Alice and the Spook will always be a very fond part of growing up for me. Having spent a lot of time in Lancaster the last couple of years I can see why they are set in that beautiful county. Great series and I really cannot wait to finish the series, if only to re-read them. Thanks for the memories.' *Stephanie Swann*

'I think the Spook's series is the best I've ever read! The storyline is phenomenal and the characters have amazing personalities! I think this series has an excellent structure to it and it has beautiful cover art that makes me want to read it just by looking at it! These are amazing books!' *Steven Johns*

'The Spook's book series is a very important series to me. Since I have ADD and dyslexia I never was a really good reader and reading was frustrating for me. I wanted to read books but it was too hard for me. I could never finish them and that made me sad. However when I started reading the first of the Spook's books, it was completely different. I found myself stuck reading for hours and hours and I managed to finish the book in just a few days. I was shocked and very happy. I borrowed the second book and I read that also in just a few days. I never knew that I could read that fast and that much. The books are so amazingly written that you get completely sucked into the story and you don't just read the story, you feel it. Not many writers have managed to get me this excited and involved in a book series. Thank you Joseph Delaney for making this life-changing tale. I am and will always be your diehard fan.' *Leo Lampinen*

'The Spook's books are amazing and I guess I never thought they would end. Joseph Delaney has created a whole other world in his readers' minds. *Tia Patricia Flanagan, 12*

'I first came across *The Spook's Apprentice* in a small book-shop in Devon. It was tucked between other books, but the spine immediately caught my attention. Ever since I have been immersed in Joseph Delaney's writing and the world of the Spook. Growing up with these books, alongside Tom Ward, has been exciting and spooky. It's been a pleasure to read them. Now I'm ready to face anything from the Dark.' *Sam Whitehouse*

'As a 22-year-old, who has been reading these books since I was 13 or 14, they've been a huge part of my life, and whenever one of these books is released, I'm always incredibly excited, and finish it on the day I get it. Always a pleasure to read. Thank you Joe.' *Ryan Hoskin*

I was walking down to the shop when I passed a bookstore and saw *The Spook's Apprentice* I knew straight away I wanted that book. The Spook's series even inspired me to write a short story. *Taylor Collopy*

'The reason I love Spook's is because I have been reading them since number 1 and I love the idea of the Spook and the job.' *Yeseen*

'When the Spook's books end I don't know what I will do. It has kept me entertained and on the edge of my seat and they have to be the best books I have ever read. I recommend them to everyone! Thank you Joseph Delaney for all of the books, I will be thoroughly sad when they end.' *Daniella Wilson*

'The way I discovered the Spook's books was much the same as many other people. I was on holiday, browsing a book store, intrigued by the cover and decided to buy it. By the evening I had finished the book and enjoyed it so thoroughly that I went back to the store. It quickly became one of my favourite book series of all time.' *Toby Causon*

'The Spook's series are a chilling read. They have great imagination put into them and are quite fascinating. The books are certainly not be read after dark as I found out the hard way!' *Darren McCahey*

'I like the Spook's books because . . .
1. They make me believe in witches and boggarts and all that.
2. Joseph Delaney is a great writer and has inspired me to write about creatures of the dark.
3. I have just finished *Spook's Stories: Witches* and found it the best one so far.
4. Joseph Delaney has a very wild imagination, wilder than mine even.'
Eric Murphy

'I really love the Spook's books when I start reading it I feel like I'm in the story with Tom, Alice and Bill Arkwright. I really wish I could meet Joseph Delaney and tell him that I'm his biggest fan and ask him what he will be doing next after he has finished book 13. I feel really sad that he has nearly finished the *Wardstone Chronicles* and wish they never stopped.' *Vicky Von-Hessler*

'I started reading this series when the first three books were published in Dutch here in the Netherlands and Flanders. I must say, the *Wardstone Chronicle*s are unique! The series is really wonderful! Also, I am a happy person because I'm not very afraid, so I read the books after dark – ha ha.' *Tim Hoogstoel*

'The Spook's books were originally introduced to me by my beautiful girlfriend, Hayley. Hayley has been a fan since childhood but we still like to share information on the series despite me being relatively new to the chronicles. The books have had a euphoric impact on me and have given me a more pleasant lease of life knowing we are guarded from those fearful witches . . . and much crueller and fouler things that the darkness is yet to unveil!' *Phil McCann*

'I'm 13 and I collect books on mythology and mythological creatures, and the book series not only contains accurate mythology but also a gripping story throughout the books. That's why I love the series and I just can't wait until the very last book to see what happens with the characters.' **Thomas (Anthony) Wootton**

'The *Wardstone Chronicles* is the best and most interesting series I have ever read. I loved the way *The Spook's Destiny* was set in Ireland because I am from there. I hope you keep writing new and interesting books!' **Mark Coughlan**

'I began to fear and love the books as I read them. I've grown up loving Tom, being jealous of Alice and fearful of – yet adoring – Mr. Gregory. The *Wardstone Chronicles* are everything I love about literature and when they end I shall re-read them again and again because great stories like this one should never end.' **Hailey Tumilson**

'The Spook's series are my favourite books. At first the message on the back worried me and I was too scared to read them after dark, but then I got so into them that it was the quickest I've ever read a book (just a few days!).' *Lucy Morgan*

'I would love to get my name in the last Spook's book it will mean a lot to me. I got my first book when I was 7 and have been following them ever since!' *Samuel Livesey*

As the wind blows and night draws on
The witches lay their eyes upon
The Fiend, a monster, the one and only,
The devil himself, so evil and unholy.
The monster in the flesh, standing in all his glory.
The villain that's told of in bedtime stories,
And as he told the witches he'd rule the County
They told him of an enemy who made them quite rowdy.
Tom was the name they all despised
One witch said he'd beat him, though he's just a boy.
The Fiend was upset to later hear
If he killed this boy, his lifetime rule would disappear.
So he sent his best assassins to make sure the boy died
None returned, though he heard they all tried.
So the Fiend got an idea, if he joined the boy
The places they could rule, the enemies they'd destroy
But Tom refused for his heart was pure
He stopped the devil there and then and said he'd hear
    no more.
So he went on with his apprenticeship to the local spook.
This is the plot summary of my favourite books.

A Spook's Poem
By Nathan Prunty, Age 14

Joseph Delaney is a retired English teacher living in Lancashire. He has three children and nine grandchildren, and often speaks at all sorts of events. His home is in the middle of boggart territory and his village has a boggart called the Hall Knocker, which was laid to rest under the step of a house near the church.

Most of the places in the Spook's books are based on real locations in Lancashire, and the inspiration behind them often comes from local ghost stories and legends.

You can visit the *Wardstone Chronicles* website at www.**spooksbooks**.com where you can find Joseph's blog and more information on the books.